I0663179

Alien Blood Wars

SLAVE DANCE

SAMANTHA CAYTO

Slave Dance
ISBN # 978-1-78686-373-7
©Copyright Samantha Cayto 2018
Cover Art by Cherith Vaughn ©Copyright October 2018
Interior text design by Claire Siemaszkiewicz
Pride Publishing

SLAVE DANCE

Prologue

Transylvania, 1205

"You waste your talents."

Emil ignored both the remark and the man who made it. Instead, he tasted his stew with critical taste buds and decided that more thyme was in order. "Supper will be ready soon," he said, still not bothering to look at his unwelcome visitor.

Dracul, as was his want, acted as if he had every right to be there, hovering over Emil's pot. He sniffed ostentatiously. "Human flora. Disgusting."

"Some of it is quite tasty, I have found. Regardless, the stores of hydroponics that we were able to salvage are nearly depleted. We need to conserve them if we have any hope of cultivating them here."

Dracul scoffed. "As if I care. Plants are plants. There's no meat in there. Why don't you add some lamb?"

Emil held his temper. Nothing good came from confrontation. There were too many squabbles, large and small, within their own group and in the world around them. "I have no interest in slaughtering those adorable creatures to feed us when beans and vegetables do the trick just as well."

"Well, I need flesh to be satisfied."

"I am aware." The man loved his blood and gore overly much, in Emil's opinion. "Go and kill what you want. I'll have no part in it." He looked at Dracul for the first time and narrowed his gaze. "I will have no part in *any* scheme you concoct."

It was as close as he'd come to acknowledging that his compatriot was courting open rebellion against their captain. Why Alex hadn't killed the man already was a source of concern. The captain was too honorable, in Emil's estimation.

Dracul did not take the hint. If anything, he got closer, more conspiratorial. "We're going to have to leave this place soon. These stupid humans and their religious crusades are making this area untenable as a home base."

Emil went back to stirring his massive pot of stew. "This planet is large enough for us to find a safer place to lie low."

"To what end?" Dracul bit out. "We are stranded here. No one comes to rescue us. We must make of our new life what we can."

Stilling his large ladle, Emil eyed the irritating man. "That is what we are doing. I, for example, have mastered a new skill. I find great satisfaction in cooking for our people."

"Female work in this miserable place." Dracul's tone dripped with contempt.

That was enough to bring Emil's anger to the fore. He whirled from his task and braced for a fight. "You overstep the bounds of decency when you speak of females as if they hold no importance. Anything that I am able to accomplish even half so well as a woman, I would take pride in."

He stepped closer and felt a spark of satisfaction when Dracul drew back. Emil didn't like to throw his size around, preferring the quiet life of a scientist. But, he wasn't one to run from a fight, either. Far from it. Reining in his temper had always been something he struggled with.

"I care nothing of your opinion of me or what you consider worthy. If my cooking offends you, find your own food. You'll do as you wish, regardless." He turned back to the bubbling pot again, ignoring his growing urge to beat Dracul to a bloody pulp and drain him dry.

"You're right about that," the man conceded. "I am done with squatting among dumb animals. Here, we can be rulers. These human are puny primitives. Why not take what's laid open before us?" He leaned in, his breath hissing against Emil's ear. "You could live like a queen, with as many pretty boys at your beck and call as you could ever want. Think of the power. Think of the blood!"

Because it was hard these days to think of anything else but the taste of salty, warm blood dripping down his throat, Emil's self-control snapped. This time, when he turned to Dracul, he did so with a raised fist. He smashed the man in the face, sending him flying away, although Dracul flipped to his feet the second after he fell.

"I am *not* a queen! The very notion is obscene. I was a worker and a drone for my hive—and gladly so. Here, I can't be as I was, yet I'm still useful to what hive we have. This"—he emphasized by jabbing a finger at this pot—"is what I do. I am content with that, and I am loyal to our captain. Go peddle your poison somewhere else."

Dracul stared daggers at him, wiping the blood from his cut lip with the back of his hand. Then he licked it before saying, "Very well. You would have been a fierce ally, but I'm not worried about your being an adversary, either."

With deliberate steps, Dracul approached. Emil kept his gaze on him, although he needn't have worried. Dracul wasn't spoiling for a fight, the coward. Instead, he spit some blood into the stew.

"There. Now at least it has something in it worthy of a warrior."

Emil watched the man stalk off and returned to his task of finishing the stew only when Dracul was out of sight. The peace he found in his cooking was gone. And now he knew for certain that Dracul was mounting a mutiny. Alex would have to be warned. Emil could only hope that enough of the others stayed loyal to their leader and hadn't been courted successfully by Dracul.

No matter. If it came to a fight, Emil would gladly die by Alex's side rather than live Dracul's promised life as a conqueror. Not even the temptation of someone for his own could sway him. Better to live his life alone than take pleasure with a slave. And in a world where Emil's size and strength caused fear among the native peoples, could he ever trust that a human was with him out of genuine desire? No, he thought not. So, he'd find his pleasure in his food.

That was the one sure way he could make someone happy.

Chapter One

Boston, 2017

Emil entered his empty kitchen just as the eastern sky started to turn rosy. He liked working before others typically came looking for freshly prepared meals. The peace appealed to him. He liked cooking on his own, too — not that he didn't appreciate the staff that Alex provided him. Sometimes it was nice to go back to his roots of concocting massive quantities of food for his shipmates. He took great satisfaction in pleasing them, even in this small way. It certainly was more attractive than fighting some bloody human war beside them. He did that as well, of course, yet he simply enjoyed stuffing them with canapes more.

And this day was particularly important. It wasn't only his own kind he would be cooking for. It wasn't some ordinary meal or even a big feast to celebrate a victory. This was a unique event for them. After a thousand years on this planet, this was the first time any of them were getting married. Not even Harry and

Lucien had been afforded the opportunity to go through this most human of rituals, having made quick work of their marriage at city hall years after they'd produced their son. Val and Mackie were treading new ground, and Emil was determined that their big, important day would be perfect.

Everything was set, the main floor having been closed to the members and turned into a kind of natural church. Not that Emil had had anything to do with that. No, Quinn and the other boys—under Mackie's critical eye—had set it all up complete with beautiful decorations that gave homage to the humans' many holidays at year end. It looked like something out of a human fairytale and Emil wasn't surprised. Mackie loved beauty, and Val loved Mackie. The bratty boy was getting his way in all things, and his joyous appreciation belied his label. Mackie was no bridezilla. Having come from so little, he valued how much he was given.

Emil wanted his contribution—the food and wedding cake—to be as perfect as he could make it. He grabbed a big mug of the pre-brewed coffee and entered his enormous walk-in refrigerator. The five-layer chocolate cake with hazelnut cream filling stood right where he'd left it the night before. He eyed it critically, checking to make sure the fondant was flawless. He'd sprayed it a light silver and festooned it with red and black icing roses. The flavor had been Mackie's choice, but he'd left the decorating to Emil. Honoring the colors favored by his people had been an odd choice by human standards, but Emil believed that Val deserved them. It was his wedding, too, and despite his show of indulging only Mackie, the man's nerves were easy to spot.

Poor Val.

Fortunate Val.

In less than twelve hours, he was going to stand in front of family and friends and pledge himself forevermore to his beloved boy. He would have someone to warm his bed, source his blood and eventually bear his sons. It was hard not to feel envious, except Emil knew how hard their journey had been. To find a human who could accept a lover who was an alien vampire was extraordinary. Some of his compatriots had been lucky in that. Others, like Dracul, had simply taken whatever they'd wanted. Emil had long ago made peace with the idea that being alone was better than being a monster.

He took a long gulp of his coffee, enjoying the almost instant buzz it gave him. He studied the cake some more, tempted to fuss over it. It was perfect, however, even if he said so himself. Best to get on with marinating the tenderloins and prepping for the side dishes and the hors d'oeuvres. Returning to the kitchen, he set about doing just that. He turned on the radio to listen to classical music. The variety of human music delighted him and he enjoyed the often raucous genres that normally infused the club. Here in his domain, however, he liked soothing, and there was no one to even roll their eyes at his choices.

Mise en place. There was an order and a rhythm to cooking that he welcomed. Everything needed to be laid out for him to begin to build the components of his menu. He had his lists and utensils. There was almost nothing available in the world of cooking that he didn't possess. There was one long stainless-steel prepping table that only he used. It was spotless because he had made sure it was. He wasn't one to delegate menial tasks to others. Pride forced him to scrub and order his work space as if the queen herself would walk in and do an inspection.

Not that she existed on this puny world...or ever would. He'd met her only once and could still conjure up the exquisite pleasure of the one time he'd serviced her as a good drone should. That memory served him well in the hours when he lay in his big bed all by himself, making do with his hand. But he didn't bring it out often. No, he would never disrespect the woman in that way. Instead, he liked to imagine a pretty human boy in his bed. He'd always liked them, even though he avoided such entanglement for the most part. They were too delicate and he was too hulking and strong. He worried that his big hands would crush them like they sometimes did with small foods.

Unlike the little amuse-bouches that he intended to prepare for the wedding, however, he didn't try to navigate humans. One could always toss away damaged food. Not so, damaged people.

"Hey, Chef."

Emil looked up from what he was doing, surprised to find his sous chef, Damien, sauntering in. The guy looked like he'd come straight from a night out clubbing. "What are you doing here so early?"

The kid gave him a tired smile as he headed straight for the coffee. "Seriously? This is...like, the big day, right? I knew you'd be up before the birds, cooking your heart out. No pre-made sandwiches or cold salads for the happy couple, right? Thought I'd come give you a hand."

Damien filled a mug and came over. His short, dark hair stood in gelled spikes and his neck tattoos showed above the collar of his too-thin jacket. The boy didn't take nearly good enough care of himself. "Holy crap,

Chef! I knew you'd go overboard, but you do know that the entire city *hasn't* been invited, right?"

Emil stared down at his prep table. "I want to make sure there's plenty of variety and no one goes hungry."

Damien snorted. "You could pass this out to everyone at Fenway Stadium and still have leftovers."

Emil sniffed. "It's the wrong season for baseball."

Damien grinned over the rim of his mug. "Okay, so make it Gillette Stadium. Same dif." He shook his head. "Is that the marinade for the beef?"

"Yup." He had two big bowls filled already. While he'd never gotten over his reluctance to slaughter animals for cooking himself, he wasn't above making do with the sanitized version found in supermarkets. And everyone did enjoy a nice cut of well-seasoned meat.

"I'll get the tenderloins soaking for you." Damien reached for one of the bowls.

"You don't have to. You look dead on your feet. Go home and get some sleep then come in at your regular time."

"Come on, Chef. Don't be a control freak. I've got this. I may have been up all night and got fucked silly by this totally hot construction worker…but I'm young. I can sleep when I'm dead." He shot Emil a cocky grin. "Besides, I like helping you out. I haven't forgotten how you gave me a chance when I was just some snotty-nosed kid with zero training."

That reminder of Damien's difficult past and how much the boy appreciated the opportunity Emil had given him was what allowed Emil to let go. "You're right," he said, holding up his hands. "I've got other things to do and I appreciate the help. After you get the meat marinating, start killing the lobsters. You know how I hate that," he added with a sigh. Lambs or crustaceans… Emil had a soft spot for them both. It was humans and his own kind that he could kill when necessary, because they gave him reason to, unfortunately.

Damien grinned broadly. "You're just an old softy, Chef."

It also made him uncomfortable being called something that he officially wasn't. Much as he'd wanted to, he'd never had the chance to attend a culinary institute. As a self-taught cook, he shouldn't answer to the title of 'chef' but he'd long given up correcting his staff. Maybe someday when Dracul and his minions had been permanently destroyed, he could indulge himself by going to school. There was always something new to learn.

In the meantime, he could strive for such normalcy as the internecine war permitted. Today was the most important cooking day of his life. Everything had to be perfect. With the two of them working, the time passed quickly. Emil was ultimately grateful for both the help and the company. It was breakfast before he knew it, so he started on the more mundane task of cooking eggs, bacon and toast for the hordes that were about to descend from the living quarters.

Mackie was the first to come flying in, with Demi in his wake. He had some kind of green goo slathered all over his face. "Emil, I have to see the cake! Please say I can." He rushed over to the counter. "Ooh, bacon."

"Mackie!" Demi cried out. "Don't eat yet or you'll crack your mask. You're not even supposed to be talking."

Emil picked up a slice of bacon and handed it over. "Here. We can't have you fainting at your own wedding. And what's the stuff on your face supposed to do, anyhow?"

"Clean and tighten his pores," Demi huffed. "It's his big day, after all."

"Your skin is perfect already," Emil told the groom with a smile, which broadened as he watched the boy consume the bacon with a blissful look. "And of course you can see your cake. Come on."

He led him over to the walk-in refrigerator and opened the door with a flourish. For a few seconds, Mackie said nothing. He simply stood and stared. Then he gasped.

"Oh, it's gorgeous." He turned moist eyes toward Emil. "It's like something you'd see on TV."

"Oh my God," Demi moaned. "Don't cry. That will ruin your mask, too."

"I don't care." Mackie flung himself into Emil's arms. "Thank you so much. If I weren't already madly in love with Val, I'd marry you instead."

Stunned by the praise and affection, Emil awkwardly hugged him back. "It gives me great pleasure to make you happy." He tried not to worry about the green stuff getting on his whites.

"Am I going to have to kill you, Emil, for stealing my boy?" Val drawled out the question as he sauntered into the kitchen and headed for breakfast.

Both Demi and Mackie shrieked. Mackie jumped away from Emil and turned his back to his fiancé. "Val, what are you doing here?"

"Yeah," Demi chimed in, using his body to shield Mackie from Val's line of sight. "You're not supposed to see him before the wedding starts."

Val paused with a piece of bacon halfway to his mouth. "Why the fuck not? I just spent the night with my dick up his ass. Doesn't that count as 'seeing him'?"

"Don't be crude," Mackie called out as he inched his way over to the door. "I can always change my mind about marrying you."

Val snorted. "I don't think so. Try it and I'll be forced to add a paddling into the ceremony."

There was another gasp from Mackie and a giggle before he and Demi left the room. "Come back and get your breakfast when Val is gone," Emil called after them with a shake of his head.

Val grabbed a plate and started filling it with food. "I'll pile on enough for the two of them and take it up." He shook his head. "Do you understand any of this nonsense?"

"No," Emil replied, shutting the refrigerator door. "But your fiancé does and that's all that matters, right?"

Val shrugged. He shot Emil a wistful expression. "Yeah, I guess that's right. I want this day to be perfect for him."

"Me too. So get your food and theirs, then scram. I need room and no distractions if I'm going to get everything done in time."

"Got it." After pouring himself a mug of coffee, Val took the meal and himself out of the room, except he paused in the doorway and looked over his shoulder. "Thanks, Emil. You have become as a brother to me, and I don't think I've ever told you how much I truly value you."

The sentiment caused Emil's heart to squeeze a bit. Their kind wasn't much for expressing emotions, at least among males. "Thank you, Val. I return the feeling. Now get the hell out of my kitchen."

* * * *

The dance floor had been converted into a nave with an enchanted bower running along the edges, complete with a canopy of greens where Val and Mackie would recite their vows at one end. The stripper poles were festooned with colorful ribbons, reminding him of the maypoles of long ago. Emil stood to one side, trying not to tug at the collar of his Canali tuxedo. He hated formal wear and was never so happy as when he was lounging around in a T-shirt and jeans — or his chef's whites. But Mackie wanted formal and the kid had gone through a lot of misery, much of it in the last few months. He deserved whatever he wanted. One didn't have to be head-over-heels in love with him to want this wedding to meet his dreams.

That included Alex officiating through some Internet certification that mystified Emil. And he was also surprised to find himself standing for Val as his Best Man in the time-honored human tradition. He had been stunned to be asked and terrified he'd fuck up his one role in the ceremony. For the umpteenth time since getting dressed, he felt in his pocket to make sure the wedding bands were there. Then he eyed the long table set at the far end where the cake sat proudly for perusal. It was a knock-out, if he said so himself. Once the ceremony was over, he would dash back to the kitchen and start laying out the food.

All of the staff, including the go-go boys, were in attendance, as were a few club members that Val and Mackie especially liked. Kitty stood nearby, gorgeous and stately in a skin-hugging red strapless satin gown. She looked every inch a queen, which was probably why he and his compatriots felt such an affinity for her. And on the other side of the room was the cop, Duncan, looking uncomfortable in a natty, pinstriped suit. Demi circled around the poor man, like a minnow harrying a shark. Emil's money was on the minnow, if it came down to it.

He craned his neck to check out the dark corners of the room and was relieved to see Logan lurking there. Although she was a grown female, perfectly capable of taking care of herself, he still worried about her. The colder it got outside, the more he wanted to keep her safely within his orbit. She was stubbornly resistant to the idea, although she did sometimes sleep in the done-over storage room he'd presented her. She had openly dismissed the invitation to attend the wedding. Yet, here she was, and it allowed Emil to breathe just a bit easier.

The music started, getting everyone's attention. Voices stilled and all eyes turned to the end of the bower where Val and Mackie walked hand-in-hand to the strains of Pachelbel's Christmas canon. Val wore a Victorian-era charcoal-gray tuxedo, complete with a champagne jacquard vest and jabot. The outfit would have been considered vintage if not for the fact that he'd bought it himself more than a hundred years earlier. Mackie wore pants in a matching shade of gray, but his jacket was a tunic-style white damask with a Mandarin collar. The ruffles of his white regency shirt cascaded down his front and peeped out from the end of his sleeves. Their combined beauty stunned Emil and caused a strange longing to rise inside him.

There was no time to dwell on his reaction, however. Soon the ceremony started with Alex reciting age-old homilies about why they had all gathered together. Then, first Mackie, followed by Val, recited the old English vows they'd agreed upon.

With a clear, yet shaky voice, Mackie said, "I, Mackenzie Andrew Fraser, take you, Valeriu Stelalux, as my wedded husband, to have and to hold, from this day forward, for better, for worse, for richer, for poorer, in sickness and in health, to love, to cherish and to obey, till death us do part."

There was a little snickering by some of the attendants at the 'obey' part, but it was good-natured. Everyone knew Mackie was Val's boy. Then Val pledged nearly the same and in only a slightly more controlled voice that made Emil smile. Alex turned to Emil for the rings, which he managed to liberate from his pocket without dropping. He breathed easier now that his role was over.

A few more traditional words were spoken, but the ceremony wasn't quite over yet. Val pulled a narrow, supple black collar out of his pants pocket with a gold tag hanging off the D ring. The tag was etched with their new monogram as a married couple — a stylized S bracketed by a V and an M. There were gold lines tooled all around the leather that looked simply like a pretty design, except that Emil and all his kind would recognize them as their language. It spoke of devotion and protection that meant more to Val than the human vows he'd given. The way Mackie gasped at its sight and looked at his husband with tears in his eyes, it was obvious he hadn't expected his wedding would also serve as a collaring ceremony for a Dom and his sub.

Val presented it. "Will you wear this, Mackie?"

The boy nodded and whispered. "Yes. Yes, *Master*."

Val buckled it around Mackie's neck, laying the tag on the ruffles of his shirt for all to see. He took the boy's hand, turned to their guests and held their arms up. Everyone clapped and cheered. Val swung Mackie into his arms, bent him over and kissed him silly. When they finally came up for air, Alex was the first to congratulate the married couple. Quinn hugged them both, and soon everyone crowded around them, giving their best wishes.

Emil used the opportunity to slip away and into the kitchen. He was tugging off his bow tie before he hit the swinging doors. There would be time enough to express his happiness to his friends. For now, his duty was to get the food out. Everyone was in the mood to party and there was no reception without plenty to drink and eat.

He took a second to pause and appreciate the quiet space he considered his domain. He loved this kitchen and he loved cooking. There was nothing he wanted so much in this world that he'd been forced to adopt than to pursue this simple pleasure in peace. If only he could. For now, there was a lull from the fighting. But how long would it last? Not long, by his experience. Tonight, though, he could let go of his worry, and it started by getting the hors d'oeuvres into the oven.

Chapter Two

"I'm happy to confirm, Mr. Washburn, that your membership application has been accepted."

"That's excellent news, Mr. Stelalux." Master's voice had that booming, happy tone that he always used when he got his own way. Joining Club Lux had been important to him, crucial even, as he focused on establishing himself in a new city.

Jase was careful to keep his perfect pose — knees shoulder-width apart, back straight, hands clasped behind it and head bowed. His job was to show what a wonderful job Master had done molding the perfect slave. He was a testament to how lucky the club would be to have a new member like Master, although Jase suspected all the club owner really cared about was the strength of Master's financials. The big, scary man sitting behind the massive desk didn't look like someone who was easily impressed by anything or anyone. Jase hoped that the man wouldn't insist on having a taste of Jase to seal the deal.

"Please call me Alex. We're informal around here."

Master chuckled. "I'm glad to hear it. People call me Wash, as it happens. I'd be delighted if you would, as well."

"Wash, then. Welcome to Lux. If you'd be so kind as to write out a check for the initial dues, I'll have your club card and key to you in the next day or so."

"Of course. As it happens, I have it here." Master made a show of taking the check out of his inner breast pocket and handing it over. "I'm optimistic by nature, so I came prepared."

Jase's view of the goings-on was peripheral, but he was used to seeing his world that way. Master—and the ones who'd come before him—liked Jase to mind his manners and not anyone else's business. All he had to do was keep his ears open and obey on command, except he'd also learned that if he didn't try to pay more attention, unpleasant surprises occurred.

He had no idea what to expect of this new city and the club. Master was happy to finally be able to settle down and parade his boy out in the open. With Jase's eighteenth birthday had come liberation from the dirty and often illegal secret of keeping an underage sex slave. There was no more hiding necessary, unless one counted that Jase had never given himself freely to the man—or any man—and that he stayed out of the sure knowledge that escape was impossible. Trying to do so meant horrible pain. Being a good and obedient boy was the best he could hope for.

"Does your boy need a membership card and key?" the club owner asked, which surprised Jase. The man was acting as if he were a person and not Master's toy.

Master's heavy hand came down on top of Jase's head. He tried not to flinch. "No. Thank you. Jase goes nowhere without me. We're in a committed twenty-four-seven Master-slave relationship, you see." A pressing of fingertips warned Jase to be good.

"Indeed." There was a pause before the owner continued. "I saw the copy of his birth certificate in your application file. He's only a few months into his eighteenth year. That was a fast courtship."

Jase couldn't help tensing. He could hear the skepticism in the man's voice. He needn't have worried. Master was a smooth liar, having years of practice that spanned more than Jase's lifetime.

Master patted Jase's head. "Well, my boy is precocious. I can't deny it. He knew what he wanted and went after it as soon as he could. I was helpless to resist."

Oh yes, Master was a fantastic liar. If Jase hadn't known better, he would have believed every word.

"Well then," the club owner said with a hint of false cheer. "Welcome to the club, Jase. I hope you enjoy our playrooms. If you have any questions, the go-go boys will be happy to assist you."

"Thank you, Alex. What do you say, Jase?"

"Thank you, sir." Jase was careful to show just the right amount of deference, yet not so much as to indicate he had any interest in the owner. Master was a jealous man.

"Feel free to use the facilities now, if you wish." The offer was a dismissal.

Master understood it for what it was and, snagging Jase's leash, he stood. Jase followed suit without prompting. "I'll see you around, Alex."

When Master turned to leave, Jase couldn't resist glancing at the club owner. The man startled him by already having his gaze fixed on Jase. Beautiful violet eyes bore into him as if the man could see right through the carefully constructed persona of a collared slave that Master had cultivated in Jase. Although the look made Jase cringe, it also held some kind of reassurance. Here was a man who would bend to no one. If Master thought he held some control over this man, he was wrong. Of course, Jase didn't harbor any desires of being taken by the man for his own slave. As miserable as life was with Master, how much worse would it be with someone who looked like he could kill without compunction? Still, it was somewhat comforting to be reminded that Master wasn't the omnipotent being he portrayed in Jase's life.

A tug on his leash was a reminder that he wasn't keeping within the required two paces behind Master. He hurried to correct the mistake, knowing that there would be consequences. There always were, even when he did everything right. There was no fun in it for Master if he couldn't subject Jase to some amount of pain.

When he stepped past the threshold of the office, however, he bumped into a rock wall. No, it was only a man—a broad-chested muscular man who reached out to steady Jase by grabbing him by the shoulders. Jase gasped in surprise and accidently looked into the man's eyes. Violet, like the owner's, except these held a softness, a kindness that Jase hadn't seen in any man...ever.

"I'm sorry. I wasn't paying attention to where I was going. Are you okay?"

Jase opened his mouth before remembering that he wasn't supposed to talk to anyone without permission. He couldn't look away, though. And the coolness of the man's hands seeped through the thin leather of Jase's jacket to his naked skin beneath it. It made him shiver.

The man frowned. "Are you cold? You should have more on. It's January in Boston, you know."

A 'sorry' was on his lips before he could stop himself, as if he had any choice in what he wore. Only Master did, and yeah, Jase had been cold walking from Master's condo down to the car then into the club. A fleeting and dangerous thought crossed his mind that if this huge bear of a man wrapped him in his arms, Jase would never be cold again.

A vicious tug on his leash had him pulling away from the man and into the less-warm embrace of Master. "Sorry. This is my slave. He's not allowed to speak to you without my permission." There was a steely tone underneath Master's matter-of-fact apology.

The man folded his arms. "Oh yeah? I'm not in the lifestyle, so... He should have more on." The audacity of the reprimand would have thrilled Jase if he didn't know that Master's anger would be taken out on his hide.

"I appreciate your concern. As a brand new member, I haven't had a chance to meet everyone." Master didn't offer his hand.

Neither did the man. "I'm Emil, Alex's cousin and the cook around here. You might want to order some food for the kid along with the clothes. He's too skinny."

The man Emil didn't wait for a response. He merely continued into the club owner's office, shutting the door behind him. A split-second later, Master was hauling Jase back to the main area of the club and up the stairs. Being daytime, practically no one around. Jase kept his head down and didn't bother checking out the beautiful surroundings.

Master stormed into the first empty playroom he found and closed them in with a kick of the door. Next, he unhooked the leash, waves of fury flying out of him. "Strip and get your ass on that spanking bench."

Jase did as he'd been told, trying not to worry about what was to come. He knew...and couldn't do anything about it. He just had to endure. It had been the same for years. Kneeling on the bench, he spread his legs wide while clenching his hole to hold in his butt plug. He stared down at the plush carpet. At least the surroundings were lovely. That wasn't always the case.

Master rattled around the room, open and shutting drawers and undoubtedly looking for the right things with which to torment Jase. He thudded over, his fury marked by each heavy tread of his feet. Master's moods swung violently these days. His cocaine use was not helping matters. He loomed in front of Jase's bowed head, yanked his chin and shoved a latex penis into Jase's mouth without preamble. He sent it hard and deep enough that Jase would have choked if his gag reflex hadn't been trained out of him. He worked his mouth to hold it in without drooling.

Next came the beating. Master wasted no time in walloping Jase's bare ass with a wooden paddle—Master's favorite instrument because it was both painful and easy to use. "Did you like it, boy? The way that man touched you and leered at your naked chest, fussing over your being cold and hungry? Did it make you feel special and wanted? Do you wish he were here instead of me?"

Every question, all of which were really accusations, was punctuated with a brutal swat of the paddle. The jarring smack layered upon old bruises was agony. Jase lurched forward with the force and cried out around the gag. He didn't try to hold back his fear and pain. That was what Master wanted to hear, of course. It was proof that he, and only he, owned Jase, body and soul. It was nothing new—the same old thing—and Jase weathered it with the meager comfort that it wouldn't last long. Master didn't have that kind of control.

Soon, the beating stopped. Master yanked the plug from Jase's ass and replaced it with his cock. There was no lube. There never was, but the plug helped keep his channel open. The burn was a familiar sensation and nothing like the pain from paddling.

As he shoved his way into Jase's battered body, Master muttered and swore incoherently. Except Jase knew the words by heart and they came down to one thing. He was the property of Master and always would be.

* * * *

"Who was that asshole I ran into out there?" Emil asked the question as he plopped down on Alex's office couch. The visitors' chairs were too narrow for his comfort.

Alex twirled his chair around and crossed his feet on the top of his desk. "The man or the boy?" When Emil merely glared in response, Alex replied, "Of course, the man. Washburn is his name and he's a new member. He's also an asshole, isn't he?"

"I just said so, didn't I? You admitted him to the club?"

"I did. I had to. His references from three club members were impeccable—and so is his bank account. He appears to be an upstanding businessman, although new to Boston. He lived in Miami for a few years prior to this, apparently."

"He's got the kid on a leash," Emil felt compelled to point out. The sight of that pretty, young boy improperly dressed for the season and being treated like a pet had bothered him. *A lot.*

"So he does. This is a club that caters to the BDSM community, remember?"

Emil folded his arms and huffed. "Yeah. I don't get it."

"You don't have to, as long as it's consensual."

"That kid looks too young to consent to anything." *And scared.* He didn't add that observation, but it was true, nevertheless. Beneath the silky fringe of white-blond hair had been bright blue eyes with a haunted look shining through.

"According to the paperwork submitted, he's eighteen. Val confirmed its authenticity."

Emil snorted. "I don't care. Eighteen is young."

"Quinn is eighteen," Alex reminded him with an icy stare.

"My point still stands. Everybody is too damn young around here. Or," he added, tipping his head back, "maybe I'm old."

Alex chuckled. "That's possible. I certainly am feeling my age these days, despite the refreshing cold of the season."

"It's Dracul. He's making us crazy, all the more so for lying low these past few months."

"That expression the humans have about waiting for the other shoe to drop comes to mind."

"Except this is like waiting for the thousandth shoe." He exhaled noisily. "I'd like it to be over."

"As would I. Never more so now that I have Quinn to lose."

That was a minor blessing for Emil. He didn't have someone he loved to worry over. But that wasn't true. He didn't have a lover, yet he did love his compatriots and their families. He worried about Kitty and Logan and Damien. There was a lot Dracul could take away from him that would break his heart.

For some reason, he pictured the boy from the hallway again. "What's his name?"

"I told you, Washburn."

"No, the boy."

"Oh…Jase." Papers rustled. "Jason Purdue. Washburn called him Jase."

"Jase," Emil repeated. "He needs fattening."

"You think everyone does," Alex retorted. "If you could, I swear you'd feed the world."

"True that. I don't understand how humans can allow their own to go hungry. There's so much I don't get about these creatures, even after all this time."

"You have a big heart, Emil."

He sighed. "For all the good it does me."

"It does others good, and that's one of the reasons why I appreciate that you stayed loyal to me more than I can say."

Raising his head, Emil looked his captain in the eye. "Why are you always surprised by those of us that stuck by you? It's the ones that were bent by Dracul who are unfathomable."

Alex smiled. "You are a treasure, my friend. I don't say that enough."

Emil grunted and rolled his eyes. "I'm a cook and sometimes a soldier. That's all." He sat forward. "Do you think if I bring them sandwiches, he'd let the boy eat them?"

Alex dropped his feet with a thud. "No! You don't disturb couples when they are playing. You should know that by now. If you need a refresher on BDSM etiquette, check in with Val. He'll tell you that disturbing a scene is one of the worst things you can do to practitioners."

A growl popped out of his mouth before he could stop it. Something about the idea of that boy being hurt brought out his protective instincts. "What if he's hurting him?"

"*Emil*, that is rather the point. The boy likes being in pain the same way Mackie does—or, at least, I assume so."

Emil leaned forward, unable to drop the subject for some reason. "What if he doesn't? Did you talk to him? The asshole said the kid couldn't talk to me without his permission. I suppose that's another part of the lifestyle I don't get."

"Hmm." Alex rubbed his chin. "I didn't, as it happens. Technically, Washburn is the member. We only asked for ID for Jase because he's going to be a recurring guest of a member. I confess I didn't speak directly with the boy at all. He didn't appear to be in distress. His heart rate was normal and I scented no sweat. If he was afraid, he hid it well."

"He would, wouldn't he? If Washburn controls him, has trained him, he'd act as if everything was fine, yeah?" Emil narrowed his gaze. "He was fearful when I bumped into him, although I think it was the sight of me that did it," he added ruefully. Sometimes his enormous size was a liability when it came to interacting with humans.

He didn't add how much of those few seconds as he held on to the boy, listening to the rapid tattoo of the human's heartbeat and catching his sweet-and-salty scent, had captured his attention. Even now, minutes later, he recalled the power of the interaction.

"I wish there were some way to check on them."

"You know we don't spy on our members. There's no security cameras in the playroom, only a panic button. Everyone deserves their privacy, and we aren't voyeurs."

Watching the boy being beaten or whatever was the last thing Emil wanted to see. He understood Alex's point, but the club had also been conceived with the expectation that everything done was consensual. "He can't ask for help if he's incapacitated."

"Good Lord, Emil… Why are you suddenly worried about what our members are up to?"

Emil shrugged. "I can't say. I just am." It was this boy, naturally. For some reason he'd gotten under his skin within the span of a minute of minor interaction.

Alex sighed. "Very well. Would it make you feel better if I ask Val to dig deeper?"

"Yes."

"And maybe I can have Quinn and Mackie befriend Jase and get their take on his situation?"

"I'd like that," he said with a nod. "If the asshole will let him talk to the boys."

"I'll see what I can arrange, and we really need to stop referring to our newest member as 'the asshole', don't you think?"

"No." With that, Emil rose and left Alex's office. He had work to do, and if he spent his time thinking about the boy while he did so, that was his business. And his problem.

* * * *

"Jesus H. Christ, these old warehouses go up like kindling."

"Yeah, and they always seem to do so in the middle of the night."

Trey didn't care that his fatigue and weariness could be heard in his tone. He and Karl had been partners long enough that they could relax and be themselves at o-dark-thirty in the morning. And with a biting winter wind cutting through his coat, he simply couldn't be indifferent to being called out on a possible homicide through arson. He didn't even have a cup of coffee to ward off the chill or brighten his outlook.

"I got to tell you I'm glad I didn't have plans last night. I was feeling sorry for myself, but falling asleep on my recliner means I'm not quite a zombie right now." He gave Trey a sideways glance. "Looks like you can't say the same. Had a hot date last night?"

Trey grunted. "If you call getting sucked off by a rando in the hallway of a club a date, then yeah." And so what if the guy had been way younger than Trey was and sporting long dark hair. "He was hot, though."

Karl snorted. "God, you've got it great. It's easy to find guys who'll do that for you. I'm thinking of turning gay to get more sex."

"Right, Karl. 'Cause that's how it works. All you have to do is change your orientation." He kept his tone light and teasing. He knew his partner's remark was his way of confirming he wasn't freaked out by some of the explicit things that popped out of Trey's mouth, especially when he was dead on his feet and caffeine-deficient.

He caught sight of Benson, the local fire chief, already on scene and heading in their direction. "I don't know what we're doing here. It's just going to be kicked over to the fire marshal, who will bring in the Fire Investigation Unit. We're ancillary at best, if this was deliberately set."

"But we're still closest, and you know how much Benson loves us. Hey, how're they hanging, Bennie?"

Benson pulled off his hat and swiped his sooty brow with the back of his hand. "I swear, Anderson... You always sound like you're out of some seventies mafia movie or something." He grimaced and looked back at the smoldering wreck. "Fuck, this is a bad one. We had to call in two other houses to help us put it out."

Trey stamped his feet in a pointless effort to unthaw them. "Still only the two DBs?"

"Yeah. It's too unstable to look further right now, but based on the statements from the survivors, it was only the two we found left inside."

Karl snorted. "That thing occupies practically a city block. There could have been dozens of homeless spread around it."

Trey eyed the group of people huddled by the ambulances, wrapped in blankets and sipping cups of coffee. *Lucky bastards.* "I don't know. They tend to stake claims and form, if not tight-knit groups, at least familiar ones. Big building or not, I bet they'd know everyone squatting in the place."

"That's what they claimed," Benson confirmed. "They said the two vics were a couple and went into another part of the building for a little privacy. Next thing anyone knew, there was an explosion close enough that it knocked a few of them flat. Then they had trouble finding their way out, due to thick smoke.

They were kind of helping each other by the time we got here."

Trey eyed the group by the ambulance again. "Are you sure they didn't accidently start the fire themselves?"

Benson nodded. "I've already determined that the fire started in a different area than where we found evidence of their squatting. They had a small, home-made brazier kind of thing lit, but that's not ground zero. The bodies were under debris near the epicenter. Poor bastards never stood a chance. The smoke alone would have gotten to them before they could make it out."

Karl yawned loudly. "Sorry. Didn't get my eight hours last night. You're sure it was an explosion?"

"That's what I'm putting in my report. The fire marshal can take it from there."

"Right," Trey confirmed and stifled his own yawn. "We'll go take official statements from the witnesses. Thanks, Bennie."

The fire chief gave him a two-finger salute before donning his helmet and walking off. Trey headed over to the homeless group with Karl by his side. He idly wondered if he could snag some coffee from the Red Cross person who'd rushed on-scene. Interviewing people who were naturally suspicious of the police took an extra amount of patience, and he wasn't sure he had any at the moment. His stress level dealing with his alien-vampire friends was on the rise, and that was despite the fact that he was truly starting to think of them in that way. When you attended someone's wedding, it strengthened a bond, whether you wanted it to or not.

The huddle caught sight of them quickly and they pulled in their ranks somehow without actually moving. He tried to convey a nonthreatening demeanor with only his expression. He doubted it worked.

Flashing his badge, he said, "Good morning, everyone. I'm Sergeant Trey Duncan and this is my partner, Detective Karl Anderson. We'd like to ask you a few questions about the fire."

No one said anything. They merely looked at him suspiciously over the rims of their Styrofoam cups. He put his badge away and took out his notebook and pen.

"So, Chief Benson tells me there was an explosion and you barely made it out okay. What can you tell me about it?" Still, no one spoke, so he decided he needed to single out one of them and speak directly. "Sir?" He nodded at the closest man, someone of middle age with wisps of white hair among an otherwise-black beard.

"What?" The guy glared at him.

Trey dug deep for that elusive patience. "What can you tell me about the explosion?"

"It was loud. Shook the whole place. Damn near choked to death on the smoke." There was a general murmur of assent among his brethren about that unhelpful answer.

"Yes, sir. The fire chief explained that to me, but I'm hoping you can give me more details, such as whether any of you heard or saw anyone or anything out of the ordinary before that?"

The man took a noisy sip of his coffee. "Nah, it was a typical quiet night." He shook his head. "If we'd thought something was wrong, we never would have just let Bobby and Carrie go off on their own." There was more general confirmation. "Don't know what you all think we can tell you more than that."

Trey tapped his notebook with his pen. "Well, sir, what can you tell me about Bobby and Carrie, then. Were they into drugs?"

"What kind of question is that?" The man's anger seemed real.

"They want to know if they was cooking meth, I bet," called out a younger man behind him.

Trey glanced at Karl before addressing the guy. "Yes, sir, that is frankly something I have to consider." It was the easiest explanation, and these days, he was looking for straightforward, terrestrial kind of crime.

The first man glared at him. "You've got no call thinking that. They were good people. You cops think just because we're on the street that we're all criminals."

"No, sir, I don't think that. But I have to pursue every possible lead. Two people did die and I want to know how and why. I assume you do, as well, and cooperating with us will help make that happen."

The first man gave him the finger.

Karl took a step forward. "Hey, you show Sergeant Duncan some respect."

"Oh, yeah? Or what, you going to arrest me?"

"Maybe."

"Karl," Trey warned. This escalation wasn't going to do them any good.

"Wait a minute," an older woman sitting off to the side called out. "Are you Duncan? Logan's cop friend?"

Trey turned his attention to her. "Yes, ma'am, I know Logan." Calling her a friend would be a bit of a stretch, but he had seen her the other week at the wedding and they'd exchanged a brief greeting. "I hope she's said good things about me." He flashed her a smile that he hoped fell somewhere into the charming category.

"She said you're all right, and that's good enough for me. Give him a break, Freddy."

The man scoffed. "Damn, woman. I've told him all I know, which is nothing." He looked around at the others. "Am I right? We was sitting around, minding our own, and suddenly, boom!" He slapped his knee for emphasis. "That's it. And Bobby and Carrie were not cooking meth. I know that, too."

There was a chorus of "yes" and "that's right" with a few "fucking As" thrown in, except the woman didn't stop in agreeing about their lost companions. Instead, she said, "You know that's not all. Tell them about what you saw when you went outside to piss."

Freddy waved her away. "That was nothing."

Trey leaned in. "Sir, sometimes the simplest things turn out to be important. Please tell me."

"I don't know." The man shrugged. "Just a shadow, that's all. A trick of the light on the roof."

"The roof?" Trey looked over at the smoldering remains of the warehouse. What was left of it was about three stories high. "Someone was up there?"

"Nah, I don't think so. I mean, who'd bother to use the roof when there are plenty of places to get inside. Maybe it was a bird."

Or a bat. No, that was crazy. Thoughts of vampires had infested his mind. If things continued, he'd need to see a shrink, except he'd still end up in a psych ward. No one could ignore the fact that someone who carried a gun thought monsters were real. It was his aforementioned tired brain running amok.

He scratched at his chin and glanced at the building again. "Could you tell where the loud sound came from?"

Freddy shrugged. "Somewhere behind us."

But the woman who knew Logan had a different take. "Above us and behind us."

Trey focused his attention on her. "Are you sure, ma'am? You think it came from a higher floor?"

"Something like that."

Trey remembered what Benson had said about the victims being buried by debris. It could have been something to do with drug production or a natural gas leak in one of the upper floors. Or… He stared at the top of the building. "The roof," he muttered.

There was no time to dwell on his half-formed theory or even question the witnesses more. With a wail of a siren, the fire marshal arrived. The guy was going to want to be debriefed, and while Trey had little to add, he understood the pecking order of arson. As a homicide cop, he'd just been demoted or soon would be on the case. His job was to provide whatever aid the marshal required.

It was going to be a long morning.

Chapter Three

Emil took a step back to eye his brunch buffet table. He loved this part of his week, in particular. It gave him a chance to do a spread of freshly-prepared food that he liked making, and the club members really seemed to enjoy having easy access to a meal that could be light and healthy or hearty and filling, depending on what their Saturday night had done to them. He could have let them make do with the kinds of pre-made sandwiches and salads that he kept stocked behind the bar, but that kind of lazy service didn't sit well with him, nor did leaving it to Damien and the other kitchen staff to offer basic diner fare. People didn't join Club Lux for the food, but he still wanted to offer them something special as a matter of pride. Most of the guys who would soon descend on the buffet hadn't left the club. They'd stagger over from the dance floor where some still rocked their dates or go-go boys to the slow jazz Kitty had put on. Others would come out of playrooms to load plates to take back to their hard-used partners. Why should they have to go somewhere else for a fabulous meal?

Emil made sure he had something for everyone — from fluffy scrambled eggs to rich eggs Benedict, thick slices of bacon or healthier turkey sausage, fresh fruit and sweet jams, biscuits, toast, bagels and lox. Damien stood at the ready to make omelets with a variety of fixings, carve roast beef au jus or whip up classic waffles. Pots of strong black coffee stood next to carafes of mimosas and Bloody Mary's. He mixed it up a bit from week-to-week, depending on his mood. There was never a complaint, and, in fact, some members made a special trip to the club simply for the brunch. It was gratifying that the table always looked within hours as if locusts had descended. Not a crumb was ever left.

A flash of white caught his attention. The boy, Jase, approached with quiet steps. He wore the same leather outfit he'd had on the day before, testament to how he'd never left the club. He kept his eyes down the whole way, although he navigated the room with an appealing grace. As he got closer, Emil could see the dark circles under his eyes, not surprising given the paleness of his skin and how he'd been awake all night. The sight irritated Emil. He wanted to bundle the kid up and put him to bed. He flashed on a vision of doing just that — only not some generic bed, his own. The thought startled him.

He took an involuntary step back when the boy was upon him. "Um, hey, Jase, isn't it?" *Smooth.* "Oh, sorry. I'm not supposed to speak with you, huh?" *Yes, that's it. Make things more awkward by asking questions he can't answer.*

Jase stopped in front of the buffet. "Your pardon, sir. It's me who's not allowed to speak." His long, pretty lashes fluttered. "Except I have leave to ask about the food. May I please fix a plate for my master?"

Emil grimaced and folded his arms. "Sure. It's for all the members and open for business as of now. Help yourself." He stepped back more, in case his proximity made the boy nervous. "Take some for yourself, too."

Jase paused in the act of taking a plate. "Thank you, sir. My master will feed me from his."

"I see." Emil had a feeling that meant the kid got whatever was left once the asshole had stuffed his mouth. He couldn't say why he believed that, yet he knew it was true. "In that case, pile it high."

Jase paused again in the middle of scooping an order of eggs Benedict. "Sir?"

Emil couldn't resist getting closer. "Take two of everything. Seriously," he added, pointing to the table at large. "Tell the as— Tell your *master* I insisted. I like new members to try out my cooking and let me know what they like. This way he can eat as much as he wants of the food that pleases him and can ignore the rest." *Or give it to you.*

"Th-thank you, sir." The breathy, stuttering reply warned Emil that he was making the kid nervous.

He forced himself to give the boy some room, although he couldn't help hovering, nevertheless. From his place behind the table, Damien flashed him a smile. Damn, Emil's interest in Jase wasn't unnoticed, apparently. He glared back at his sous chef and made a motion for him to go ahead and carve a couple of slices of beef.

Jase startled when Damien reached out to put them on the boy's plate. "Oh, thank you, sir." *God, this poor kid is too skittish by half.* If there had been any doubt about how he was being treated by the asshole, spending a few minutes in Jase's company had erased them. If what these two did was consensual, why was Jase such a nervous wreck?

When the plate held as much as the law of physics permitted, Jase stopped by the spot where the drinks were. He was obviously trying to figure out how to balance his plate and pour a drink. It wasn't rocket science, but the boy was clearly having trouble thinking. He was tired—exhausted really—and visibly flustered about being in a strange place.

Emil couldn't resist stepping in. "Here, let me help. What do you need? Coffee?"

Jase flashed him a look from under his lashes. "No, sir. Master likes mimosas, if that's what's in the carafe."

"Yeah, sure it is." Emil filled a wide flute to the brim. He wanted to carry everything to whatever playroom the asshole waited in while his living toy catered to him. But he worried that would work against Jase's interests, so he forced himself to merely hand over the glass to the boy.

"Thank you, sir." Jase was still looking down. Emil wished he'd raise his pretty eyes so that he could see them again.

"You're welcome." He grunted to clear a suddenly tight throat. "And my name is Emil."

There it was, a flash of baby blues that caused Emil's heart to enter a quick tripping beat. A slight quirk of Jase's lips gave Emil a little lift, as well. He'd bet that almost-smile didn't happen often. Or maybe he was simply projecting. Maybe Jase was happily committed to the asshole and would be stuffed full of food in no time.

Nope, he couldn't manage to buy that.

He watched as the boy navigated his way back to and up the staircase, anxious like a mare with her newborn colt taking his first steps. It would have been laughably ridiculous if not for how much he was truly worried.

"Is that the boy Val wants me to cozy up to?"

Emil didn't spare Mackie a glance. He couldn't shift his focus away from Jase. "Yup, that's him. What do you think?"

"He's gorgeous."

"No kidding. Anything more useful?" He still kept staring at Jase until the boy walked out of sight.

"He's hurting."

That got Emil's attention. He swung around and glared at Mackie. "Seriously?"

Val's bratty husband cocked a hip. He was dressed for his new role as the go-go boys' wrangler. His skinny black jeans hugged his lower half, while a red silk shirt lay open to halfway down his chest. The collar Val had placed around his neck was on full display. Mackie twirled the monogrammed tag with his thumb and forefinger.

"Now, don't burst a blood vessel or anything. He's been playing hard all night, probably, and feeling it the next day is half the fun. I didn't mean to imply his pain was a bad thing."

Emil grimaced. "I don't understand any of this."

Mackie patted his arm. "It's okay, sweetie. I know you don't. But trust me. Although it's obvious to me that he's feeling some hurt, I'm not alarmed by it. Not yet. He does look awfully tired," he allowed with a sigh.

"I'm sorry if I'm acting like an old mother hen. There's something about that boy that disturbs me."

Mackie fluttered his lashes. "No kidding," he said, throwing Emil's words back at him.

"I mean, I'm worried about him. That's all."

"Uh-huh. Don't worry. I'll try to befriend him and get the low-down for you." He straightened and turned away. "Hey, Sergeant Sweetie, to what do we owe this visit?"

Emil followed his gaze in time to see Duncan shuffle in like the walking dead. Emil's figurative finger hovered over the panic button. Nothing good could come from the cop's unexpected visit. "What's wrong?"

"Maybe nothing," Duncan replied with a wave. "Mind if I fuel up before I get into it?"

"Sure, help yourself." Emil jerked his thumb toward the buffet.

Duncan was already steering in that direction, although he hit the coffeepot first, filling a mug. He held it in two hands as he gulped down what Emil knew to be a hot brew. He winced at the way the man must have been scalding his mouth. The cop didn't seem to mind. He looked to have finished half before coming up for air.

"Christ Jesus, I needed that. You planning a party or something?"

"No, this is Sunday brunch. I put out a spread every week."

Duncan raised an eyebrow. "Oh yeah? I'm going to have to stop by more often. Let me fill a plate, then I'd like to talk to Alex and the rest of you."

"Sure, so long as it's not urgent."

"Not in particular. Maybe not at all," the cop replied around a piece of bacon. He was piling on as much food as Emil had forced Jase to. "I may have an overactive imagination." He paused and gave Emil and Mackie the fisheye. "Hanging with you guys has certainly stimulated it these days."

Emil gave what he hoped was a subtle nod at Damien, who was mixing an omelet for a wobbly member clearly suffering from the previous night's exertions. "We can hold on until the others are available."

Duncan nodded. "Sure. Wish I'd thought of that," he added with a roll of his eyes.

"I'll go let Val know," Mackie chimed in. "I think Alex and Quinn retired a few hours ago, so it may take them a few minutes. I'll see if it's okay to meet in their suite."

"That would be the best place," Emil confirmed. "And thanks. We'll head up as soon as Duncan's ready."

"Got it." Mackie threw Emil a worried look then took off.

"Oh, man, eggs Benedict. I haven't had this in years. I'd like to speak with Logan. Is she around?"

"In the kitchen, last time I looked." Emil held back his worry, so as not to alarm Damien or any of the other members who'd wandered over now that the feast was obviously available.

Duncan sidled up to him with a topped-off mug and plate of food that looked like the Leaning Tower of Pisa. "Don't worry. She's not in trouble. I just think she might add some perspective to what I want to talk about."

"Fine. Let's start with the kitchen before heading to Alex's apartment. Here," he added, reaching for the mug. "I'll carry this so you can start stuffing your face."

"Thanks." The cop wasted no time digging into his breakfast as they walked. He moaned like he was getting the best blow job on the planet. "God, I could marry you for this bacon alone. What did you do to it?"

"I sprinkle a little brown sugar on it right before it's done. And no offense, Duncan, but you're not my type."

"Yeah, same here. We'd fight over who got to top. Still, I might happily bottom for the rest of my life for food this good."

Emil snorted. "Maybe I'll teach Demi what I know. That would solve your problem."

Duncan tripped over his own feet, almost dumping his plate on the floor. He swore a blue streak. "I don't know what the fuck you're talking about."

Emil chuckled. "Sure you don't. I saw you dancing with him at the wedding."

"The kid dragged me out onto the floor."

"Of course he did."

"He's stronger than he looks," the guy muttered around a mouthful of biscuit and gravy.

"I am aware."

They entered the kitchen and found Logan right where Emil had left her. She sat at the table the family often used for private, late-night meals. She'd cleaned her own plate and was nursing a mug of coffee. She stiffened ever so slightly at the sight of Duncan before relaxing once more. The fact that the mostly homeless vet trusted the cop went a long way toward allowing Emil to do the same.

"Hey, Logan," Duncan called out, "mind if I ask you a few questions?"

The woman's hackles went up immediately. "What about?"

"Nothing I think you'd be unwilling to tell me," the cop was quick to reassure her.

Emil interceded. "We're having an impromptu gathering in Alex's suite. Do you mind tagging along?"

It was important for Logan to always feel like she had a choice. It had taken a lot of patience to convince the woman to hang around the club and not out in the streets. She didn't trust easily, so the fact that she seemed to trust him a little was a point of pride. Plus, the selfish part of him couldn't help worrying about her. When he could see she was fine, it took one thing off his emotional plate for a while.

Logan didn't respond for a few long seconds. She sat staring back at him and Duncan, clearly assessing whether she was in the mood to indulge them. To his credit, the cop said nothing more. He simply scarfed down his food and waited for her to make up her mind. Emil appreciated how he understood the best way to approach someone who had lived on the streets and suffered from mental health problems. The human was all right in Emil's book, proving himself more and more each time they interacted.

"Fine." Logan stood with her mug in hand and walked over, not too slowly, yet not in any hurry, either.

Emil led the way to the elevator and the penthouse suite that his boss shared with his human lover. They were the last to arrive. Harry was sitting in a living room chair, appearing like an intense professor ready to listen to a student's presentation. Lucien and Demi, of course, were not around. Harry always tried to keep them out of the fray and was still fretting over how he'd been forced to involve Lucien briefly the last time they'd all convened.

Val and Mackie sat at the kitchen counter, wolfing down large plates of food. Apparently they'd had time to visit the buffet. Quinn perched on Alex's lap on the sofa, eating a bowl of cereal while Alex sipped at a cup of coffee. They all homed in on the trio as they entered.

Emil gave his attention first to his boss. "How come you're not eating?" It might have seemed an inconsequential topic, but food had become Emil's reason for being. He took it almost as a personal affront whenever his efforts to provide for his family went unused.

Alex gave him a pained look. "Emil, dear friend, I'm barely awake. Please take some pity on me. I promise to gorge myself on your bountiful feast once my synapses are fully functioning."

"I'm eating," Quinn mumbled.

"Cereal." Emil couldn't keep the derision from his tone.

The boy stared at his bowl. "Sometimes I'm in the mood for Froot Loops, you know?"

Alex pressed a kiss to his head. "You may have whatever you want, darling boy." He shot a warning glance at Emil.

The guy is way too protective of his lover. Then again, Emil wouldn't have liked if he weren't. Alex's boundless capacity for compassion and care was what made him the kind of leader Emil was happy to follow.

Nevertheless, he threw up his hands and said, "Fine, whatever... Maybe I should accept Duncan's proposal so I can cook for someone who appreciates it all the time."

Every pair of eyes turned to stare at the cop, who slouched down on the chair opposite Harry. He paused in his eating long enough to say, "It was a joke, although I don't know how any of you can pass up this stuff."

That reminded Emil that he still held the cop's mug. "Here," he said, setting it down on an end table. Then he stood with his legs braced and arms folded. "So, what's going on anyway?"

Duncan slurped some coffee. "Yeah right. Sorry. I forgot for a second why we're all meeting. I just came from the site of an arson that left two people dead."

"Unfortunate," Alex replied. "What does that mean for us?" His gaze narrowed in the next instant. "You think it has something to do with Dracul? *Val.*"

"On it." The security chief was already putting down his fork and picking up his phone.

"You're not going to find much in the way of details," Duncan warned. "The fire marshal is investigating still, and he'll pass it along to the Fire Investigation Unit, which is part of the state police. Nothing official has been concluded yet, but Karl and I were out there earlier this morning."

"According to the news feed, two homeless people were killed," Val added.

"Yeah, about that…" Duncan turned to Logan, who lurked by the door. "It was Bobby and Carrie, according to the ones who made it out. I'm sorry if they were friends of yours."

Logan shrugged. "I knew them. Sort of." She didn't elaborate or show any emotion. It was hard to tell what she was thinking or feeling.

"Well, the witnesses I interviewed were more cooperative than usual because one of them recognized my name. Apparently, I have some street cred, thanks to you."

Logan shrugged again. "You're all right…for a cop. So what?"

51

"So, thanks. I appreciate your vouching for me. It helped me get a better picture of what happened, and without the witnesses' cooperation, we wouldn't be as far along with the investigation."

"What exactly did they say?" Emil asked. His stomach was already aching from the mere hint that Dracul was back at it again.

"The fire appears to have been started by an explosion. One of the people in the warehouse said he thought he saw someone on the roof a few minutes before it happened. And the witnesses all seem to think the explosion came from above. Now, whether that means it occurred on a higher floor or on the roof is something investigators will figure out, once the building cools off sufficiently to go back in."

Emil said what he supposed they were all thinking. "That's it?" His tension eased down a notch.

"That's it," Duncan confirmed. "I warned you from the beginning that this was probably nothing."

"So you did." Emil decided he needed more coffee. He went to Alex's kitchen area to pour a cup. It wasn't as good as his, but good enough.

"It's just... I don't know. A three-story abandoned warehouse with multiple entry points? Why does someone bother to blow it up—and why from the top?"

"Insurance," Val called out, still searching his phone for news.

Duncan slurped and nodded once more. "Sure. They're looking into the owner and fraud is always a front-runner explanation. Plus, if you go high, it's harder for anyone to see you from the street, not that it's a well-traveled area of the city or anything."

Emil returned to the living room and sat down on the steps leading from the front entryway. He took a few sips of his coffee while he considered the situation. "There's no obvious reason to believe that Dracul is involved. Our species doesn't hang out on rooftops, as a rule."

"Right. Right." Duncan speared a piece of melon, the only healthy thing he'd taken from the buffet. "I'm just being paranoid, right?" He heaved a sigh, chewed, swallowed. "So what if all of the fire escapes had been taken down? I mean...there's other ways of going up three stories. Maybe the perp came in through a door and climbed up and out. For some reason, that doesn't occur to me, no matter how hard I think about it."

Alex hummed. "You've gained my attention more, Duncan. Is there any word on the type of explosive used?"

The cop shook his head. "They'll be working on it for sure, though."

"That information might prove very illuminating."

The ache in Emil's stomach flared. "You're thinking of Marius."

Alex pressed his mouth against Quinn's head before replying. "He does have quite the penchant for making things go boom."

"I thought he'd left the party, as it were," Emil offered, hoping that there really was no connection between this terrible event and Dracul. "He was done with the fight, wasn't he?"

"I never thought so," Val replied. "He was licking his wounds, that's all. I can't believe he'd settle down for a quiet life among the humans."

The bottom of Emil's stomach dropped. "Neither can I, I'm afraid." Marius had been another botanist on the ship, a job he'd been ill-suited for and probably pushed into by his family.

"What happened to him, exactly?" Mackie asked.

Val pulled him in for a sideways hug. "Nothing he didn't deserve. One of his bombs exploded too soon and it blew his arm off."

"Ha!" Mackie crowed. "Serves him right."

"I always thought so," Emil agreed. He hated being mean-spirited, but Dracul and his boys always brought out the worst in him. "I truly hope it's not him, though. In his own way, he's worse than Dracul."

"Is that possible?" Quinn asked in a quiet voice. His bowl of cereal sat forgotten on his lap. Yeah, this was a topic that could put almost anyone off their feed.

Alex cuddled him even closer. "He has all of Dracul's psychopathy without his self-control. It's strange. Onboard the ship, he was always so quiet and awkward. I suspected his mother sent him on the voyage just to get him out of her social orbit. It took centuries after we crashed, but eventually he came out of his shell under Dracul's careful tutelage. He's *unstable*, I'd say."

"He's out of his fucking mind," Emil felt forced to remark. The coldness in the man's expression the last time Emil had seen him still sent a shiver down his spine. He looked at Duncan. "When will we know more?"

"I can't say. I promise to keep you in the loop, of course. I'm not going to be anything more than on the periphery, I'm afraid."

"If it is Marius," Val added, "it's going to get worse very quickly. I expect the warehouse was a test case for him. He'll escalate to bigger targets with more carnage. A warehouse fire that killed a couple of homeless people won't gain the attention and create the kind of panic that Dracul is looking for." He glanced over at Logan. "Sorry… That's the hard truth."

Emil turned in time to see the woman toss her head. "It's nothing I don't already know. Those people didn't matter to whoever did it, alien or not."

Standing, Emil faced her. "To Dracul, all your people and everyone in this room are nothing of consequence."

She gave him a cynical grin. "Is that supposed to make me feel better?"

"Not in the least." He spoke to the room at large. "I guess there's nothing we can do except wait. I hate that."

"As do we all," Alex said. "We can only focus on what we can control, for now. Val, would you please pull any files you have on Marius' previous activities? It has been a while since we've dealt with him. We might find something useful. And please keep in touch, Sergeant. Our doors are always open, and food is always in the offing."

The cop grinned. "Thanks…and will do."

"If we're done, I'm going to go see how Damien is doing with the buffet." That at least was something useful he could do. And there was the boy, Jase. It might not be any of his business, but if that boy needed protection, he was going to give it. He might be able to save at least one human, even as he worried that Dracul was about to unleash misery on the rest of the city.

* * * *

Jase ignored the stares as he walked over to the bar. There weren't many members, given that it was the middle of the week and most people had jobs that made playing at a club until late at night difficult. Master didn't seem to work, at least not that Jase had noticed in the few years that he'd been enslaved by the man. Oh, there were 'business trips' filled with meetings that somehow ended with Jase kneeling before some strange man, sucking his cock to help Master's cause. But if there was a product being sold or a widget being manufactured, Jase had never seen it. Sometimes it felt as if *he* was Master's business — and perhaps it was true.

The few club members lounging about didn't bother to hide their interest. One even winked at him, as if Jase could somehow be lured away to another man's side, as if he had that choice. It made no sense, although he understood why he caught their attention. Master had sent him down in search of food after a particularly hard 'play' session and he'd made him go wearing nothing more than his black leather jock strap with the built-in butt plug. His hole was stretched unpleasantly wide, especially after the pounding Master had given it. Every step was painful. His red ass and welted back were on full display, testament to how well he took his discipline — or, really, how brutal Master was in his punishment.

No wonder he caught the attention of everyone he passed. He kept his head down, however, careful not to give encouragement or offense. He headed for the bar where the tall, scary woman stood polishing the already spotless, shiny top. He swallowed back his anxiety, trying to remember that there'd been a time in his life when he'd been happy to talk to people.

He stopped inches from the bar's edge and locked his fingers behind his back. "Excuse me, please, ma'am."

The woman ceased her cleaning. "How can I help you?"

Her tone was gentle, unhurried and unconcerned. Jase's tension dropped a notch. "My master was hoping I could order a bacon cheeseburger with lettuce, tomato and mayonnaise?"

This new club was unlike any place Master had ever taken him—not only luxurious but also open all the time and with food and alcohol always available. Master wasn't interested in some crappy pre-made snack, however. He wanted a special meal. Jase stood waiting for an answer and hoping he wouldn't have to return with something that would make Master mad. That was not going to result in a complaint to the club's management about a lack of service. No, that disappointment would be taken out on *his hide*.

The bartender alleviated his worries with a quick answer. "Sure. I'll place the order with the kitchen and it should be ready in fifteen minutes, given that Emil is still on duty. Would you like French fries with that?"

"Yes, ma'am. Thank you." Fuck, he'd forgotten that part and Master would have skinned him for it.

"You're very welcome. You don't ever have to be shy around me, honey," she added.

He dared to glance up and saw that she was smiling at him. Her expression appeared genuine, so much so that he returned it before he could catch himself. He dropped his gaze a split second later, and his cheeks heated in embarrassment—and fear. That was his constant companion, regardless of where he was and with whom. Experience had taught him that you could never tell whether someone was actually nice or only biding their time before they showed their true colors.

The bartender moved away to punch something into a computer. Jase relaxed a fraction now that no one's attention was centered on him, at least not that he could tell. Despite his pain, his stomach felt hollowed out. His last meal had been hours ago and not that much, either. He could only hope there would be enough of Master's meal leftover that he could scarf the rest. If it was the big, scary chef making it, there was every chance of that. The man frightened him more than anyone ever had, except he also had this kind way about him that almost caused Jase to let down his guard. Almost.

"Hey!"

The sudden greeting made Jase jump. He whirled to his left to find the redheaded boy who was part of the staff leaning against the bar. He hadn't heard the guy arrive and yet suddenly he was within a foot of Jase.

The boy grinned. "Sorry. I didn't mean to startle you."

Not sure of how to respond, Jase fell back on silence. He curled his fingers tightly around one another while keeping his eyes on the floor.

"I'm Mackie Stelalux, by the way. I've seen you around the last few days but I haven't had a chance to introduce myself." His tone was light and breezy.

Jase wasn't sure what to make of it. He did understand that the pregnant pause was his cue to say something. "I'm Jase, sir."

Mackie laughed. "You don't have to call me sir. I'm like the least 'sir' kind of guy around. In fact," he added with a flick of his finger at the base of his throat, "I'm the one who calls someone else sir."

Oh. Right. He hadn't focused on how the boy was also a collared slave, although his collar was of beautiful quality. It didn't look like it chafed or anything. Plus, a monogramed tag hung from the D ring. Mackie was a boy who was loved.

Jase still wasn't sure what, if anything, he should say, so he stayed silent. That didn't seem to bother Mackie at all. He started chatting away.

"Yeah, see? I'm married to the head of security, Val. He's my husband," he added for extra clarity, flashing a wedding set on his left ring finger. One of the matching bands was paved with diamonds, testament to how much his master valued him.

Marriage and a husband were something that Jase could only dream of. "You must be a very good boy." It was all he could think of saying.

Mackie laughed again, a trilling kind of giggle that held real mirth. "Oh, no… I'm a very *bad* boy. Val has to constantly correct me." His gaze roamed down Jase's body. "Looks like you've been playing hard."

Jase shivered at the reminder. It was cold in the large room, but really, it was the visceral memory of how much he'd endured in the last few hours that caused the reaction. "I'm not a very good slave," he admitted. "I need a lot of correction, too." His voice sounded pathetic and strained to his own ears.

Mackie inched closer and placed a hand on Jase's arm. "Are you okay?" The touch was oddly cool, even though the tone of voice was warm.

Jase nodded his head jerkily. "I'm getting better at pleasing my master." Or he was maturing sufficiently to accept Master's discipline without collapsing or too much sniveling. He'd gotten stronger with age.

Mackie squeezed his fingers briefly before letting go. "You know, if you ever need to talk to someone… I live here with Val and I manage the go-go boys, so listening and helping with problems is kind of my job."

Jase didn't know how to react to the offer. He sensed it was a trap, a way for Master to see if he was bad when out of sight. Telling tales, complaining, seeking a sympathetic someone to help him escape... These were the worst things he could do. Nothing made Master angrier than knowing Jase wasn't devoted to him. Jase had learned that lesson a few times in ways that had left him howling in agony and both wishing and fearing he would die from it. He wouldn't, couldn't, make that mistake again.

He said nothing, standing there silently and pretending that he hadn't understood or didn't care about the offer being made. Then it didn't matter because both of their attentions were taken by the scary chef barging up. He held a plate piled with two cheeseburgers and a mound of fries. Jase took a half-step back before remembering that avoiding punishment was one of the worst offenses.

The chef's angry gaze swept Jase from head to toe. The expression on the man's face turned extra grim. "I figured the special order was for the asshole, so I doubled it to make sure there was enough for you, too."

Jase was too stunned by the declaration to say anything, even if he'd been expected to. Mackie made a small noise in the back of his throat and looked away. The chef slammed the plate on the bar counter and, with a huff, strode off.

Jase swallowed past the lump of fear clogging his throat. "I'm sorry. I didn't mean to make him mad."

Mackie patted his arm before picking up the plate and holding it out. "Oh, sweetie, you didn't. Emil — and believe me when I say I love him like an uncle — is on a mission to fatten up the world. He takes it as a personal affront if everyone isn't stuffing their face twenty-four-seven. Here... Take this to your master before it gets cold."

"Oh, right. Thank you." He grabbed the plate and appreciated the warmth that seeped into his hands. He turned, still rattled, yet mindful that only one man in the world could truly hurt him.

"You're welcome, and please remember I'm here if you need me."

Jase nodded in appreciation. Surely there was no way that small gesture could be interpreted as disrespectful or traitorous to Master. Then again, he should have learned by now that Master was far cleverer than Jase would ever be. He knew everything and was good at laying traps that led to Jase being hurt more and more. The presence of an extra burger, even though all meals were included in the club fee, could set Master off. He would likely think Jase had wrangled it out of the kitchen.

He thought briefly of stuffing it down before he returned to the playroom. But no, Master would smell it on his breath and the punishment for eating without permission was brutal. Jase was trapped. No matter what he did, it was going to be the wrong thing. He should know that by now. He should be resigned to his fate. Nothing and no one was coming to rescue him. His only option was none at all. He simply had to endure until Master killed him.

Death was his one way out.

Chapter Four

Dracul's Castle, Wales

"Excellent! I knew Marius wouldn't disappoint." Dracul kept his gaze glued to the flat-screen across the room.

Dafydd looked away. There was only so much carnage and the misery that came with it he could tolerate. The suffering of people in a city across the ocean barely registered, in any event, compared to his own existential and personal issues. He rubbed at a stitch in his side caused by his rapidly swelling belly. The daily vomiting had ceased, but the discomfort of his body accommodating something it wasn't designed for had ratcheted up. This time around, he knew what to expect, which made it worse somehow. He couldn't pretend that anything other than a pregnancy was happening.

His skin rippled as the alien being inside him writhed in its fluid-filled sack. He tried to summon, as he had before, some paternal affection for what would be his son. He couldn't. It was only the one, thank God, not the twins he'd carried the first time. Enough of Dracul's genes polluted Earth as it was. Dafydd had loved his boys at first. It was only human to do so, after all. Eventually, the fact that they were wholly Dracul's offspring had killed his feelings for them. Not that he'd seen either of his sons for months... They still hid from their vicious father's ire somewhere deep in the bowels of the old castle—out of sight and out of mind, most likely. Dracul had turned his focus to an almost-son, someone as psychotic as he. Marius' dead eyes always sent a shiver through Dafydd that rivaled the kind elicited by Dracul's attention.

"Ha!" Dracul crowed. "Look at them scurrying about like the vermin they are. A little explosion, a few dead bodies, and they act like their world is coming to an end. Invading this miserable planet in force would have been an easy conquest."

The madman could barely contain his glee, jerking about on his stomach like a landed fish while poor Brenin did his best to provide a massage. The boy hadn't quite become accepting of his situation. He'd ceased fighting off the rapes and had gained proficiency at pleasing Dracul's sadistic needs. He had adapted more easily in that regard than Dafydd had. But this evidence of Dracul's murderous bent was proving too difficult for the poor boy to accept. He kept his gaze averted to the dreadful news flashing in front of him.

Petru lurked to one side, like the ghoul he was. "Yes, sir. Marius has elevated the fear over there in quick order. I think his plan of small explosions in various locations in quick succession shall prove more disruptive than one large one."

Dafydd knew nothing of war strategy—less than he did about the way Dracul's mind worked—but even he understood the plan was an ingenious one. A big, traumatic event would cause the people of Boston to mourn for a long time, but they would recover their normalcy quickly, as they had before. Small disasters that struck without an obvious pattern would put them on edge as they anxiously went through their days wondering if they would be at the center of the next one. Yes, that would serve Dracul's interests very nicely indeed.

Dracul hummed in agreement. "Marius is the best of all of you. It's a pity he has such a short attention span. I could use him more consistently if he were stable and reliable. It would also help if he could stop blowing off body parts."

Dafydd nearly grinned internally at that remark. He'd only seen Dracul's crazy acolyte a few times, yet on each occasion some extra bit of him was missing. His endless experimentation with explosives was proving to be almost as problematic for him as for anyone else. In his more morbid reflections, Dafydd wondered if the guy was self-harming in an effort to slowly remove himself from a place he'd never wanted to be. Too bad he was taking many innocent lives with him, if that were the case. There was nothing amusing about Marius.

"It's true, sir," Petru allowed. "He will grow weary of this game. We can only appreciate how much the Stelalux clan must be aggrieved by all this."

"Yes, there's always that." Dracul sighed before turning his head sharply to glare over his back.

"Careful, slut. Your nails need trimming. See to it before you touch me again or I'll have your useless fingers cut off."

Brenin paused for a moment, head bowed. "Yes, Master. Sorry, Master." He glanced at Dafydd once Dracul's attention was back on the screen.

Dafyyd tried to reassure him using only his eyes. It was cold comfort, he knew. They were almost never able to speak with each other without Dracul or Petru or someone else listening in. Even then, Dafydd still didn't dare share his plans with the boy. He simply couldn't trust Brenin not to betray him. No matter what scruples someone held, Dracul had a way of making good men bad. Besides, he thought with another rub at his side, there was time. Nothing could happen until Dracul's spawn was cut out of him.

He just hoped the birth would be the beginning and not the end.

* * * *

Emil fled Alex's office, unable to continue watching the horror playing out once again on the television. Five dead, a dozen injured… It was too much to bear. A peaceful wintery night at a local club had turned into a battlefield. If there had been any doubt about the warehouse explosion being some isolated and random event, it was gone now. The newscasters were already speculating about it being a terrorist attack. And it was…just not the kind they thought. After a few months' lull, Dracul was back in action. The city was going to suffer yet again.

Because of us. Emil couldn't help the guilt swamping him. He knew the others felt the same, and if they didn't already, Duncan would be by at some point with his understandable anger. If it would help, Emil would gladly hide away somewhere in a corner of the globe where others wouldn't be hurt. Alex and the rest would, as well. But, as they'd told Duncan and those allies who'd come before him, they weren't the reason Dracul sowed havoc. They were the check on him. Leaving Boston wouldn't make things better. It would only allow Dracul a clearer shot to harm the people here or wherever else the man chose to focus his attention.

They were caught in an ever-tightening net with the only way out being the total annihilation of Dracul and his minions. The question was how? After centuries of trying, they hadn't managed to achieve it. Maybe they never would.

Strategy was not his role. He was a scientist by training and a cook by choice. So, with nothing better to do, he went to his happy place, as the humans liked to say. He headed for the kitchen. In the middle of the night, with his anger vibrating in his bones, his best choice was bread. Making bread took time, physical energy, and it made the kitchen smell marvelous.

He started with his favorite, a sweet almond-flavored braided bread. Into his large mixing bowl, he put a packet of yeast, warm water, a small amount of sugar and flour. After a few minutes of gentle mixing, he let it sit with a cloth cover draped over the bowl. He spent the time while he waited heating milk and melting butter, something he should have done first. With his frustration level rising, he didn't have the patience to *mis en place*. It might not be the best way to bake, but it suited him at the moment. He could work faster than a human could, although he was careful not to be indiscreet about it. Damien was known to come in when he couldn't sleep in the dead of night. Like Emil, the human used cooking as a form of therapy. It wouldn't do if he found Emil flittering about the kitchen at supersonic speed.

He uncovered the bowl to see the bubbling yeast and took a deep sniff. There was something so delightful in that smell. He never tired of it. After carefully mixing in the rest of the ingredients, he turned the dough onto a floured surface and began to knead it. He loved this part of the process. There was something satisfying about the rhythm and physicality of working the dough. Once again, he took care to use human speed. It was better that way, a controlled expression of his anger and worry. He pressed down with his palms, rolled the dough, pressed again. Occasionally, he whacked it against the surface to switch the kneading method.

He didn't stop until the dough was as soft as a baby's bottom. Not that he'd had much experience with how that felt, but somehow he just knew when he'd reached the right consistency. Cooking came naturally to him, and if there was some good to come of being stranded on this strange world, it was that he had the chance to cook. On the home world, much of food processing was automated and it was rare for a male to make it a hobby. His mother would have nixed the idea regardless. That much he knew.

Next, he placed the ball into an oiled bowl, covered it to give it a nice warm place to rise and started on the next loaf. This one would be a dense, multi-wholegrain with fruit and nuts. He'd learned it centuries ago and it nourished and stuck with one for hours. Entire armies had marched on such bread. He'd already made the poolish that would serve as the mother dough and make the end product more complex in flavor and last longer. It would be reserved for family only. The club members liked refined food and never quite appreciated his more rustic efforts.

Emil worked through the quiet of the night, away from the angst and debates about what to do going on in Alex's office. The club was too far away from the carnage of the bombing for him to hear anything even with his ultrasensitive alien ears. He liked the quiet, not bothering with turning on music. The hours ticked by unnoticed as he moved from one type of bread to another—sourdough, pumpkin, corn... It was all good and much of it would enhance the omelets he intended to make for breakfast soon.

The kitchen became enveloped with a myriad of smells. Emil lined up each loaf as they came out of the oven. In a way, they were his soldiers in this war, the one thing he could muster to help others in the battle. He turned away to start a pot of coffee. Without looking at the clock, he could tell dawn was breaking and that Damien and those club members who'd never left would be looking for a hit of caffeine to jump-start their days.

The sound of footsteps caught his attention. They were human, yet not any that he recognized. There was no Mackie-bounce or Quinn's sure tread. These were hesitant, fearful even. The scent followed a moment later, and Emil closed his eyes briefly against the wave of tension that washed over him. Even with the kitchen filled with the smells of freshly baked bread, the sweet one that he associated with the sad little human cut through easily. Emil was careful to turn slowly, so as not to scare the already easily spooked boy.

Jase approached with hunched shoulders and a downward gaze. Like the last time Emil had seen him, he was naked, except for a tight jockstrap that crushed his cock and balls and invaded his ass with an obvious plug. And as always, his satiny pale skin was marred with angry red welts and dark bruises. Emil frowned at the sight and had to bite back a growl. Jase's fringe of blond hair flopped down over his eyes, so he couldn't see Emil's reaction, not that he looked at anything other than the floor.

With hands balled into fists, Emil pushed a quiet question past his pressed lips. "How can I help you?"

The boy still jerked at the sound of Emil's voice. His Adam's apple bobbled before he answered. "I'm sorry to disturb you, sir, but my master was hoping for breakfast, and the bar only has late-night snacks."

Emil really wanted to say that the asshole could fuck off, but twenty-four-hour food service was part of the membership. Special orders outside of normal mealtimes were permitted if kitchen staff was available, which obviously he was. Plus, he wouldn't do anything that could lead the man to take his anger out on the boy.

"Of course," he said, careful to keep his tone neutral. "Is there anything in particular he'd like?"

"Two poached eggs, please, on rye toast with some fruit on the side. If you please, sir." It didn't take an alien's senses to tell how nervous and tired the boy was. His voice quavered and his body trembled. Fine goosebumps showed all over his exposed skin, although it wasn't necessarily from feeling cold. It had to be unnerving to stand essentially naked in front of a stranger. The boy's dignity had been stripped from him as surely as his clothing had been.

Once again, Emil wanted to wrap him in his arms and carry him to bed, not that he had any plans about what he'd do once he put the boy there. His first instinct was to protect and coddle. Any more carnal interests needed to be shoved down and out of sight. That they were there at all scared the crap out of him. Yet, he made an involuntary move to scoop up the human before catching himself.

Instead, he nodded once in quiet acquiescence, an effort lost on someone not looking at him. "Sure," he said, "no problem."

He started to go get the eggs then changed his mind. The asshole could wait. Just because Emil couldn't whisk the boy away to the safety of his bedroom didn't mean he couldn't make his stay in the kitchen better. He went to where he kept a clean set of whites hanging and grabbed them off the hanger. It wasn't much, but it was better than nothing. He approached the boy slowly with the jacket outstretched.

"Here. Put this on."

Jase jerked his head and blinked a few times before tipping his chin down again. "Um, no thank you, sir. I'm fine," he added.

Emil stood staring at the top of the boy's head for a few seconds, debating whether he should push the issue. It really wasn't any of his business whether this boy played rough games with an asshole who didn't appreciate him. Not Emil's concern, either, if the games were getting out of hand and hurting the kid. Nope, Emil was a cook, not a babysitter or a knight in shining armor coming to the rescue.

Fuck it.

"Put it on." He made it an order, leaving no room for refusal.

Jase quivered some more, obviously uncertain how to react, before putting his arms through the proffered jacket. As he turned, it gave Emil a chance to see his back. It was worse than the front and it seemed impossible for anyone to want that kind of harm inflicted on himself. Hardening his heart for the moment, he helped Jase tug the jacket on, buttoning part of it to keep it closed. His fingers brushed the boy's chest, proving that it was smooth and silky where it was unmarred.

The sleeves were comically long, so Emil rolled them up to Jase's slender wrists. It was like dressing a child, except young as he was, Jase had a certain maturity to him, physically anyway. It was impossible for Emil to ignore the tug he felt, much as he tried. That urge to move them both into the bedroom reared again. Worse, his cock rose from its usually dormant state to take an interest. Thank God his whites hung long and loose enough to cover that inconvenient truth.

Stepping back from temptation, he nodded. "There…that's better. It's too cold in here to be naked." It was a ridiculous statement given the heat from the baking, yet he knew Jase would never gainsay him.

The boy stood with arms hanging down straight, his thin legs now the only part of his body other than his head and a bit of neck and fingers showing. It was good. It gave the boy some privacy, although Emil's memory of what was covered did little to cool his heated reaction.

Don't be like the asshole. Don't exploit him.

The admonishment helped a little, as did the idea that the boy was probably hungry. He was certainly way too skinny. Feeding him would be the next thing to do.

Emil pointed to the table in the corner. "Go sit down. I'll bring you something to eat."

"T-thank you, sir, but my master will feed me from his plate."

Yeah, Emil could only imagine what little scraps the asshole bothered to throw Jase's way. "Sit," he ordered, before turning to his line of bread soldiers.

He didn't bother to make sure Jase was obeying. The light patter of feet told him as much. Emil cut a thick slice of the fruit and nut loaf, slathered butter on it, and put it on a plate, along with a scoop of fruit salad he had ready in the fridge. He also poured a large glass of milk and carried it all over to where Jase sat nervously on the edge of a chair.

Emil put the plate and glass gently in front of him. "Here, eat and drink all of this."

Jase peeped at him from under his fringe. "It's a lot, sir. I don't think I can eat it all. Truly."

Emil frowned. "Nonsense. You're not Scarlett O'Hara. You don't have to pretend that you eat like a bird and you don't have to worry about your waistline. This is good, hearty fare. You know… Back in the day, armies marched with food like that in their bellies and won battles. If you're going to let some asshole beat the crap out of you, you need to at least keep up your strength."

He hadn't meant to be so belligerent about it—or judgmental. And he really should stop referring to the club member as an asshole, except—fuck it—he couldn't. The way Jase's shoulders hunched in on themselves made Emil feel like a real son of a bitch, like he'd kicked an already-whipped puppy.

"Please," he said, trying for a different, more productive tack. "Take small bites. I'm a cook, and I like to see people enjoy my food." Okay, now he was guilt-tripping the kid, but damn if it didn't work.

Picking up the slice with one delicate hand, Jase nibbled at the corner. His lips quirked a tiny smile as he chewed. "It's delicious," he said after swallowing and before he took another larger bite.

Pleased, Emil nodded. "That's it. Good boy."

That praise caused Jase to smile more broadly. It seemed like it didn't take much to bring the boy out of his shell. The fact that he needed the affirmation made Emil feel sad. There was nothing beneficial about dwelling on it, however. So, after watching Jase eat another bite and drink some of the milk, he headed over to the stove to fix the asshole's eggs.

Poaching eggs was hard to get right. He considered briefly overcooking them, but pride and concern for the boy killed that idea. So instead, he slid two perfectly cooked eggs onto equally perfect slices of toasted rye bread. He added a scoop of mixed fruit to the plate, swiped away a few dribbles and put the meal to one side.

"Does he want coffee?" he called over his shoulder, already headed for the pot.

"Yes, please, sir. Black," came the reply from across the room.

Emil thought the boy's voice sounded stronger. At least less afraid, and he counted that as a win. He poured a cup of coffee into some good china that he kept for fussy club members. It wasn't because the asshole deserved it. Emil simply wanted Jase to bring something that would appease the man. He arranged both the cup and the plate of food on a simple wooden tray. Jase should find it easy to carry upstairs where the asshole undoubtedly lay waiting like the fucking

Queen of Sheba for his breakfast. A fantasy flashed through his head where he marched to the playroom and first dumped the coffee on the guy's head before smashing the eggs in his face. *Oh yeah, that would be very satisfying.* Too bad it would give Alex fits, and again, it would only end in trouble for the boy.

He turned and pulled up short before he bumped into said boy. Jase had returned with an empty plate and glass. "I'm sorry, sir. I, um…thank you," the human stuttered through an unnecessary, yet likely automatic, apology.

"You're welcome." Emil plucked the offering from Jase's hands and placed it on the counter. "I have your… *Don't say 'asshole'*…a tray for you to take." *There. No need to even bring up the recipient.*

"Thank you, sir."

Shit. All that 'sir' business was grating on Emil's last fucking nerve, not that there was anything to be done about it. However, he had an impulsive need to keep the boy hanging around longer. He blocked Jase when he moved to get the tray.

"Hey, there's something I want you to try."

Jase carded his hair away from his face and blinked a few times. "Sir?"

"Come here." Emil slid over to where the sweet almond bread sat. Slicing a piece off, he held it with his fingertips. "Try this for me. I want to know if I balanced the flavors right." That was a lie. He'd made it a thousand times over. He simply didn't want the boy to leave quite yet.

As he held it out for Jase to take, Emil couldn't help but stare intently at his face, such perfectly formed features with high cheekbones and a cupid-bow mouth. Those lips opened while he looked at them. Instead of taking the slice from Emil's fingers, Jase took a small bite with his straight white teeth, much like a horse would a carrot or an apple. And Emil wanted to run his palm down the boy's head, just as he would a horse. He wanted to gentle him to his hand, to his touch. Except this wasn't his boy and never would be.

The look on Jase's face as he chewed was the happiest Emil had seen to date, not that he was familiar with the human at all. Still, he was gratified by the reaction, even more so when, uninvited, the boy took another bite. Then another, until there was only a small piece left in Emil's hand. With his gaze fixed on that mouth, Emil slowly fed it to him. He let his finger brush against the boy's lips and dared to swipe a crumb away with the tip of his thumb.

A slight shiver ran through Jase. Emil would have missed it if he hadn't been concentrating so hard on everything about the human. His body responded with renewed interest, his cock not only twitching but swelling within the confines of his pants. His nostrils flared in an involuntary effort to take the boy's scent in deeply. There was a heady mixture of sweetness with a hint of nervousness that might be part of arousal, yet more likely was simply fear.

Emil forced himself to take a step back. At the same time, Jase removed the whites Emil had dressed him in. He silently held the jacket out. Emil took it without saying anything. He didn't trust himself to speak. What was there to say? *Don't go. Stay with me. I'll take care of you.* He pressed his lips together to keep all those words inside. He had no business uttering anything of the kind. Who was he to interfere with a relationship that, while he didn't understand it, was something Jase had appeared to seek? Besides, nothing had changed in the last thousand years that made it any easier or more sensible for Emil to get involved with a human.

Jase picked up the tray. "Thank you, sir...for everything," he added and shot a quick smile in Emil's direction.

When the boy had left his line of sight, Emil brought the jacket to his nose and inhaled deeply. His balls nearly erupted at the hit of scent. He held himself in check with an effort that *hurt*. If he was going to function at all for the rest of the day, he needed to take care of his sudden and unwanted arousal. Usually, he waited until night, in his own bed, to satisfy this most basic of needs. He often felt a kind of Puritan embarrassment about it, testament to how he'd spent too long on this planet. No one on his home world would have thought twice about it, although back there, an endless supply of willing men ensured no one had to be alone.

Still clutching the jacket, he raced to his small office in the back of the kitchen. No one ever entered without knocking, yet he locked the door anyway. He also kept a small fridge with a homemade lock that ensured no one could ever see what he kept there. It wasn't merely sexual release that he craved. A terrible thirst suddenly plagued him, a reminder that it had been a while since he'd last fed. He pulled out a bag and, after popping its seal, began sucking down its contents as is. He was too on edge to bother with warming it in his small microwave.

The first slug went straight to his cock. Nothing goosed his arousal like the taste of the one thing that his species and humans shared in particular. They both needed this stuff coursing through their body to survive. Humans might not drink it in as obvious a fashion as his people did, yet they indulged in lots of ways, from rare steaks to blood pudding. Yeah, there was nothing better, not even bread.

He flopped into his worn leather chair and shoved his whites up with his free hand before unzipping his pants. His dick poked out of his boxers, happy to be free of its confines. Shoving away the thin material that still covered his shaft, he palmed it then sighed through his nose. He sucked and jerked in a synchronized rhythm. This was familiar territory. He had self-gratification mastered to a quick and brutal science. He knew right down to the number of strokes and sucks how long it would take for him to empty both the blood bag and his balls. No one knew his body or his needs better.

And if he pictured a pretty human boy with white-blond hair and a wan smile as he groaned his way through his orgasm, so what? Whom did it hurt? He could imagine how it might feel to press his dick into a tight and welcoming hole. Soft, silky wetness would envelope his shaft in undulating waves, gripping him with a fierceness that would prove he was welcome, not feared. He'd drape his big frame over the smaller one, covering it completely, taking it within his embrace and holding it close. They would shudder and gasp together, he and the boy, finding their release in each other's hold so that their sweat and scents mingled. He would hold the human so tightly and claim him so completely that no one and nothing would ever get between them.

Emil's eyes slammed shut as his seed spilled over his fist and the last of the blood slid down his throat. He bucked his hips into his curled fingers and wished there were something else, someone else. His hands went slack as the tension drained out of him. The blood bag dropped to the floor, and his cock flopped against his abdomen. He sat sprawled with his head back and his chest heaving. Some part of his brain urged him to get up, clean up and go back to work.

At the moment, he couldn't muster the energy and vaguely worried that he'd never be able to do so again.

* * * *

"It took you long enough, stupid slut."

"I'm sorry, Master." Jase didn't bother to defend himself. Master didn't care about reality, only about his own needs and perceptions. How much time had actually passed didn't matter. The drugs the man took warped his sense of it, anyway.

"Coffee first," Master said with a wave of his hand, as if Jase were going to do anything other than race over to where he lay on a couch.

Jase knelt by his head and placed the tray carefully on the side table. Then he picked up the coffee, held in a beautiful porcelain cup and saucer, and handed it over with as much care as he could. That didn't matter, either. Master grabbed the cup and left the saucer. He slurped noisily while he idly stroked his dick. Despite having gotten off a few times throughout the night, he was still hard. That was drugs, too. All those warnings about erections lasting longer than four hours didn't seem to faze Master at all.

"I'll have to beat you extra hard later for your slowness," Master said between swallows.

"Yes, Master." Jase wondered why the man thought he was holding back. The horrible aches and pains currently plaguing his body laid waste to any claim that he'd gone easy on him so far.

And yet, Jase felt better than usual because his stomach was comfortably full. That was the big cook's doing. The man was scary as hell, but also kind. The duality of it confused Jase. In his experience, no one was nice without wanting something in return. And there was usually a strong correlation between a man's size and his level of brutality. The bigger a man was, the more vicious. Why then had the man fed him so sweetly from his hand, and why did Jase feel safe when he was with him? Both were true, so much so that even back in the cruel orbit of Master, a warm sense of comfort blanketed him.

Master pushed to a sitting position, swinging his legs over the edge of the couch. He grabbed the fork and started eating. "Don't just sit there like an idiot," he said as he chewed. "Put that mouth of yours to good use. You have to earn your breakfast, or are you still so stupid that you've forgotten that?"

"Yes, Master." Any other day in the last few years, Jase would have approached a morning blow job with both hope and revulsion. Not this one, though. Cum wasn't going to be the first thing to hit his stomach today, and that was a minor miracle.

Inching forward on his knees, he placed himself between Master's legs and bent over to take the stiff dick bobbing between them into his mouth. The first taste was sour, naturally, having been inside Jase's ass recently and no shower in between. He suppressed his revulsion from long practice and worked his tongue around the shaft to clean it off. Then he got to sucking in earnest, taking it deeper into his mouth and eventually down his throat. He cupped the heavy balls with one hand and massaged the base of the dick with his other.

He'd become adept at taking himself somewhere far away from his horrid life where he serviced men in debasing ways. Usually he had nothing but fantasies based on what little TV he watched and books he was allowed to read. This time, however, he had a real place to travel inside his mind. He imagined being back in the kitchen, snuggled warm within the over-large chef's jacket. The yeasty smell of freshly baked bread invaded his nostrils, not the funk of a man's crotch. He could imagine being in a safe, lovely space where nobody hurt him while he filled his stomach. The thought sustained him as he worked Master's cock to completion.

It didn't take long for Master to come, his groans muted by a mouthful of food. Jase swallowed the cock all the way down so that the taste of cum never hit his tongue. He consumed every spurt before pulling back, careful to lick the dick clean before letting it go completely. He coughed as quietly as he could and, sitting back on his heels, dared to wipe his mouth with the back of his hand.

Master chuckled and tossed the fork on the plate. "I hope you liked the meal I just gave you because it's the only one you're getting for a while. Next time, tell that hulking ogre who runs the kitchen to be more generous with my meals." He gulped at his coffee. "With the dues I'm paying, they damn well should give me more."

"Yes, Master." Jase silently hoped that Master would order him to go back to the kitchen. The man who ran it was big, but he had his own kind of beauty. All that black hair, messily sticking up around his head, strong facial features and muscles that made Master look like a stringy boy... They should have revolted Jase. Somehow, they didn't. The odd coolness of his skin, the little Jase had felt, was in strange contrast to the utter warmth of his gaze. Yes, it would be lovely to bask in those eyes some more.

But Master didn't send him back. He finished his coffee, stood and dragged Jase by his collar to the St. Andrew's cross. After securing Jase in painfully tight bindings, he took another hit of what had to be cocaine. Seeing it sent fear coursing through Jase. The drugs made everything worse, and since joining the club, in only a few days, Master's use of it had escalated. As Master approached with a rubber flogger swinging from his hand, Jase wondered how much longer he could take this punishment.

Chapter Five

Jase hugged the wall for support. He'd never been in such intense pain before. He didn't think anything was truly damaged, yet he wasn't able to shake off the play session as easily as he usually did. Every step was agony and not a bit of his skin seemed to be unmarred. A deep ache inside his ass told him that he was close to the breaking point and there was even a trace of blood on his thighs, not that anyone could see anything. With Master passed out cold, Jase had grabbed one of the terry-cloth robes in the playroom. At least now no one in the club would see as much of him. He just wanted a shower somewhere away from Master's prying eyes and ears.

He'd heard there was a shower in the go-go boys' dressing room. He was hoping no one would be there, or, if so, that they wouldn't mind his using the facilities. Using the back staircase to avoid patrons, he went to the lower level and snuck along the hallway. Although he didn't run into anyone along his journey, luck wasn't entirely with him. He could hear voices as he approached what he thought was the right place. He shuffled in on quiet feet to find Mackie and another boy sitting around chatting. They stopped as soon as they saw him.

Mackie smiled. "Hi, Jase. Come on in."

He tried to return the look and knew he failed. "Thanks. I hope you don't mind. I was hoping to use your shower. I didn't want to wake my master."

"Of course, sweetie. Shawn was about to head out to dance and I'm being lazy. No problem at all."

"Thanks," Jase said again and made his way past them to the bathroom area. He was relieved to see that no one else was around and that the showers were private. He preferred to relieve what he could of his misery without concerned eyes taking stock of his condition and awkward questions being asked about it. He was aware that by the standards of the average BDSM relationship, Master used him to an extreme that most would find disturbing. He was pretty sure Mackie would, based on the questions he'd already asked.

After turning on the shower and adjusting the temperature, he quickly stripped out of the robe and stepped under the spray. For once, he wasn't wearing even his jockstrap and plug. Every inch of his body was free to be washed, but the sting of the warm water then the soap, had him biting back grunts and moans. The pain was nothing, however, in the larger scheme of things, and getting clean overrode all other considerations at the moment.

Although it was tempting to stand under there in both pleasure and pain, he feared Master waking before he returned. The man's habits and schedule had become very erratic since he'd joined the club. With the drug use added in, Jase was having a hard time predicting his actions and his moods. Jase would be in trouble for leaving to shower without permission, as it was. There was no need to add to Master's ire.

Jase washed quickly so as not to be a nuisance, either, for the boys who depended on this bathroom. Although the club wasn't all that busy from what he'd seen earlier in the night, they must work up a sweat dancing, regardless. And with the club members constantly pawing at them at a minimum, he could imagine they were almost as desperate to wash as he was, not that he'd ever seen any of them other than with a smile on his face. They seemed happy in their work. Then again, Jase put up a good front, too. He'd learned never to show how unhappy he was. Honesty and sincerity only got him more punishment. Perhaps the boys here were as trapped and miserable as he was.

With his shower done, he dried off with a nearby towel and slipped the robe back on. All he had to do was rush back to the playroom without attracting any more attention. His luck still didn't hold, however. Mackie remained sitting in the outer room, although the other boy had left. The redheaded boy looked at him with too-knowing eyes.

"Are you okay?"

"I'm fine." Jase tried to give an upbeat tone but feared he failed.

"Huh." Mackie stood, his gaze roaming up and down Jase. "Are you sure? Seems to me you and your master have been playing pretty much nonstop for, like, a day now. You look kind of beat-up."

Jase grimaced before the expression morphed into a too-bright smile. "That's the idea, right?"

"Not necessarily." Mackie took a step closer. "There are limits. It's supposed to be fun for both of you." His gaze pierced Jase. "You are into this, right? You understand what you've agreed to and how this is supposed to work, using a safeword and everything?"

What's a safeword? Jase actually did know what that meant, although he'd never been allowed to use one. His stray thought had been a snarky one. It had already been asked and answered years ago. *Safewords are for poseurs, boy. You're a real slave.* That particular lesson had been delivered along with a vicious beating and fucking that had left Jase incapacitated for days. Jase had never dared raise the issue again.

He tried to act nonchalant. "Yeah, sure. I know the drill."

Mackie looked skeptical. "Do you? How long have you and Washburn been together? I mean, you must be new to the scene."

Jase huffed, chafing at the amount of time the pointless conversation was wasting and worried that the delay was going to be taken out literally on his hide. "Not really. I've been Master's slave for years." He knew the moment the words were out of his mouth that he'd said the wrong thing. Exhaustion and pain had loosened his tongue. Mackie's eyes were wide as he stared at him.

'Never tell people any detail about us, boy. That's up to me. You keep your pretty, slutty mouth shut. Understand?' he'd said.

Swallowing hard, he struggled for a way to backpedal. "I mean, we've been together for a few months. It kind of seems longer, you know? Because it's so awesome, I've kind of lost track of time. And I've been away from home for years, though. Same old story… No one wants a gay kid polluting the family."

The lie came easily because it was so often true, just not in his case. He backed away as he spoke. "Thanks again for the use of the shower. I'll see you around."

He turned and fled, fear making his pain a distant second in his mind.

* * * *

Emil sat with his head lying on the back of Alex's office couch and stared at the ceiling, not that there was anything remotely interesting about the white expanse above him. It was just that there were only so many times he could listen in on the endless speculation about what Dracul was up to and the best way to find his latest rabid dog set on the city of Boston.

"The FBI, Homeland Security and even the AT-fucking-F is involved," Duncan was saying.

Emil had to give it to the guy. He was running back and forth between his job and keeping the family abreast of the progress of the investigation. He was looking more and more like the walking dead and had waved aside the food Emil had brought in favor of a healthy glassful of Scotch.

"They're analyzing the composition of the explosives. It doesn't seem to be anything run-of-the-mill."

"Marius is very inventive," Emil chimed in, not bothering to move his head.

"He was the first to figure out a way to produce gunpowder using refined saltpeter," Val added from where Emil knew he still stood by Alex's desk, never far away from his captain.

"I thought that was the French," Duncan remarked. "Damn, is there nothing you guys haven't had your fingers in since you arrived?"

Emil lifted his head and stared at the cop. "Very little, I'm afraid, despite the best efforts of those of us in this room. At least all Marius' tinkering eventually cost him his arm for his troubles, along with a few other less-noticeable parts."

"You don't mean…" The human waved in the general direction of his lap.

"I do." At the look of horror on the man's face, Emil chuckled. "No more than he deserved. He has also lost part of an ear and a fingertip or two. Maybe other stuff. Marius doesn't care. He's that weird by any species' standards."

Duncan frowned into his glass. "You can't regenerate your body parts or anything?"

Emil smiled at the question. "We're not amphibians."

The cop shrugged. "Just wondering. I suppose it's good news you aren't that indestructible."

The bit of humor already draining from him, Emil would have returned to his lazy position except Mackie came rushing in.

Val went on high alert. "What is it?"

Mackie went straight toward him and wrapped his arms around his waist. "I think something's wrong with Jase."

"What?" Emil jumped to his feet, all trace of ennui gone in a flash. His heart raced and blood pounded in his head. "What's wrong with him?"

Instead of answering him directly, Mackie looked at his husband. "What have you learned in your background check of him and Washburn?"

"Nothing of note." He ran his palm down Mackie's head. "What has you concerned?"

"Jase just told me that he and Washburn have been together for years. I mean, he backpedaled and said he meant months, but I'm not buying it."

Years. Emil didn't have to do much math. "He's only eighteen." He was surprised at how calm he sounded, given the fact that his fangs were starting to descend.

Val shook his head. "I don't know. According to my deep dive, Jase is who Washburn says he is and was born a little more than eighteen years ago in a small Louisiana town. His father died when he was young. His mother remarried then died some years later. I couldn't find any record of his graduating high school, but lots of humans don't finish their education."

"He said he'd run away because he was gay," Mackie informed everyone.

"If that's true, there was no police report of his being missing."

Duncan stood. "Maybe his stepfather didn't bother reporting it. If he didn't like Jase's orientation, he was probably glad to see the back of him. It's an all-too-common tale, and I'm preaching to the choir, I know," he added with a scratch of his head.

"I think he was telling the truth the first time," Mackie insisted, his face becoming pinched. "And I think things are getting out of control with Washburn. That boy is *hurting* and if he's a happy slave… Well," he huffed, "I'm not buying it. He's in trouble, I'm telling you."

That was all Emil needed to hear. His fangs dropped and he yanked off his jacket as he tore out of the room. He heard his name called as if from a distance. He paid no mind. His focus was on getting to Jase. With this blood rushing through his veins, he let loose his natural strength and speed. He took the back stairs to the second floor without thought of any humans possibly seeing him. Nothing mattered except getting to the boy and stopping whatever horror was happening to him. The primitive instinct to protect had taken over him, body and brain. His vision was clouded with images of tearing a man to shreds.

He bounded up the stairs in a blur and punched through the hallway door. Scent carried him unerringly to the right room. He kicked this door open hard enough to send it hanging off its hinges. As he entered the room, the roar he'd been holding back escaped past his lips. A tableau froze in front of him. A naked man stood holding an equally naked and kneeling boy by his hair. They both turned startled eyes on him that quickly turned into terror.

Emil's gaze homed in on a red blotch blooming on Jase's cheek. The sight robbed him of whatever rational thought was left in his head. Going straight for Washburn, he was on him in a millisecond, grabbing the guy by the throat and yanking him away from Jase. A squeal was cut short by Emil pressing his fingers into the soft flesh and lifting the human to eye level. He opened his mouth and hissed, letting his fangs and his fury show. Washburn's eyes bulged and his lips flapped in a noiseless blubber. The acrid smell of piss hit Emil's nose, but he was too focused on the scent of fear and the panicked pounding of the human's heart.

I will kill you. I will tear your flesh from your bones and eat every bite with relish.

The primitive thoughts flickered through his mind as he propelled his enemy back against the nearest wall. He didn't bother to expose the man's throat, having no interest in ingesting his blood. He only wanted to make it flow and send the sadist to his death so that he could never again touch the beautiful boy and make him hurt.

"Emil!" Alex's voice barely cut through the fog of Emil's righteous anger.

Multiple fingers encircled his arms and tugged in an effort to get him to let go. He hissed even more and twisted, batted at the men attached to the grasping fingers with his free hand, to no avail. Then he lunged forward to take a bite out of the man's reddened face. An arm got in his way so he latched on to cloth instead of flesh. With a growl, he shook free like an enraged animal and tried again. More hands and more shouting and too many people pulling his arms and waist, prying his fingers loose... He fought them all until a quiet sobbing somehow cut both through the noise around him and clambering inside his head.

Emil opened his hand and let the human drop from his grip. He stumbled back, vaguely aware that not only Alex and Val had been wrestling him, but Duncan and Harry, as well. None of that mattered. His attention was taken by the sight of Jase curled on the floor in Mackie's arms. The boy was staring at Emil with wide, bleary eyes that spoke of horror and misery — and fear. Fear of Emil, of course, because he stood there as he really was — the alien, the vampire. There was no hiding that fact anymore.

"Jesus fucking Christ, he's gone into cardiac arrest." That was Duncan talking about Washburn, although Emil hardly cared.

Emil barely spared the cop and the others a glance. They had Washburn laid out and there were efforts at chest compression and mouth-to-mouth. He could have told them not to bother. If the man survived, Emil was only going to pick up where he left off and kill him. He would simply make sure to do it somewhere Jase couldn't see. He kept his gaze on the boy, who wasn't making any sound, although tears ran down his face — a face marred by signs of violence visited upon it. He stared back at Emil in the most forthright way he'd ever done since they'd met. But it was the kind of attention a prey animal gave to a predator, making sure he knew where the danger was and what it was doing at all times.

Emil wanted to go reassure him that he was safe, yet knew his touch was the last thing the human wanted. Besides, Mackie was on the job, making soothing noises as he held Jase. Val's husband didn't bother to hide his ire at Emil, giving him a look that would have made the strictest of teachers envious. Although he internally grimaced at the fair rebuke, Emil wasn't going to regret what he'd done. *Never.*

A hand landed on his arm. "Emil."

"What, Alex?" He didn't take his eyes off Jase.

"Washburn is dead."

"Good."

There was a deep sigh. "Yes, well…I appreciate your feelings on the matter, but it does raise some problems."

"Yeah, I'm sure it does. He's cold," he added when he noticed goosebumps raised on Jase's thigh.

He went over to the couch and grabbed a blanket lying on it. Rows of white powder were on the end table, along with a bottle of some kind of pills and a mostly empty fifth of vodka. He ignored them and carried the blanket over to the boys. Jase flinched at his approach, which hurt Emil to see, even though it was to be expected and was entirely reasonable.

He held the blanket out to Mackie. "Cover him." He waited until the boy had complied before turning to Alex. "I didn't think I'd managed to choke him."

Duncan stood over the splayed body. "You didn't, although the finger marks are going to be hard to explain. His heart gave out."

Emil grinned with bitter satisfaction. "I'd like to think I frightened him to death, but the drugs over there probably had something to do with it."

The cop raised his eyebrows before going to the end table. He peered down at the powder, picked up the medicine bottle and sighed. "Cocaine and boner pills with a whole lot of booze thrown in. I suppose that would do it, especially if you add it all with a monster attacking you with murderous intent as the final chaser."

Emil nodded then looked at Alex. "I will not apologize. He's been raping that boy for years. He got what he deserved."

With raised eyebrows, Alex said, "We don't know for sure about that. You jumped the gun before we could get to the bottom of it."

Emil folded his hands in front of himself, mostly because he'd only just realized that his fury had made him hard and he didn't want to flash that thing in front of Jase. "Ask him, then."

Alex didn't have to. It was Mackie who did. "Jase, sweetie," he said in a gentle voice. "Please tell us how long you were with Washburn. You're not in trouble, you know. We just need the truth."

A few seconds ticked by. Emil didn't think the boy would respond. He didn't dare look at him for fear of terrorizing the traumatized human more. Then came the answer, barely audible.

"Three years."

A shudder ran through Emil, hard enough to make his bones ache. He walked over to where Harry still knelt beside Washburn. "Are you sure he's dead?"

Harry blinked at him. "I am."

"Pity. I would have liked to have killed him."

Val placed a hand on his shoulder. "For all intents and purposes, you did, dude."

"Not in a way that was satisfying."

"Yeah, but in a way that at least hasn't sent the kid completely into a catatonic state. You really should be focusing on cleaning that shit-show up rather than wishing for bloody justice." Val stepped back and looked pointedly where Jase still sat curled in Mackie's arms.

"Fair point." Emil took a few deep breaths to calm himself. He wasn't going to help Jase by allowing his thoughts to be clouded with fury. That had already landed them in a difficult predicament.

He turned to Duncan. "Can you do something about this?" He jerked his thumb toward the body.

The cop wasn't wearing a happy face, nor should he be. So far, he'd only been asked to cover up the war with Dracul, something that didn't sit well with him, yet was justified because it helped humanity. This time, it was a personal matter. Emil couldn't explain away what he'd done on the basis of it serving a greater good. It didn't, although Washburn's removal from society was definitely a positive. Could Emil really expect the man to sweep this event under the rug?

With a grimace, Duncan replied, "If you'd killed him outright, I'd be in a fucking quandary about this. As it happens, I can twist the facts a bit. I mean he was a middle-aged guy who looks like he was a good friend of saturated fats and rarely hit the gym. If an autopsy confirms that he was ingesting cocaine, et cetera, right before his heart gave out, I can't see that your frightening him is all that relevant." He huffed out a breath. "And I can probably keep the kid out of my report, too. His involvement is ancillary at best."

That last part relieved Emil as nothing else had. "Thanks, Duncan. I appreciate that. He's...ah...been through enough," he added with a quick glance at Jase. Those wide eyes were still locked on him.

"Yeah, well...get him out of here, please," Duncan said, taking out his phone. "I need to call the coroner." Before he punched in the numbers, he also glanced at Jase. "Hey, kid, you understand I'm a cop and I'd have you out of here in a heartbeat if you were in any danger, yeah?"

Jase didn't answer. He didn't even look at Duncan. His focus remained on Emil in a way that was starting to freak him out. It was as if the boy's whole universe was centered on Emil's face.

Harry approached. "I should check him out. He's taken a beating to his cheek at a minimum and is probably in need of something to calm his nerves, given everything that's happened." When he took another step toward Jase, however, the human shrank back into Mackie and whimpered. There was almost a pleading look in his eyes, as if he expected Emil to protect him. That made no sense. Emil was the monster here. In comparison, Harry held the appearance of a kindly uncle.

Nevertheless, Emil blocked Harry with his arm. "It's okay. I think an exam can wait until tomorrow. He needs rest now. I'll take him to my room, and if you can bring me something to give him, like a pill, I'll see that he takes it."

"Very well," Harry murmured.

Emil stepped forward with his breath held. It was a crazy idea to think he could simply sweep Jase up and take him to his room. Being with him — the freaky monster with the red eyes and long fangs that had come close to sinking into a man's face — had to be last thing the human boy would want. As far as he knew, the monster was coming for him next, the reassurances of a cop in the back pocket of the monsters notwithstanding. Yet, instinct had Emil slowly advancing toward the boy. He kept his arms to his side and made his face blank, trying to appear as safe as possible.

He stopped about a foot away, still not making any moves to touch Jase. "Can you stand?"

When Jase continued to stare at him mutely, Mackie interceded. "Here, sweetie, let me help you." He tried to get both of them to their feet and failed. Jase's limbs were floppy and the boy's glassy-eyed look confirmed that he was leaving himself as dead weight for Mackie to manage.

"Thanks, Mackie," Emil said with his gaze remaining on Jase, "I've got him."

Although Mackie shot him a dubious look, he nevertheless backed away. With the slowest, most careful movements he could muster, Emil bent down and slid one arm around Jase's waist and the other under his knees. The parts of the boy's skin that were exposed were cold and clammy. His heartbeat was jackrabbit-fast, a rapid tattoo that caught Emil's attention, despite his resolve to rein in his own needs and wants. Saliva pooled in his mouth at the sound of the beating pulse and the rush of blood through the boy's veins. Against the paleness of his skin, they showed a deep and tasty-blue to Emil's vision. His fangs itched to punch down at the same time as his dick punched up.

It was hard to angle the human's stiff and trembling body to prevent him from feeling the erection pressing from behind Emil's fly. He worried that the boy could hear his own pounding heart, too. The good news — because, Christ, they needed some — was that Jase didn't fight him or shrink away. He simply sat curled within Emil's embrace, soundless and with a vacant stare focused somewhere in the distance.

"It's okay," he tried to reassure the boy. "I've got you and you're safe."

"Yes, Master." It was the first words he'd spoken since confirming how long he'd been with the asshole. His voice was soft and quivering, testament to the fact that while he was resigned to his situation, he wasn't happy with it. *Of course he isn't.*

Emil frowned at being called 'Master' when he was no such thing. He started to say as much then stopped. If the boy had been enslaved in the very real sense of the word since the age of fifteen, or, God forbid, earlier with some other guy, he likely only knew this one thing. Any man that claimed him and controlled him physically and financially was the master. The poor kid likely thought he had no choice in what happened to him or what man owned him.

Sadly, in all actuality, at that moment he was right. Emil couldn't let him go. Not only was Jase vulnerable, he was now privy to what Emil and the others were really like. If they simply cut him loose, he'd talk and maybe people would listen. They couldn't take that chance — not yet, not without first trying to co-opt him to their side. It was a terrible situation for all concerned and the fault lay squarely at Emil's feet.

And yet, he didn't regret a thing. Washburn, that predatory piece of shit, had deserved to die. If Emil hadn't intervened, the worst that would have happened to the man was arrest and incarceration. As dismal as human prisons were, it didn't seem like a sufficiently fit punishment for a man who'd preyed on and abused an underage boy. Eighteen might have been an arbitrary and relatively new age for consent among humans, but the very fact that someone was willing to ignore the societal norms that were intended to protect children made the asshole worthy of violent retribution. Worse, Emil felt sure Jase's abuse hadn't started a mere three years ago. He worried that the boy had suffered longer than that. Recovery from such a thing would be difficult and needed help from someone knowledgeable and patient.

Emil was full of the latter, not necessarily the former. Right at the moment, however, he was what the boy had. He carried him to the family living floor, taking time to walk no faster than a human would, and headed straight for his own room. He didn't think his decision through. It wasn't even true that he had no other choice. The room that both Quinn and Mackie had occupied, then left for their lover's and husband's beds, was currently vacant. Emil could have taken Jase there. He didn't. His primitive self was still driving his actions. Jase needed to be safely ensconced in Emil's private space, and that was that.

The door was open, and he carried Jase inside without bothering to shut it. Harry would hopefully be coming soon with something to relax the boy. Besides, he didn't want Jase to feel trapped. He briefly noticed and regretted that his bed was unmade and rumpled from his night's sleep. Although he was always careful to keep his kitchen and pantry in pristine condition and order, his bedroom was different. It seemed silly to make a bed that no one was going to see all day, only to unmake it later. It proved useful in any event, giving him a clear path to place Jase onto the sheets.

"There now," he said because the silence between them was deafening and he was desperate to reassure the boy. "You're safe here." It was dumb to keep saying it when everything that had happened in the last fifteen minutes indicated otherwise.

He flattened his lips at the sight of the blanket from the playroom still wrapped around Jase. It had been necessary at the time. Now it reminded Emil, and perhaps Jase as well, of what had happened in that room. Leaning down, he peeled it away with care. Jase didn't so much as flinch, which would have been gratifying except his stillness reminded Emil again of an animal paralyzed with fear.

Emil tossed the blanket aside and pulled his comforter up. He tucked it around Jase's curled form. "There… That will keep you warm." Every word out of his mouth struck him as being inane, yet he couldn't think of anything better to say.

To Emil's surprise, the boy seemed to unclench in subtle ways, almost sinking into the bed. Then he let out a shuddery sigh and blinked at Emil. "Thank you, Master."

Emil cleared his throat and scratched at the back of his head. "I, um…would prefer you call me Emil."

Jase blinked rapidly some more before saying, "Yes, Master Emil."

"Ah, no…" Before he could get out more than that, a knock at the door caught his attention. Harry stood there with a pill pinched between thumb and forefinger and a bottle of water in the other hand.

"Oh, thanks." He was pathetically grateful for the distraction. Being with Jase left him floundering out of his depth. He'd never had a human boy in his bed before—or his care. With his blood cooling from his confrontation with Washburn, his natural inclination to lie low and stick to his lane was resurfacing. Outside of stuffing food down people's throats, he had no experience in taking command and being responsible for others.

Harry handed him the pill and the bottle. "This will knock him out for a while. He needs rest. I can tell he's exhausted just by looking at him."

"Thanks. I'll see that he takes it." He really wanted to ask Harry to stay, but he hadn't missed how the man's entrance had caused Jase to stiffen again.

He managed to open the water without dropping the medicine and squatted down by the side of the bed. "I need you to sit up a bit and swallow this, baby." *Baby? Where the fuck did that come from?*

Jase didn't seem to mind the endearment, or if he did, he was good at hiding his feelings. Of course he was. The boy hesitated only a moment before propping himself on one arm and reaching for the pill. He popped it into his mouth as if he were well-trained in taking what was given to him without complaint. That led to a new worry that Washburn had forced drugs on the boy. Emil vowed to himself that this would be a one-time thing, especially when Jase only needed a small sip of water to toss back what he'd taken. Then, he slid down again and stared off into space.

"You can trust that Harry picked something safe to help you sleep. I promise you won't have to take anything more after this."

When Jase said nothing, Emil impulsively reached out to card the boy's fine hair away from his face. Jase flinched in a barely perceptible way, sufficient for Emil's sharp eyes to notice, but not so much that Emil wasn't able to do what he wanted. It was as if every flight instinct the human had was on lockdown. *Beaten out of him.* The thought caused Emil's fingers to close convulsively around the bottle, crushing the plastic and sending water shooting over his fist.

"Shit." He sprang away from the bed to keep from getting it or Jase wet. Putting the bottle in his free hand, he wiped the water off on his pants. Then he set the bottle on the nightstand. "I'll leave this here in case you want more later."

Jase nodded as his eyelids drooped and he yawned. It was the first natural thing he'd done since the nightmare of Emil's doing had begun. A small, almost animalistic noise escaped his briefly open mouth before he went completely silent. The sound echoed inside Emil's head. He heard it for what it was — a cry for help.

He reached down to brush the boy's silky hair once more. This time, Jase didn't react at all to the touch because his eyes were closed. He'd fallen asleep, his pulse beating in regular fashion, still enticing. It would have taken nothing to drop to his knees before sinking his fangs into the tender neck. Jase would likely not even fight him, not given how broken down he was by his abuse. Except even if he'd wanted to, the tight leather collar blocked the way. Emil angrily fumbled around to find the latch. He had to crush it when he found that it was held in place by a small padlock. It came apart in his hand and he had to force himself to go carefully when he removed the collar.

The marred skin beneath it brought his fury to the fore again. Damn Washburn anyway for keeping that lovely neck encased in chafing confines. Emil promised himself to never again allow it, not that he would have a say in the boy's life forever. Of course he wouldn't. But while he did, there would be only tenderness and care. The sight of the exposed, slender neck didn't tempt him to drink at all now. Emil would have rather pulled his teeth out and bled himself dry before abusing the boy in any way.

"I promise I'll take care of you," he vowed in a quiet voice. "Nothing and no one will ever hurt you again."

He hadn't gone looking for a boy, didn't want one. Jase was his now, though. There was no denying that.

Chapter Six

Red eyes. White fangs gleaming with saliva. The monster chased Jase through his dreams. He couldn't move fast enough to avoid the big, hulking creature who was coming and coming. No matter how much he tried, Jase couldn't put any distance between them. His limbs were like lead and his heartbeat thrummed with the kind of fear that made words and breath catch in the back of one's throat. A roar, like the kind a wounded King Kong would make, surrounded him. It made him shiver and quake, and he wanted to sink into oblivion and never resurface. There was no escape. There never had been. He'd been doomed from the very first to be trapped by monsters.

Jase's eyes popped open on an almost-scream. He took a deep, shuddering breath and immediately smelled something wonderfully calming—sweet and spicy at the same time. He recognized it as homey and comforting. It was the covers surrounding him that the scent clung to. Of course...Chef Emil. This was his bed.

No, not Emil…the monster, the one with the red eyes and the wickedly sharp fangs. The one who made horrible sounds and picked up a grown man as if he were nothing more than a ragdoll.

Jase should have been swamped by a fear greater than any he'd ever known, except that he still smelled sugar and spice and everything nice. "That's what gigantic monsters are made of," he whispered into the dark room.

"I'm sorry, sweetie. What did you say?"

Jase started at the sound of Mackie's voice. He hadn't realized he wasn't alone. A sudden bright light shining from the nightstand had him blinking before he turned his head and looked at the redheaded boy. He remembered in a rush of memories how he'd held Jase in those first few nightmarish minutes when Jase had learned that there were worse things in the world than men preying on boys.

"Are… Are you a vampire, too?" he dared to ask.

Mackie, his hand still lingering on the lamp he'd turned on, grinned down at him. "No. Not exactly," he added with a wrinkle of his nose. "It's complicated, but I *am* human."

The answer only made Jase more confused. Still, he latched on to the one thing that he understood. "You're like me, then…a slave to a vampire."

Although he hadn't had time to truly process what had happened, he'd been passed around enough by men to understand that he belonged to Emil now. And, apparently, the chef was actually a blood-sucking creature like something straight out of a horror movie. The absurdity of it all would have made him laugh if he weren't so terrified. His life had taken a decided turn for the worse. Washburn had been brutal, but no more powerful than the average man. How could Jase survive being dominated and played with by a far stronger inhuman being?

Mackie's eyes softened. "I'm not a slave. I'm a submissive, and while there are boys like us who are in a Master and slave relationship, you haven't ever been exposed to what that really means. Washburn's treatment of you isn't how it's supposed to be. That was abuse, not the least of which was because he started when you were too young to give consent."

Jase licked his lips. "Oh, okay." He had no idea what Mackie meant and whatever his new master had forced him to take the night before had left his brain fuzzy still. "I guess Master will teach me what I need to know." Master, whoever he was at any given time, always did. There was something liberating in knowing that he didn't have to figure things out on his own. Obeying was easy, even when it was scary and painful.

Mackie wrinkled his nose. "About that. It's not really my place to say, but Emil isn't your new master."

Alarm shot through him. Jase shoved to a sitting position. "What? Who has he given me to?"

Oh God. He hadn't had time to consider that he might have already been sold to someone else. Emil might be a vampire, but at least Jase knew him. If nothing else, the guy fed him the most amazing food. And did this mean that he belonged to some other vampire? What kind of games would a creature like that play? He jerked his fingers to the base of his throat. He felt around for a scab or other indication that someone had sucked his blood.

"Hey!" Mackie plopped down beside him and grabbed him by the wrist to stop his frantic search. "It's okay. No one fed off you. They don't do that without permission."

That was only somewhat comforting. "But they do it, right?"

Mackie's eyelids drooped in a sexy expression. "Oh, yeah, and it's like the best orgasm enhancement ever."

"Seriously?" Jase dropped his hand. "Someone's going to suck all my blood while they fuck me?" The idea was ridiculous, yet he couldn't deny what he'd seen. He knew Mackie wasn't pulling his leg.

"No, silly. Not dry, just enough to make you come harder than you've ever done before."

"Yeah, right." Jase replied dully, too distracted with worry about who his master was. "I don't usually do that—come, I mean. Master doesn't like it. And I'm almost always in chastity anyway. My cock doesn't expect anything different."

The reminder made him aware that he was completely nude, with nothing cinching his cock and balls or stretching his ass. He couldn't remember the last time he'd woken in such a liberating state. With a gasp, he cupped his throat again. He hadn't noticed before that his collar was gone. He looked around as if he'd find it nearby. "Where is it?"

Mackie fiddled with the beautifully engraved tag dangling off his own collar. "Oh, Emil took it off last night, I believe. You're going to need some cream to soften all that chafing," he added with a nod toward Jase's throat.

Dropping his hand onto his lap, Jase sank back into his pillow. "What's the point? I'll only get a new one soon."

"I don't think so. You're actually not someone's slave anymore. Emil isn't in the lifestyle and he didn't give you to someone else. He doesn't think you're his to control in the first place."

"I don't understand." Jase's confusion was mounting. "He effectively killed Washburn for me. If I don't belong to him, I have to be someone else's. I'm a slave. That's who I am. Who do I belong to?" Panic, irrational and destructive as it was to his well-being and sanity, welled within him. He couldn't stop it.

"Yourself, of course. You are your own person." The answer didn't come from Mackie.

Jase's heart leaped into his throat and he turned to look in the direction of a new source of light. The door to the bedroom was open and standing in the middle of the threshold was the monster, except he didn't look like one. He looked the way he usually did—the kindly chef in a white jacket, a ready smile and a tray piled high with awesome-smelling food.

If he tried hard, Jase figured he could pretend the horrors of the previous night hadn't happened at all. But he couldn't, because despite everything that had occurred since his mother had died, he hadn't been able to find some happy place inside his own head. He'd often wished he could fool himself into believing that pain was pleasure and being subjugated was a gift. Something stubborn about him had made that impossible. As miserable as it continued to make him, he always faced matters head-on.

With his fingers gripping the covers, he sat up again. He worked his throat to press down his fear and raise his courage to ask questions. Nothing came to him. He opened and closed his mouth in an aborted effort, only to fall back on old habits. He slid his gaze to the floor and silently waited for whatever was coming. The sound of heavy tread and flashes in his peripheral visions told him the monster was coming toward him.

No…Emil. It's Emil, the man who is so nice to you. Picture him baking bread in the kitchen, not trying to murder Washburn.

Mackie left the bed. "Here, Emil. Let me take that."

"No, thanks. Jase and I need to talk, and he may as well get used to my being around, given the circumstances. Thanks for watching him."

Mackie huffed. "Fine. Be careful with him." The fierce boy's tone brooked no disagreement.

"Always."

It wasn't until the door shut that the food tray was placed on Jase's lap. He stared at it, saying nothing. He was kind of disappointed that it held mostly healthy stuff, like oatmeal and a glass of milk. There was a bowl of fruit, though, and something baked sat under a napkin. He sniffed quietly and thought he detected chocolate. His stomach growled, making him jerk with embarrassment and fear that his need for food was indiscreet.

"You're hungry. That's good." Big hands approached him. Jase froze even more, although nothing happened other than his pillows were piled behind him. "There now… Sit back so you can eat without spilling stuff."

Jase obeyed instantly. He reminded himself that he'd been in this position before—learning the rhythms of a new master's whims. He was a quick study and could only hope that a vampire was no different than any other master. With his back propped against the pillows and the tray balanced on his lap, he waited for instructions. No eating without permission was slave rule one-o-one. No matter what had been said to him in the last few minutes, he knew he was a slave, not a free person. That was a lesson he wouldn't forget, and if his new master wanted to play some game where Jase pretended that he gave himself freely, well fine. He could do that. He was good at giving men what they wanted.

"Go on. Start with the oatmeal. I figure your stomach is probably a little upset from, um…you know…everything. If that sits well, then there's fruit and after that, a little treat is waiting for you."

Jase didn't need to be told twice. Hesitation in obedience was forbidden for one thing. And for another, he was starving. The oatmeal was a good choice. It slid down into his stomach easily enough, not too hot and sweetened with something. He made sure to eat slowly, so as to not spill and because concentrating on putting food in his mouth allowed him to ignore the large body hovering over him.

That didn't last long, however. Once Jase had consumed a few spoonfuls, his not-your-master moved away from the bed and sat in the chair by the door. The way he flopped down into the thing, making it creak with his large weight, made it seem that he was tired. And how did that work, exactly? Didn't vampires sleep during the day, assuming it was day? Jase was certain he'd seen the club's chef during the morning, so maybe all that stuff about vampires being nocturnal was nonsense. Of course, the existence of monsters was supposed to be crap, and look where he was. Someone had gotten something right along the years. Some myths were true, apparently.

Damn, he had so many questions.

"I bet you have a lot of questions."

The observation startled him sufficiently that his normally obedient mouth opened and he spoke without thinking. "Can you read my mind?"

A chuckle crossed over to him, the sound warm and genuinely mirthful. "No. I can't do that. There're lots of things I can't do." There was a sigh, sadness replacing cheerfulness in an instant. "I'm sorry I scared you last night. My temper got the better of me." There was a pregnant pause. "I can't apologize for precipitating Washburn's death, but I hope I haven't hurt you by it."

"Hurt me?" The concept was so foreign to him that he wasn't sure he understood it.

"Yeah, I mean, did you love him?"

"Fuck no!" Jase dropped his spoon with a clatter against the tray before freezing. His tongue would be the death of him.

There was no admonishment, however, only another chuckle. "That's good. He was an asshole. But maybe it's still scary for you that he's gone. It's okay to tell me the truth. It's vital to me that you do, actually."

Jase bided his time, a risky yet necessary thing, by taking a sip of his milk. The coolness of the liquid slid mercifully down his dry throat. "I'm only scared of not pleasing you, Master." There, the truth and flattery mixed in one.

"Emil, remember?"

Right, some of the details of the previous night were murky. "Sorry, Master Emil."

"No. I mean… Never mind. We'll let that go for now. Is there someone you'd like me to get in touch with, like your stepfather?"

Jase shot a look in Master's direction. "No, please." He couldn't hold back a whimper. The original monster in his life was someone he couldn't face. Vampires were better…much better.

Master held out his hand. "Okay. That's fine, and I'm not surprised. When you're ready to do so, you can tell me what happened there. Or, maybe you'll want to talk to Harry or Mackie." He dropped his hands between his knees and stared at the ground for a second. "Keep eating and I'll tell you *my* story. Okay?"

Jase did as told, returning to the surprisingly yummy porridge. Soon, though, he barely noticed what he was eating as he became absorbed in Master's strange tale. Aliens, not vampires, except they were the origin story — a thousand years, marooned, just trying to make a life on a new world. Blood was good but not essential, unlike secrecy, which absolutely was.

Jase ate his way through the food on his tray, utterly fascinated with the story unfolding. By the time he dared expose the treat under the napkin, Master had finished speaking and was sitting in silence. Jase bit into what was a chocolate croissant, still slightly warm and obviously homemade. Flavor exploded on his tongue while his brain tried to accept what he'd been told. It was utterly unbelievable, although, compared to the idea that undead blood-suckers roamed Earth, perfectly plausible.

He chewed, swallowed and finished his milk, staring at where his feet pushed up from under the covers. If there was something he was supposed to say to all of it, he couldn't imagine what that was. So, he fell back on being a good, silent little slave and waited for instructions.

"Jase?"

"Yes, Master Emil?"

"Do you have any questions?"

He realized that of course he had one. In all the fairy-tale telling of his Master's nature, he'd forgotten for a moment who and what he was. He picked up the tray and placed it beside him on the bed. "Yes, Master Emil."

"What are they?"

"Only one, if you please." He glanced at him with a flutter of eyelashes that he hoped would be appealing. "Would you like your morning blow job now?"

* * * *

"So, I need you to peel all ten bags of potatoes and put them to soak in this pot of cold water. That will keep them from oxidizing before I have a chance to roast them. Don't worry about cutting them. I'll do that later."

Jase nodded like the dutiful slave he was, even though he already understood what he needed to do and why. "Yes, Master Emil."

"Jase, remember what we discussed." Master's tone was infinitely patient.

Jase cringed anyway. He didn't like fucking up, and not only because he feared punishment. There was something about this new master that made him want to please him. "Sorry. Yes, Chef." In the kitchen, Master was always to be called 'Chef'. Master was for the bedroom, at least he thought so. The rules for that place were murky at the moment.

No blow job or sex of any kind had happened since breakfast. Instead, Jase had been ordered — kindly — to bathe in Master's house-sized shower with four spray-heads beating down on his tired, creaky body. Big, fluffy towels had dried him quickly and like a soft hug.

Toiletries had been brought by the ever-helpful Mackie, because apparently alien vampires didn't have body odor quite like humans. It made Jase a little self-conscious. He'd have to be extra careful to stay clean and fresh. The boy had also brought a brush, because Master merely ran his fingers through his hair with some gel to create his spiky look.

Clothes and sneakers had come from Quinn, because he was closer to Jase in size, and Jase didn't have anything other than leathers to wear at the club—or anywhere, really. His lack of clothing had made Master mad. Lots of weird things did, like offering the blow job. Master's face had gone all red and Jase had been sure he was in for a beating. But no. Master had only refused and said no more offers of that kind needed to be made. Jase had wanted to ask if that meant never, except he'd figured he'd used up his quota of questions, and the idea that his new master would never want sex from him was absurd. This master wasn't the same as others had been. His wishes would be harder to determine, and Jase would have to watch out for that.

So, no sex, at least for now. Instead, Master wanted him to help out in the kitchen and Jase was actually excited to do something new and useful. It didn't matter how boring or menial it was. It served a purpose other than getting some slobbering man hard and off. And for this work, he didn't have to be naked. Over his T-shirt and jeans, he wore a jacket—'whites', Master called them—the way he'd done when he'd sat in this nice, safe place eating bread. This time, though, a jaunty white cap sat on his head to keep his hair away from the food and the jacket fit because it had been supplied by a quirky guy named Damien. Damien was a human and he didn't know that Master was an alien vampire, so mum was the word on *that*.

There were lots of new rules for him to learn. That was fine. Of necessity, he'd become a fast learner. Secrecy was also something he was well used to. Jase had had years of practice both obeying and hiding the nature of who he and his master were, both in absolute terms and relative to one another. Nothing much had changed. Really, one type of monster over another hardly mattered, although this new twist on that theme wasn't as scary as it should have been.

Everyone at Club Lux had treated him kindly so far, the Stelalux family in particular. He was still learning who was what, but it didn't take any effort to understand that anyone tall, pale, black-haired, violet-eyed and male fell into the category of vampire. While Master had emphasized how important it was not to talk about the family's unusual nature, he had also said that the bartender knew the secret. And the cop from the playroom obviously did, as well. That didn't surprise him, actually. He'd spent the last several years of his life discovering that lots of men in powerful positions lived within the tight circle of men who liked underage boys. He'd made the mistake once of thinking he could confide in a man with a badge, only to end up being his toy for the night. Lesson learned. So, yeah, a cop hiding a group of vampires didn't faze him.

"Jase, are you listening?"

His heart skipped a beat. "Yes, Chef."

Master nodded. "Good. I don't want you to tire yourself out. If you need a break, take it. Make sure to sit on this stool if your feet get sore."

"Yes, Chef." Jase was kind of touched that Master showed any worry about him. He could stand for hours if need be — had done so often in a corner for being bad, and after a beating. At the moment, given his full night's sleep and the fact that his body was free of restraint, he felt better than he had in a long time.

Master didn't look convinced. "Hmm... Remember what Harry said about not overdoing it and how the effects of the pill I gave you will linger for a few more hours."

Jase nodded. The kindly vampire, who was apparently a doctor, had gently examined him at Master's insistence after the shower. It was way weird that a blood-sucker also healed people. Weirder still, when Jase tried to give him a blow job as a thank you, the man had refused with a look of such utter pity that Jase had felt ashamed. The rules of this place definitely mystified him. Like cops, doctors played with young boys all the time. Patching them up always came with a price, too. If Jase wasn't valued here for the sex he could provide, what was his worth?

What was his purpose?

Master held out a peeler. Oh, right...potatoes. Taking the wickedly sharp thing in hand, Jase stepped to the first bag. He opened it and started working. Master hovered nearby for a minute or two until Jase proved trustworthy with the simple task, then he left. Normally, Jase would have felt relief. Oddly, he missed the guy's presence as soon as it was gone. He pushed aside the feeling, though, and concentrated on the job. It was easy and rhythmic and soon his worries fell away and he settled into a groove.

Being open twenty-four-seven to its members, the club played music nonstop. It was piped into the kitchen and Jase appreciated how it accentuated the sounds of chopping and whisking around him. It was almost as if the kitchen staff, himself included, were part of a rhythm band, keeping time to the beat of the song. He hadn't had much chance to listen to rock or hip-hop or any kind of modern music. Washburn had preferred classical, which was nice. This newer stuff, though, seeped into him. He found himself nodding his head and shaking his hips. It helped to pass the time.

"You like to dance?"

Consumed with what he was doing, Jase hadn't heard Master return. With a jerk, he fumbled the potato in his hand, and when he stopped it from falling, he nicked his fingertip with the peeler. He hissed and pulled his hand back so as to not bleed on the food. A rush of warm air bathed his face, and Master grabbed his hand with his much larger one. Jase looked at him and gasped.

Master's eyes had gone from their unusual violet to a deep black, which was way better than the red of the previous night. His nostrils flared and his breathing was labored. No fangs protruded, but he licked his lower lip while he stared intently at the bead of blood welling up on Jase's finger. His grip tightened almost painfully around Jase's palm and wrist. In a flash of understanding, Jase figured black had to do with passion, as opposed to anger, which was red. That had to be it. Master wanted Jase, at least in this way. Maybe the guy wouldn't want sex, only blood.

He's going to suck it. He's going to suck my finger!

Jase held his breath as he waited for Master's lips to close around the wound and tug. What would it be like? Would it hurt? The idea of pulling his hand away barely registered as a thought before he tossed it aside.

The worst sin of a slave was to fight the attentions of a master, no matter how frightening they were. Yet, he wasn't so sure he could say he was scared. More like curious.

A second passed, then another and another. Master didn't suck Jase's finger into his mouth. Instead, he pulled back and turned his head. His gaze met Jase's only for a heart-stuttering moment before he looked over his shoulder.

"Hey, Damien, please bring the first-aid kit."

"Sure thing, Chef."

"I'm sorry," Master said to Jase. "I shouldn't have startled you."

Jase was still trying to process how a master had apologized to his slave, when he noticed that Master's eyes had gone back to normal. He found himself curious again about the color change. *Red has to be for anger, and black must mean lust?* These aliens were sort of like chameleons, except only their eyes changed, and it was based on feelings, not environment. That had to be it. But was it simply the blood that had made Master feel so, or was it Jase's blood in particular that appealed to him? Wow, that was a completely strange and random thought. Jase had long ago surrendered any idea that he might actually be attracted to a man and want his attention. Those thoughts and feelings had just started to waken within him when his stepfather had dirtied them forever.

Or at least Jase had thought they were gone for good. Perhaps not. For a brief second before Damien trotted over with the kit, Jase imagined what it would be like to have Master feast on his blood. Mackie had said it made one come extra hard. That was assuming, of course, that one was already hard. Or, again not. Maybe alien vampires could arouse someone simply by the act of sucking a fingertip or a wrist—or a throat. A shiver ran through him at the very idea of Master's mouth pressed against his exposed neck.

Master obviously felt the slight tremor because Jase could feel his eyes boring into him. "Are you all right?"

"Yes, Chef." He wasn't sure he'd told the truth. The small cut didn't bother him, but Master's proximity and touch did, though not in the usual way of a master. This was different, much different, and it disturbed Jase. His unfettered dick twitched a bit, as if it were trying to rise from a long slumber. For a second, he actually worried that he might become hard. Then, the idea of coming in his pants in front of bags of potatoes amused him.

A giggle escaped his lips before he could bite it back. The sound startled him and Master both. He hunched in his shoulders, expecting admonishment. Instead, Master smiled. The expression poured down on Jase and filled him with a lovely feeling. He couldn't help smiling in return.

"This is kind of weird," Master said in a low tone. "I'm glad you're not scared."

Jase had nothing to say to that observation, not that he expected his opinion to matter anyway. Damien arrived with the kit, and Master asked the boy to play nurse while Master doctored Jase's finger with ointment, a bandage and a surgical glove to keep the potatoes from contamination. When he was done, he politely thanked Damien for his help and sent him on his way.

"There...all done now." He released Jase's hand. "Do you need a break?"

Jase perversely missed the contact as soon as it was gone. "No thank you, Chef." He dared to look, and that's when he realized how tense Master was. Not angry, yet clearly trying hard to keep his shit together. That massive chest rose and fell on labored breaths and his lips were held in a grim line. And while the man's jacket hid his groin, Jase expected he was aroused. The signs were there. Jase knew them well.

Master stepped back. "I'll leave you to it."

Why wasn't he acting on his desire when Jase was his for the taking? A better question was, *"Why do I care?"*

* * * *

"I suppose we should be grateful that we're invited to this debriefing at all."

Trey spared Karl a glance. They were propped against the back wall in a room filled with federal, state and local law enforcement, and in a line-up such as that, he and Karl were definitely part of the kids' table. "Yeah, makes me wonder why, too. We've been kept in the dark since the second explosion. They obviously think there's a connection between that one and the warehouse, but sharing would be nice. We know how to keep our mouths shut."

The complete irony of that last statement wasn't wasted on him. He'd spent the better part of the previous night hiding what had happened at Lux. Although the autopsy was pending, he was sure Washburn had died from a combination of what he'd ingested, not simply because a vampire had bared his fangs. And keeping the kid out of it was still the right thing to do. Trey didn't worry about how he hadn't contradicted Val and Harry when they'd given their statements. As far as the official report was concerned, Washburn had been playing with a random that he'd picked up somewhere before keeling over from an apparent heart attack. The random had left right after sounding the alarm, without giving his name. Trey had happened to be visiting his friend, Val, when it had all gone down. Blah, blah, lie, lie. It held because no one really cared about a guy like Washburn.

Trey's conscience was clear, certainly. Jason Purdue had obviously been a victim of sex trafficking. When the time was right, and when Emil in particular didn't look like he'd rip Trey's throat out for approaching the kid, he'd see if he could learn enough to give another report to vice or the FBI. In the meantime, the kid was in safe hands. Emil had the biggest heart of anyone Trey had ever known. His obvious attraction to the boy notwithstanding, Emil would protect him—even from Emil himself.

So, yeah, Trey was the epitome of discretion. What bothered him most wasn't that he was doing it. It was how easy it was and how used to it he'd become. Standing there, waiting for the debriefing to begin, he just knew down to the very marrow of his bones that Dracul was behind these bombings. And yet, he wasn't going to say a goddamn word about it. No, he would bide his time until he could get to the club and update a group of aliens who had somehow become his masters, if he were honest with himself. It was the best course of action if he really wanted to protect his own people. He understood that intellectually. It still sucked.

"Okay, everyone, let's get started." A tall man, successfully rocking a Vin Diesel look, had stepped up to the podium. "For those of you who don't know me, I'm Agent Franklin of Homeland Security. I am leading this investigation."

He made eye contact around the room, asserting his dominance, although not in a dickish way. "I appreciate how all of you have been working diligently together on this tragic event. Once again, Boston has been the scene of terrorism. Only this time, we can't say who is behind it. No organization has stepped forward to claim responsibility, which in itself is surprising. We haven't heard any chatter, either, about it on the usual sites that we monitor. At this point, we're working on the belief that our unsub — unknown subject — is both not currently in our data base for previous bombings and acting alone. That, of course, could change.

"What we do know," he added, starting a PowerPoint presentation, "is the two recent explosions — one at the warehouse and one at the nightclub, which have claimed a total of seven innocent lives and have left another half-dozen hospitalized — are connected."

He went through a series of photographs, side-by-side from both cases to show comparisons in damage. "The material itself that caused the detonation and the subsequent fire is organic-based." He brought up a picture of some charred mass. "It's vegetation, but not your usual basic fertilizer. The labs are working on further analysis. At this time, however, its nature and origins match no known plant. It's alien to this area. That much has been established."

Fuck! Even though he'd known it was coming, it still hit Trey low in the gut. Whatever was being used was something Dracul had either created on this world or brought with him from their place of origin. That was something he'd have to ask Alex. That thought had barely settled in his brain before the next slide made his heart stop.

"This remnant of what looks like a credit or membership card was found at the second scene. As you can see, the lettering is almost completely charred, leaving only two, maybe three characters that are readable. We've got analysts researching if they have any particular meaning, although that's a stretch, given the possibilities."

Karl stirred. "Hey, Trey, isn't that — ?"

"Yeah." There was no hiding this. If he didn't step forward, Karl would. He raised his hand like he was back in middle school. "Excuse me, sir. I think I can help you out with that one."

Chapter Seven

Agent Franklin was not an idiot. He had listened to what Trey had had to say about Lux and the Stelalux family without immediately jumping to conclusions. His questions had been equitable and reasonable. He'd raised his eyebrows when Trey admitted that he'd developed something of a personal relationship with them, something that Trey believed fell into the category of necessary confession. His word and his ability to steer this investigation in a safe direction depended on his remaining in the know. If Franklin decided he was a liability, he'd be out of the loop and no good to Alex and company. Karl, bless his big, loyal heart, had claimed that he, too, had been invited to Val and Mackie's wedding and had been unable to attend. That lie lent credence to Trey's claim that it was more gratitude than real friendship that allowed him to go to the club. The look his partner shot him afterward said they'd be having a private conversation later about it, however. Oh well, worse come to worst, Trey could blame Demi's infatuation for his invite.

Franklin had also decided that only he would go with them to visit the club and interview the people there. He could have just as easily brought a cast of thousands and a search warrant that would have perhaps not held up in court. It would have nevertheless uncovered stuff in which the violation of Fourth Amendment rights would have been entirely beside the point. The constitution was designed to protect the rights of people. Technically the aliens weren't homo sapiens, so the Supreme Court would have quite the thorny issue to navigate. Trey could only imagine what the immigration arm of Homeland would make of actual aliens as opposed to undocumented immigrants. How would one deport when a rocket was needed? The idea of it almost made him smile.

Almost... Because along with being pragmatic and smart, Franklin was also very serious. His expression as they entered the dark luxury of the club was best described as *grim*.

Despite the relative earliness of the weekday, quite a few members lurked about while boys twerked their way around poles. Franklin's human and hetero nature came out when his steps hitched at the sight before he turned his gaze away. The guy was obviously working at not showing his surprise and maybe disgust as he headed for the bar. Kitty was at her usual post, polishing glasses and giving them her haughty look. Val was nowhere to be seen, which was a blessing, because easing anyone into the orbit of the Stelalux family with the scariest version of them would be a trial. Not even Alex was around, but Emil came around the corner the moment when they reached the bar.

It said something when the sight of the chef made Trey relax a hair, although he wasn't sure what. The big guy had this Zen quality about him that was comforting, notwithstanding the major way he'd lost his shit the other night. Trey had no doubt the guy would have killed Washburn if circumstances hadn't beat him to it. That should have worried Trey, but instead, he liked Emil better for it. Anyone who preyed on children deserved what they got in his book. And, speaking of which, Demi sailed up with his usual baiting grin. Trey's nerves set on edge in a heartbeat. Fortunately, he didn't have to figure out the best way to respond. Emil did it for him.

"Demi," the chef said sharply, "this is grown-up stuff. Go back upstairs."

Oh, the kid didn't like that. His grin vanished, replaced with a frown. He didn't argue, though. "Yes, Cousin Emil." He bit the words out before turning and flouncing away.

Emil fixed his attention on Franklin. "How can I help you, sir?"

Franklin flashed his badge and identified himself. "I'd like to speak with the owners about a national security matter."

"There's only one owner of this club—my cousin, Alex Stelalux."

Franklin nodded. "Then I'd like to speak with him and all of his relatives who are onsite."

"That can be arranged, although, unless you press the matter, my cousin Val and Uncle Harry will want to keep their husbands out of whatever is going on, as well as Demi, Harry's son. As you have seen for yourself, the boy is a child."

God, Trey wished that were true, but it was more complicated than that — not that he should be focused on anything other than Franklin's reason for coming.

"That's fine," Franklin agreed. "Is there somewhere we can go that's private?"

"Sure." Emil turned to Kitty.

"I've already texted everyone, and Alex says to go straight to his office. They should all be there in a few minutes." She narrowed her gaze at Franklin. "Do you want me there, too?"

"Not at the moment, ma'am."

No surprise there. As a woman who was a naturally born American, she didn't check any of Homeland's usual boxes for this kind of thing. Nor should she, except he knew from experience that she was no one to underestimate.

"Please follow me." Emil headed back the way he'd come, his large frame showing surprising grace. If he was concerned about Franklin's arrival, he didn't show it. But the mere fact that he didn't offer his usual hospitality told Trey the guy was tense. Trey wanted to ask him how the kid was doing. Now wasn't the time, although he might not be able to return at all. His movements would likely be scrutinized from here on out, and he didn't want to give Franklin or anyone else the idea that he was playing on a team other than the one labeled US of A. He might have to trust that Emil was keeping the kid safe, which he did anyway.

Ushering them into Alex's office, Emil said, "Please make yourselves comfortable, gentlemen." So saying, he took a standing position in the far corner to the right of Alex's desk.

Franklin, then Trey and Karl, sat on the sofa, all lined up like school children waiting for the principal to chew them out, except Franklin was not someone who would let Alex or anyone else control this little meeting.

A few seconds later, the Stelalux boys came parading in. Trey tried to imagine what Franklin must be thinking at his first sight of these unusual men. Knowing what he did, Trey couldn't believe he'd ever seen them as anything other than completely alien. The sheer size of them, the pale skin, the unrelenting black hair with widow's peaks and long tails, or in Val's case, that skull-hugging Mohawk... It all gave the appearance of otherworldliness. They looked like ruthless killers, as well. Franklin had to be assessing them in that exact way.

Then Alex smiled and his smooth, guileless expression reminded Trey of how good these creatures had become at seducing humans. "Agent Franklin," he said, extending his hand, "I'm Alexander Stelalux. This is my uncle, Horatiu, my cousin, Valeriu, and you've already met my cousin Emil."

Franklin rose and shook. "Mr. Stelalux, gentlemen," he added to the room at large. "Thank you for speaking with me."

"Not at all. We are always happy to help out law enforcement, as I hope Sergeant Duncan and Detective Anderson have attested."

"Yes, they have spoken of your cooperation in past inquiries." Butter wouldn't melt in Franklin's mouth. He wasn't giving an inch.

"They are too kind," Alex demurred as he sat behind his desk and relaxed into a sprawl. He gave every appearance of being unconcerned about Franklin's presence—a man with nothing to hide. Then again, he'd had a thousand years of practice dealing with humans who might make trouble for him. Given the obvious wealth the aliens had amassed in addition to their superior *everything*, they probably had an escape plan that could get them gone within hours.

"They also helped save my husband's life," Val chimed in, taking his usual folded-armed stance by Alex's side. "We owe them for that alone."

Franklin shifted his gaze to the bouncer. "I've read the report about your encounter with the serial killer that is assumed to have drowned. As I recall, you were the one to save Detective Anderson's life that night."

Val merely shrugged at the observation. Karl, though, cleared his throat and said, "Yes, sir, that's right. Mr. Stelalux saved me, at great risk to himself."

Trey gave a surreptitious nod to his partner. Good old Karl knew that something was up with Trey and this group. He was trying to do his bit to smooth things along, even without understanding fully what was going on.

"Well, we certainly appreciate citizens' help," Franklin said.

"But?" Alex prodded.

"No buts, sir. We're here on a completely unrelated matter. I'm sure you're aware that there have been two fatal bombings in less than a week in this city."

Alex's face went very serious. "Of course. I've asked Val to increase security at this club. We are all too sensitive over how gay men can be a target. We take such threats seriously."

"I'm not going to suggest you shouldn't be concerned. We are still trying to determine who is behind these events and what their motive is." He paused significantly, and Trey wondered how much the guy was going to share with his quarry.

Franklin pulled out a folded piece of paper from his inner breast pocket and stood to hand it over to Alex. "Would you please take a look at this?"

Leaning forward, Alex stretched his long arm to take the offering, open it and do as asked. His expression barely changed, except for a narrowing of his eyes. Wordlessly, he passed it over to Val, who did the same with Emil.

It was the chef who spoke. "It looks like a photocopy of a piece from one of our membership cards." With a flick of his wrist, he gave it to Harry.

Franklin nodded his head. "That's what Sergeant Duncan thought."

Emil's gaze switched to Trey. He couldn't be sure, but he thought the guy was trying to convey reassurance. Not surprising. Of all the aliens, Emil seemed to be the kindest, even more so than the doctor. Trey had to look away before he could be accused by Franklin of communicating with witnesses who might be suspects in an unsanctioned way.

"Naturally," Alex interjected, "the sergeant is familiar with our club. I've offered him a complimentary membership, as it happens. And although he's refused, he knows he's welcome here any time. I'm not surprised that he recognized the card, even in its damaged state. Are we to assume it was discovered at one of the bombing sites?"

Franklin didn't seem surprised by the deduction, nor should he have been. It didn't take a lot of brain power to connect the dots. Alex's massive intelligence was overkill here. His nonchalance was impressive, for sure. He, and all the Stelalux boys, could have given the Homeland agent lessons on how to play it cool. They stood and sat in various poses of relaxation, or I-don't-give-a-fuck in Val's case, their poker faces in place. They gave the impression that they'd wait until the end of time for Franklin to respond.

Which he did. "Yes, actually. That's exactly what happened. We were hoping you might be able to give us some useful information. We need to catch this guy before he acts again."

"Of course, I—all of us—want to help however we can. Unfortunately, if you expect us to know the identity based on that picture, you are destined for disappointment. The member's name is never on the card. Discretion is critical. I'm sure you'll understand. The number on the card would tell us the man's identity, but as you know, that part is burned, not that its presence at the bomb site means one of our members is involved. Was it found at the nightclub, for example?"

"I'm afraid I can't answer that, sir."

Alex's smile was brittle. "Naturally. I only ask because if one of our members was there as a potential victim, perhaps he dropped it in the chaos of trying to save his own life."

"That's a possibility, certainly. I wonder, sir, if all of you could think hard if anyone strikes you as suspicious? I know you haven't been in this country for too many years…" Whatever innuendo Franklin was going for, it was the first thing he'd said that rankled Alex.

He sat straighter and shot Franklin a cold smile. Trey well-remembered from his own efforts at questioning these aliens that they played the profiling card well. "I trust you're not suggesting that I or any of my family might be involved with this horrific event simply because we are foreigners. I believe Sergeant Duncan

can advise you about how well that worked for the FBI a few months ago, hmm? And I assure you all of our documentation is in order."

Franklin nodded. "Yes, sir, I know. I've reviewed it myself and I didn't mean to imply otherwise. I have to explore all avenues, you understand."

Alex flashed his teeth. "Vividly. I expect you'll want to know where we all were the nights of the bombings."

Now Franklin affected a sheepish air, as if he were doing a thankless task that he didn't really believe in. "Yes, sir. That would be very helpful, just to cross one more thing off our list. I would like Sergeant Duncan and Detective Anderson to remain here to take statements from everyone—a formality, and a voluntary one." Yeah, no one was really buying that assurance.

Alex inclined his head anyway, like the grand chess master he was, already five steps ahead of the agent. "Very well. As I've said, we're happy to cooperate with your investigation."

"Thank you, sir." Franklin stood. "I'll call for a patrol car to pick me up," he added to Trey. "Take your time with the interviews. Make sure you get the boys and the members who are here now."

"Yes, sir." Trey wasn't sure what to make of this turn of events. Part of him felt as if it were some kind of test of his loyalty. If that were the case, the guy would be disappointed. Trey would conduct interviews in the usual way, knowing that Alex and the others would back him up to keep him in Franklin's good graces. It was in their best interests to have their man on the inside in good stead.

Right before Franklin walked through the doorway, he stopped and snapped his fingers as if he'd just remembered something. No one was fooled by this show, either. "By the way, I almost forgot to ask, what did you do in your native country of Romania?"

It was Emil who answered. "We were farmers. Why?" It was the most direct and rude Trey had ever seen the man be.

Franklin gave a tired smile. "No reason...just curious. I guess you worked with plants a lot, huh?"

"I think that's the textbook definition of what being a farmer means," the chef deadpanned. Who knew the guy had it in him?

"Sure." Franklin knocked on the side of his head. "Of course. I'll see myself out."

The room was quiet for almost a minute afterward. If Karl hadn't been there, Trey would have given in to his impulse to slouch down on the sofa and beg Emil for something to eat. His stomach had been in so many knots since the briefing had produced the remnants of the membership card that he hadn't had lunch.

Karl broke the silence by tapping Trey's arm. "Hey, Sarge, how about I get started on the interviews out in the main room? I can begin with the bartender, if that's okay?" He asked the question to Alex as much as Trey.

"Certainly, Detective Duncan," the club owner said. "Kitty is always happy to see you." That sounded like a stretch, given how frosty the woman acted around them. "She'll help you with rounding up the boys. And I'm sure I don't have to ask you to be delicate with the members?"

Karl stood. "No, sir, you don't. I understand. No one ever likes it." He glanced down at Trey. "Meet me later out there when you're finished here?"

"Yeah. I'll take the kitchen staff," he added, thinking that the boy he wanted to check on might be hidden away in Emil's domain.

"Right." Karl left, closing the door behind him. Damn, the guy was way too savvy for Trey's own good.

Emil relaxed a fraction. With Anderson gone, only the family remained. And yeah, Duncan already felt like he was one of them. Pushing away from the wall he'd been holding up, he crossed over and sat in the space the detective had vacated. "Well, that was unexpected."

The cop angled his body toward him. "Really? You didn't think this Marius psycho would pull that move?"

Emil shrugged. "It's more that I didn't think Dracul would. After the drubbing his boys took, I bet he wants to make this agony last longer for us. Our being on the radar of Homeland Security hardly accomplishes that. We're no fun if we're sent to detention."

"Perhaps he's decided that he'd best get us out of the way quickly — and once and for all," Alex mused.

"He must know we won't allow ourselves to be locked up." Even as he made the observation, the idea of having to leave Boston sat like lead in his belly. He'd come to love the place. Plus, what would become of Logan? Or Jase?

Not that the boy was his problem in the long term... He was only helping him get back on his feet — at least that was what he told himself. Jase needed time to heal emotionally, and teaching him the basics of cooking would give him a marketable skill. All of that would take time, and if Marius was determined to frame them for the bombings, they wouldn't have it.

You can always take Jase with you.

He told the voice in his head to shut up. The idea was ridiculous. Jase had already been captive to another man's whims for too long. He deserved freedom—of choice, of destiny. He might think he wanted to obey Emil and call him Master, but that was only because he didn't know any other way. Emil needed time to show him that he could have more, that he deserved more.

"I don't want to run," he heard himself saying. Looking over at Alex, he added, "We have to hunt down Marius."

Alex inclined his head. "Agreed. What do you think, Val?"

"Yeah, I'm on board with that idea, of course, but we can't track him by scent. Even if I dared scope out the site of his next explosion, the strong, acrid smells of the fire would overpower my sense of smell. We need to determine some other way to find him."

"He's using some kind of as-yet-unidentified plant as the basis for his explosive," Duncan said. "Remember last time we convened on this I said they were analyzing it, and now they've narrowed it down to something organic—and non-native. Franklin actually used the word 'alien', although he didn't mean it the way I do."

"Oh shit, I should have known," Emil replied, feeling like three kinds of a fool. When the cop raised his eyebrows, Emil explained. "We managed to salvage some of our food stores before blowing the wreckage of our ship. During long voyages, we grow our own food to process onboard. We held on to them with the hopes of being able to seed some part of this planet. It would have been a taste of home, you understand."

His species wasn't immune to the concept of what humans called homesickness. "We have a small amount of them here, you see. Occasionally I cook with them, and Harry employs some medicinals. We never did any real planting because we quickly understood we wouldn't be able to contain them. Your world might have been overrun with something you couldn't consume. Some of it would be deadly to your species and other animal life."

Duncan sat straighter. "Are you saying you have explosive plants right here?"

Emil nearly rolled his eyes at the suggestion before remembering how frightened the human must be for his people and his city. "No, they aren't inherently dangerous in that way, but Marius was playing around with mixtures involving Earth-based elements to create something powerful. He may have perfected what, so far according to our knowledge, had only caused him to lose his arm."

"I thought that was gunpowder."

"No, sorry if we gave that impression. His foray into that only cost humans their lives. Marius has been careful with his own, despite his, um…hobby costing him bits and pieces."

"I suppose I have to be grateful he didn't figure out how to split an atom," the cop muttered. Emil couldn't help but bark out a laugh. The others did, as well, even Harry. "What's so funny?"

"Sorry. He does know how to. That's something our world did eons ago. We gave it up quickly as too unstable." He shook his head. "No, Marius is crazy, not suicidal."

"And Dracul wants to rule a livable world, not a dead one," Alex added.

"Okay, good to know." Duncan blew out a breath. "So now what? Can you guys counteract this stuff, whatever it is?"

"Possibly." Emil grimaced. "I'm a botanist by training and Harry is a whiz in the lab. We can maybe concoct something useful. We're going to need a sample, though. At least it would be helpful to have one."

Duncan threw his head back. "Fuck, I knew you were going to say that." He righted his head. "I'll see what I can do, but don't hold your breath. This isn't like conning the coroner or outmaneuvering hospital staff. The feds don't fuck around. Security on the evidence is tight as a tick."

"Don't take any unnecessary risks. Harry and I can make do with the information we have."

Alex slapped his palm on his desk. "Well, have we spent sufficient time here to convince the stalwart Detective Anderson that we've been properly questioned?"

"Yeah, probably." Duncan labored to his feet, tiredness and worry evident in the way he carried himself. "I have to question the kitchen staff to make it look good, and I'd like to talk to the kid…Jase." He shot a meaningful glance in Emil's direction.

His first reaction was to roar out his disapproval. He dialed it back in a millisecond, although his thoughts must have shown through his eyes because the cop jerked back. "Sorry, and yes, that's fine. I have him working in the kitchen."

"Yeah? That's convenient. By the way," Duncan said to the room at large, "be extra discreet in your hunt for this Marius asshole. I'm betting Franklin is going to have this place, and maybe each of you, watched. He's suspicious as hell."

"Won't you be able to warn us if that's the case?" Emil felt compelled to ask.

"Maybe. I get the feeling he thinks I'm compromised. It's the company I keep," he added with a grin.

Emil could tell it bothered him. He put his hand on the man's shoulder. "I'm sorry. We don't mean to cause you trouble."

Duncan shook off the apology. "It's fine. It is what it is, and nothing matters except stopping this nightmare once and for all."

"Come on. I'll take you to the kitchen. Damien is the only staff member working tonight. Logan might be around, too, if that helps."

"I don't want to drag her into this mess unless I have to. She has no official position here, and only Karl would know she's involved at all with the club. I don't think he's inclined to say anything at this point."

"Loyalty is a rare virtue."

The cop didn't say anything in response. Emil got the impression he felt conflicted on how he was compromising his partner with the secrets and lies that came with being involved in the war. The kitchen was pretty quiet, Emil having gone for simple and hearty beef stew for those members interested in eating. It was a cold day and would be a colder night. One-pot cooking was both easy and comforting.

His gaze homed in on Jase without his thinking about it. The boy was right where Emil had left him, sitting at the table, poking at a bowl of stew. Jase looked up instantly, aware the moment that Emil had stepped foot inside the room that he'd done so. The response saddened Emil and angered him. This poor, abused kid had learned to always know where potential danger was. He shouldn't have to be on alert like that. When

Jase's eyes went wide at the sight of Duncan, Emil hurried to reassure him.

"Hey, it's fine. Sergeant Duncan only wants to ask you a few questions." Rushing to the boy's side, Emil put a smile on his face. "I promise everything's fine."

Jase lowered his gaze. "Yes, Chef."

Christ. Chef sounded like 'master' to Emil's ears because that's what Jase meant. He was trying to give Emil what he wanted. Of course he was. He knew no other way. The really scary bit was that some part of Emil liked it. Hearing it made him puff up inside with pleasure and that wasn't right. Unlike Val, he'd never chosen to explore this Dom lifestyle where he controlled a boy with loving mastery. If he'd thought of it at all, he'd have pictured something more like what Harry had with his precious Lucien and Alex had with the adorable Quinn — someone to coddle and spoil and protect.

Not that Jase was his to keep in any form. He was like Logan, someone to help out, patch up and get back on his feet. Emil was a way station in the boy's life until he could strike out on his own and take care of himself. Emil was all wrong for him anyway. The age difference alone, even if Emil were human, made them an unsuitable couple. His chastisement of Alex and Val taking on such young lovers was real, not simply ribbing. He'd felt the same way about Harry and Lucien, although he had to admit that in all three cases, there was true love between the men and their boys. Still, it bothered him, and besides…Jase was different. He'd been abused and deserved careful treatment. He didn't need Emil salivating over him.

Like he had earlier with the sliced finger. If he closed his eyes, he could still smell the sweet scent of Jase's blood welling up and beckoning him. The willpower it had taken to resist sucking that digit into his mouth and savoring the salty treat had nearly killed him. And it hadn't been simply blood that he'd wanted. It had been Jase's in particular. Only the knowledge that he would have frightened the boy half to death and disgusted him to boot had given him the courage to resist the temptation.

Duncan's voice pulled him back to the present. "Hi. Jason, isn't it? Do you remember me?"

"Yes, sir."

"Good." Duncan sat down on Jase's opposite side. "How are you feeling?"

"Fine, sir. Thank you for asking."

"Okay." Duncan sighed. "Could you please do me a favor and look at me and tell me that again."

After a moment's hesitation, the boy did as asked but not before a quick glance at Emil first. Emil smiled and nodded in encouragement. "I'm truly all right, sir."

Duncan studied Jase's face for a few seconds before his gaze pierced Emil's over the boy's head. "How about you give us a little privacy, Emil?"

"Sure." Even as Emil spoke the word, a small whimper came from Jase. He looked at Emil with pleading eyes. "And that would be a no," he amended before sitting down at Jase's side.

Duncan sighed again. "Fine. So, Jase, is there a family member that you'd like to get in contact with?"

Jase shook his head slowly. "No, sir. There's no one."

"Really? No parents, siblings, maybe a grandparent." When Jase merely shook his head again, Duncan got down to the harder stuff. "How long were you with Washburn? I know what you said last night. I want to hear it again, now that you're in a safe, quiet place."

Jase fiddled with his half-empty glass of milk for a few seconds before abruptly stopping. He put his hands in his lap. He seemed so lost and afraid.

"It's okay, baby. You should tell Sergeant Duncan the truth." *Fuck, again with the 'baby'. What is my problem?*

Jase took a deep, stuttering breath. "Three years."

"To be clear, Washburn took you in when you were fifteen?"

Jase nodded, his face steeped in misery.

"Were you a runaway that he found somewhere?"

Jase shook his head and his pale cheeks pinked.

"How did you end up with him, then?"

Jase opened his mouth. Nothing came out. He swallowed hard enough for Emil to notice. He could hear the quickening of the boy's heartbeat. A glance at the base of his throat showed a rapid thrumming of his pulse. There was no temptation to sink his fangs into the vein, however. Emil knew only pity and empathy. And mounting fury, although he tamped that down. Obviously, the answer Jase was working up his courage to give was going to be bad.

"It's okay. I'm here. Take your time." He dared to put his arm around the boy's shoulders and was rewarded when Jase didn't flinch. If anything, he leaned into the touch.

"He, um…won me, sir," Jase finally managed to say.

Duncan's mouth formed a thin line before he asked, "You mean, like, in a poker game or something?"

"No, sir. It was an auction."

"Auction! Who was selling you?" The cop was crap, apparently, at holding back his emotions. He'd said the very thing that Emil thought and in an aggrieved tone that mirrored Emil's feelings, although Emil would have added "And where can I find the fucker so that I can kill him."

Tears formed at the corners of Jase's eyes. His lips trembled as he tried to speak. Then he launched himself into Emil's chest and held on to him with clenched fists.

"Please, Master, please don't make me do this."

Emil didn't hesitate. He picked the boy up and pulled him onto his lap. He tucked Jase's head against his shoulder and hugged him tightly. "Okay, Duncan, that's enough."

Duncan frowned. "I'm trying to help him, Emil."

"I understand your motive, but he's too fragile right now. Back. Off." Opening his mouth, he let his fangs show and hissed softly at the man.

Duncan held up his hands and stood. "Okay, okay, don't have a cow. But I got to ask, Jase. Do you want me to take you to a shelter? There's one I know for gay teens that is safe and has counselors."

The cop hadn't finished his spiel before Jase whimpered again, louder this time, and practically plastered himself against Emil.

Emil gave Duncan a pointed look. "That would be a hard pass."

"Right. I just hope you know what you're doing."

"So do I," Emil admitted. He jutted his chin in Damien's direction. The sous chef had been doing his best to pretend he wasn't following the goings-on across the room. "That's Damien if you want to interview him about *you know*."

Duncan nodded. Before he left, he placed one of his business cards on the table. "Jase, I'm leaving my contact info. Don't hesitate to call if you need me."

As there was no chance of Jase taking it, Emil tucked it into his pocket after standing. Jase clung to him like a limpet, so he hoisted the boy more fully in his arms. It felt right, natural, and that disturbed him. It shouldn't. Jase was a chore, he reminded himself. A duty, not a pleasure.

"It's been a long day already. Let's get you to bed, for a nap at least."

He realized the import of his words the moment they'd left his mouth. His cock loved the implication, jumping up — or at least trying to. It was tightly trapped in Emil's jeans. It begged to be let out. He told it to shut the fuck up.

Chapter Eight

All the way to the bedroom, Jase kept telling himself to stop being such a baby. Master had been patient so far with him, but that wouldn't last forever. He'd kindly stayed with him when the police officer had asked him hard, painful questions—questions that the man seemed genuinely interested in getting answers to. It hadn't felt like a trap, something designed to get Jase to say the wrong thing and for which punishment would be administered. The man hadn't touched Jase once, hadn't shoved his cock down Jase's throat or bent Jase over the table for a fucking. What was more, Jase believed that if the man had tried, Master would have stopped him. It was ridiculous to have such faith in anyone, let alone a monster. And still, against all reason, he did.

"Here we are." Master's voice sounded so cheery as he carried Jase into the bedroom.

A quick peek confirmed it was the same one he'd slept in the night before. Master's, not some new place where he might be alone. Again, that shouldn't be comforting because it meant sex. That was never an experience to welcome. It was debasing at best and excruciating at worst. While he had a feeling Master would be kind to him, there would be nothing to do about his size and how ill-equipped Jase's body would be to accommodate it. He couldn't bring himself to imagine what kind of huge dick Master had. Everything about him was ginormous. That part had to be as well. And Jase had spent the day without a plug in his ass to keep him stretched out. This night might be as painful for him as the very first time.

So, yeah, he should be scared and desperate to maybe run downstairs to see if the cop was still there and his offer for sanctuary was real. He wasn't, and he had no interest in fleeing, either. Part of that was years of hard-learned lessons that escape was impossible. A bigger part, though, was this perverse sense that there was no better or safer place than Master's arms.

Master didn't toss Jase on the bed as he expected. Instead, he gently set him on his feet and released his hold before stepping back. "How's that? Feeling all right?"

Jase nodded. "Yes, Master. I'm sorry I got so upset. And I'm sorry I forgot not to call you Master in the kitchen."

"That's okay. I understand. Don't worry about it."

"Thank you, Master." *Shit.* "Thank you, Master Emil," he corrected himself.

Because he had his gaze downward like a good slave, he couldn't see Master's expression. He thought he heard a frustrated sigh but couldn't be sure. It was faint and Master was already moving away.

He didn't leave, though. He went to sit in a chair in the far corner. The piece of furniture was oversized, like everything else in the room. It accommodated the large man with ease, giving him a comfortable amount of space to sprawl. There was even a spot left where a small human could curl beside him, if permitted. That stray thought surprised him, as so much had in the last twenty-four hours. Jase had spent the last few years trying to keep away from men, not get closer. So much had changed in his life in a dizzying amount of time. Standing in the dark room populated with big things, Jase felt like Alice in Wonderland—and, like that fictitious girl, he wondered who in the world he was.

"Why don't you go and take a shower? Get ready for bed. I know it's kind of early…"

Jase knew an order when he heard one, regardless of how it was phrased. With a nod, he did as told. He kept the bathroom door open in case Master wanted to watch him. Some men did. Maybe vampires didn't. He wasn't going to take any chances, and in the larger scheme of things, a lack of privacy didn't rate very highly in things that worried him.

He stripped down and was careful to neatly fold his borrowed clothes and put them on top of the hamper before getting under the spray. After a day of standing around peeling potatoes and prepping other foods, the hot water felt good on his body. The ache, though, was a welcome one. It hadn't been obtained from punishment—merely good, hard work. It gave him a sense of pride to know that he'd served a purpose during the day. Master seemed to truly value his efforts, and other people appreciated them, without his being demeaned in the process.

He was careful to clean himself thoroughly, though, because surely the next job of the day was to bring his Master pleasure. There was no enema nozzle for him to use, so he worked his hole with a soapy finger. He winced at how tight he'd become already. That was the problem with this passage into one's body. It wasn't designed to stay open and loose. Even though wearing a plug had been for the benefit of his old master's dick, it had still helped him, too. He'd hated every second of wearing the thing, but he was sure missing it now.

When bathing wasn't part of a show, time was of the essence. As much as he would have liked standing under the spray for a few more minutes, he didn't linger. The big, fluffy towels wicked the water from his skin quickly and did a decent job of drying his mop of hair. There was no hair dryer, so there was no way to remove the dampness. He hoped Master wouldn't mind his sheets getting wet. The last thing he did was brush his teeth and put on some deodorant. Masters could be stinky, not so slaves. Not that his current master smelled like anything other than the things he used to cook with.

As he stood staring at his reflection in the bathroom mirror for a moment, he tried to see what Master saw and assess whether that was a good thing. He knew he was pretty, because he'd been told that his entire life, and he looked young. Men had slavered over him for that very reason. Was that appealing to this master? Would a creature so large and strong and darkly exotic find small paleness desirable? Perhaps his very opposite nature was exactly what the vampire wanted. Of course, if it was blood he was looking for, Jase didn't have much.

The idea that he was about to be bitten and drained brought him crashing down to reality. He started to break out in a panicky sweat. Good thing he'd gone for the deodorant. If he thought he could get away with it, he would have stalled some more. That never worked. Best to get things over with. He could do this. Over the years, he'd learned he was stronger than he'd believed as a child.

Master was still sitting in the corner chair, although he'd stripped down to a T-shirt and jeans. The way the fabric stretched across his broad, muscular chest was impressive. It caught Jase's attention, despite his growing fear. He tried to focus on that and not the equally eye-catching bulge straining the denim over the man's crotch. *Don't get ahead of yourself. One step at a time.* It was the only way to stay sane.

He went on autopilot mode, letting his training take over and pushing active thoughts aside. Master's thick legs were spread wide, giving Jase the perfect spot to kneel between them. With head bowed and hands clasped behind his back, he waited to be used. A hand landed on top of his head. He stiffened for a split-second in anticipation of having his hair grasped with a painful grip, of being pulled forward, of being forced to choke down a cock. As much as his gag reflex had been trained out of him, he might not be able to swallow the dick he knew lurked just out of sight.

None of those things happened. Instead, Master patted him, like he was a small boy, then helped him back to his feet. Before Jase could register what was happening, he found himself sitting on Master's lap. Now the bulge that he'd spied pressed against him. It was hard, even through the jeans. It *pulsed.*

"Sorry about that." Master shifted Jase so that he sat more on his rigid thigh. "Pay no attention to what my dumb body is doing." His arms hung loosely around Jase for only a moment before Master moved them to the chair arms.

Stunned and confused, Jase did the only thing he could think of. He relaxed against the broad chest, tucking his head under the man's chin. He could hear the quick thud of Master's heart. It matched his own fluttering beat, although stronger in some way. It was oddly comforting. This alien monster was not so different than he was. Unlike what the legends of vampires said, he wasn't undead. He was very much alive and affected by Jase's proximity. Why then was he not feeding Jase his cock or shoving it inside him? That was what Jase was for, after all.

"I think I need to be clearer about why you're here." Once again, Jase wondered if Master could read his mind. "You are not my slave, sex or otherwise. You don't have to kneel before me, you do not need to give me blow jobs and I'm not going to fuck you. That is not what this is about. Do you understand, Jase?"

He started to nod yes then changed his mind. In this case, he believed that an honest answer was expected of him. "No, Master Emil, I'm sorry but I don't."

The chest he lay against rose and fell on a deep breath followed by an audible sigh that ruffled his hair. "Okay. Let me see if I can explain. I'm not very good with words. I don't have Alex's silver tongue, that's for sure."

Master ran his hand lightly down Jase's back. It made him shiver in a delightful way. "So much pain." He began rubbing with slow circles. "I look at you and I see the scars and the welts and bruises that haven't yet healed from whatever Washburn did to you before he died. And I know there is more, things from the past that have already healed. Worse, there are wounds inside you, physically and emotionally, that I can't see at all. It breaks my heart."

The man's tone was so sincere that Jase believed him. Touched, he snuggled closer to show that he appreciated the concern and wasn't afraid — well, not too much anyway — to be his slave. The back rub was soothing, as well. It was not so different that the ones his mother had given him long ago when he'd been a little boy and fretting over some imaginary fear. Those days seemed like a lifetime ago, and something that had happened to someone else. How naïve he'd been back then, worrying about monsters that didn't exist when the world was filled with real ones that had been beyond his imagination at the time.

"You're here with me," Master continued, "because once Washburn brought you into our orbit, we had a responsibility to protect you. We failed. And, for that, I can't apologize enough."

The words confused Jase. Masters never said they were sorry. That was a sentiment reserved for slaves. He had no idea where this was going.

Master sighed again. "So, with Washburn gone, we owe it to you to get you back on your feet, to make sure you can take care of yourself. I'm the best choice to do that. Alex and Val have Quinn and Mackie to worry about, and Harry has his family. All I have is the kitchen, and maybe Logan, although she would likely punch me for the suggestion," he added with a little chuckle. "It's my job to help you figure out what you want and make sure you get it. Understand?"

Jase shook his head. He didn't. Not really. And that word 'job' made him inexplicitly sad. Master didn't desire him? That wasn't the case. It was obvious that he did. Jase could feel how much.

"I'm sorry, Master Emil. I don't understand." He wiggled his ass. The hard length of Master's dick pressed against the back of his thigh. "You want me," he dared to say in a near whisper.

Master surprised him by pecking a kiss on the top of his head, then chuckling. "Of course I do. You're beautiful and sweet. How could I possibly resist you? I may be stronger than the average human, but I am no better at controlling my baser instincts. My dick has no scruples. Fortunately, I run the show, not it. There will be no sex, Jase. It's important that you believe me about that. You've been forced too much in your young life, in any life. Rape isn't something that my species does, and it is one of the most appalling aspects of human behavior."

He paused, and Jase could sense him tensing. "That's not entirely true. There are those of my people who have adopted the worst of what humans do to each other. I can't deny that, and while you don't need the details, I have to admit that not everyone who survived my ship's crashing has stayed faithful to our beliefs. Those of us loyal to Alex take pride in not having succumbed to that temptation. We've made it our new lives' work to combat it, in fact. I will not abuse you. I'd rather die than do so."

"I believe you." Jase said the words because he meant them and because he thought Master needed to hear them. He also dared to ask the one question that sat on his tongue demanding to get out. "What about blood? I thought you needed it."

"Need is a stronger way of describing it than is reality. We can live without it for a very long time, although we are miserable doing so. I get mine from a blood bank. I don't need yours, and taking it without consent is anathema to my family, as well."

Jase swallowed hard past a lump of fear forming in his throat. He couldn't believe he was going to say this. "I will give it to you, if you want, Master Emil."

"Oh, baby." Master pulled him closer and kissed the top of his head again. "Such a sweet offer, and I have no doubt you mean it. The trouble is, you've been programmed to give a man what he wants, even to your own detriment. I can't accept your offer, not now. And later, when you're back in complete control of your life, you'll probably regret ever making it. Humans have a primal fear about blood sucking."

Jase frowned. He didn't like the idea that his thoughts weren't being taken seriously. Then he remembered that his didn't count for anything. That part of his life hadn't changed. Still, he found the strength to persist. "Quinn and Mackie allow it, don't they?"

"Sure, but that's different. Mackie likes it as part of his role as a submissive and Quinn gave it as a gift to someone he loved. I doubt it was easy for either of them to do. In any event, you and I aren't like those couples. You didn't choose me."

I might have. His surprising and stray thought didn't have time to gain traction.

Master's back rubbing continued. "That's enough questions and answers for now. You've had a long day and I bet you're still suffering a deficit in your sleep. Relax. I've got you. You're safe with me."

Between his real tiredness and the soothing nature of Master's touch, Jase had no trouble following that order. Closing his eyes, he gave in to the pull and drifted off in the security of a monster's arms.

* * * *

"Thanks." Emil whispered his appreciation to Harry as he closed the bedroom door.

A quick glance toward the bed confirmed that Jase still slept soundly. Emil had waited until the boy had been asleep for a good ten minutes before lifting him off his lap and tucking him in among the covers. If it had been all about what Emil wanted, he would have stayed sitting in that chair the whole night. Nothing had ever felt so wonderfully right to him as cradling the human in his arms, rubbing slow circles up and down his battered back did. The mere fact that the boy had been relaxed enough to fall asleep was gratifying. It gave Emil hope that recovery from his years of abuse was possible. All Emil had to do was keep his own traitorous body on lockdown.

Easier said than done. The talk of blood had raised a thirst that he couldn't ignore. And the proximity of Jase's tempting ass had caused Emil's dick to become engorged. No amount of time or chastisement was having any effect. With Jase safely down for hopefully the whole night, he'd decided that he needed to take care of both needs before morning came. The problem was that each time he'd tried to step out of the room, some internal alarm forced him back. He didn't want to leave the boy alone was the bottom line.

So, warm blood bag in hand, he headed for the bathroom. He tilted the door shut so that if Jase needed him, there would be no chance he'd miss it. He kept the light on, as well, knowing that humans feared nothing as much as they did the dark. Their puny eyesight and diurnal natures made it scary, and that was the last thing he wanted for the boy.

Popping the seal on the bag, he began to tug down long gulps of the salty treat. Harry had been a dear in warming it for him. As he sucked, he unsnapped his jeans, then lowered the zipper. The relief of freeing his dick was intense. He bit back a groan, determined to be silent in his private effort to meet his needs. The toilet was the only place to sit, and that didn't appeal. He pressed against the wall and slid down until his butt hit the tiles. He grabbed his cock on the way with a death grip.

It wasn't very comfortable, but that was hardly the point. This was all about satisfying the primitive within him. His body craved blood, and if it wasn't the type he wanted, tough shit. His balls required emptying and, again, where he wanted to deposit his seed was irrelevant. He couldn't help Jase if he was constantly flaunting his hard-on and bloodlust in front of the boy.

That would not do.

But he was only human, in a manner of speaking. His species was more evolved than that one, yet not by much. He succumbed to many of the same weaknesses, sex and hunger being two of them. And he was no saint, either. While his intellect and sense of morality told him he should make his mind blank as he drank his blood and worked his shaft, he lacked the strength of mind or character to do that. Instead, he cast his memory back to less than an hour ago when Jase's small, cute ass had pressed against his groin. He recalled the sweet scent of shampoo, minty toothpaste and lavender deodorant. Humans were oddly worried about smelling bad. At that moment, though, he appreciated it. Part of the delightful way he thought of the boy included the odors he carried.

His dick jumped in his clasp and his balls tingled. He worked the part underneath the glans that held the sensitive bundle of nerves. His breath hitched, making him choke slightly on his blood. With long practice, he synced up the rhythm of his sucking and jerking. The salty hit in the back of his throat mirrored the pulse of pleasure working his shaft. He closed his eyes and concentrated on his growing climax along with the way the blood slid down his throat.

He imagined that his lips weren't wrapped around a piece of plastic but were sealed against skin. His fangs punched down as if piercing flesh. He drew in a long, hard pull. With his fingers clenched tightly around his shaft, he rolled his hips to fuck them. In his mind, he pushed into Jase's ass. Not the real boy, someone different—a human who gave himself freely, who looked at him with adoring eyes and urged him to thrust faster and deeper. Emil groaned at the thought.

"*Master…*"

Yes, someone who called him that because he wanted to. A whispered entreaty born from love and not fear.

"*Master…*"

The word rang in his ears, and he pumped his fist with desperate urgency. His fingers were too hard and dry. He needed soft and wet, with a welcoming heat. He sucked his bag of blood with an unquenchable thirst, as if he'd been starved for years. It wasn't going to be enough. It never was.

A tentative touch to his balls made him jerk. His movement fumbled as his eyes flew open. Jase kneeled beside him. He'd reached over and cupped Emil. The boy did nothing more than that, merely sat and waited for something. Permission, maybe, to continue — or chastisement to go back to bed.

The word 'master' hadn't been inside Emil's head. He realized the boy must have been calling to him. *Shit.* So much for being quiet and circumspect. The former slave must have developed a sixth sense about a man needing him. Or perhaps Emil had been shouting the house down without realizing it. Regardless, he needed to stop, put the blood bag down, let go of his aching dick and put that poor kid back under the covers — without sliding in with him and finishing his fantasy for real.

He couldn't do it. To his utter shame, he lacked the strength to do the right thing. Instead, he started again. This time, he kept his eyes open, staring at Jase's bowed head, savoring the simple pleasure of the boy's fingers caressing his balls. The tension in him mounted quickly. Then Jase looked up and his pretty blues eyes stared straight into Emil's undoubtedly black ones. He came with a force that had him doubling over. The bag dropped from his nerveless fingers, as cum pumped over his fingers.

A drop of blood slipped past his lips and he watched it as if in slow-motion, hitting the stretch of skin between Jase's forefinger and thumb. Letting go of his dick, Emil grabbed the boy's hand and enveloped the fold with his lips. He sucked as if he pulled on a vein. The small bit of blood he ingested was nothing compared to the pleasure of simply tasting the human's flesh. Emil was careful to keep his fangs retracted. It nearly killed him, but he wasn't going to go back on his promise and drink without free permission. He'd already sinned by taking advantage of Jase's belief that he had to help Emil's jerk-off session.

He kept sucking until the last of his orgasm subsided. Then, with a shaky hand, he let go of the boy and sat back. He was about to apologize in the most groveling way he could manage when Jase surprised him by first looking at his hand then licking it. Emil suddenly realized that he'd transferred some of his cum onto the boy.

Jase smacked his lips. "It tastes like a human's except a little spicier. It's nice," he added with a sheepish grin.

The observation sent another pulse through Emil's cock. A last bit of cum dribbled out. He worked to regain his breath and his voice. "I didn't mean to wake you."

"I sleep lightly." The confession was painful to hear because of the implication that a sex slave would have to for survival.

"You didn't have to help me. It's important for you to know that. I can't assure you this won't happen again. I don't want you to think I'm going back on my promise."

Jase peeked at him from under his lashes. "Is it okay that I did, Master?"

Emil didn't bother to correct him. What was the point, given that he clearly enjoyed being called that by this boy? "Yes. Everything you do is fine. Don't worry about displeasing me. It's impossible for you to do so." Because the sight of Jase demurely kneeling beside him gave him too many bad ideas, he looked away. "Go back to bed."

Jase didn't hesitate to comply. He rose with a grace that Emil couldn't ignore. It made the boy more appealing than ever. Emil briefly considered that he should offer a reciprocal hand job, except Jase's lovely, slender cock hung flaccidly between his legs. The fact that the boy wasn't aroused emphasized that helping Emil had been a chore, not a pleasure. Guilt swamped him.

"Thank you," he called out before Jase had reached the doorway. It sounded stupid and entirely insufficient under the circumstances.

Pausing, Jase peered over his shoulder. His naked beauty was breathtaking. "You're welcome, Master."

The boy sounded as if he really meant it, which made him more dangerous to Emil than ever.

* * * *

Wales, Dracul's Castle

"Well?" Dracul punctuated his impatient demand by thrusting viciously into his new slut. He had the boy bent over the end of the bed, inconvenienced by the doctor's examination of Dafydd's disgustingly swollen belly. He turned away from the unsightly bulge. Pregnancy did nothing for the boy's looks, his whole body distorted and his face mottled. Dracul preferred the sleek, tight one he currently gripped far better.

Drogo straightened from his examination, covering Dafydd with a sheet. The tiresome man was always doing stupid things like that. As if Dracul didn't have the right to see every inch of the human's body. But for his medical skills, Dracul would have purged the irksome drone from his ranks.

"All is well with your son, sir. A few more weeks, two months at the outside, and he will be ready to be birthed. I would recommend," he added with a slight frown, "that your consort drinks more blood. Soon he will lose a great deal of his own when I cut the boy from him."

As if Dracul cared about Dafydd's health. His life was over the moment the baby left him. It was merely a matter of how much Dracul wanted to participate. Exsanguination from the birth would be, at worst, a waste of a tasty meal.

He snapped his hips to shove his dick deep inside his new slut's resistant channel. Breaking in a virgin continued to delight him. While the human had ceased to fight him actively, his pathetic, yet pretty body waged its own war. It still took effort to invade it. The grip was delicious. He groaned with the pleasure and dug his fingers into the spare flesh.

"Do what you must to keep my son healthy," he said with a dismissive toss of his head.

Drogo stepped back with an obsequious bow. No longer restricted by the doctor's needs, Dracul refocused on his own. He pulled out his dick and slapped the boy's flank. "Crawl up."

He delighted in the human's obvious difficulty in doing so. The moment he'd landed fully prone on the covers, Dracul launched himself as well. He had his half-hard dick buried once more into the small ass within seconds. He smiled at the boy's whimper. He covered the smaller frame with his much larger one, taking his own weight on his arms only to keep from smothering the weak creature. He was enjoying him too much to waste and intended to stay cocooned inside the wet heat for the rest of the day.

As Drogo rushed out of the room, Petru passed him. "Your pardon, sir. Marius has called in with a live feed he wants you to watch." He handed over a tablet.

Dracul took it with some annoyance. Human technology could be useful but also a distraction from the simple pleasure that he enjoyed—such as a tight and unwilling hole. Knowing that neither Marius nor Petru would dare to bother him with something trivial, he took the device and tapped the video to life.

He found himself watching some kind of outdoor area with brick buildings and people milling about. Unlike where he lay, it was still daytime wherever this was. Everyone was bundled with obvious cold. Humans were so pathetically susceptible to being chilled. Then again, if he wanted to be charitable, his species hated warm weather. No, he didn't want to be understanding. His was a superior nature to humans.

At the moment when he'd started to lose patience, there was a loud noise, followed by an avalanche of smoke and debris. Then a sound that made him crow with delight—screaming.

Chapter Nine

"Haymarket is hundreds of years old. People in Boston have been buying fresh produce and fish in this place for generations. It gives you a real sense of history and it's still a great way to buy fresh, local stuff at a good price."

Emil wasn't sure if his tutorial meant anything to Jase. The boy's face was hard to see, bundled as it was in a puffy parka loaned by Quinn. Since leaving the club, he'd been taking in the pedestrian sights of the Boston streets as if seeing the world for the first time. It made Emil appreciate better how limited Jase's life had been for a long while. It made him want to extend what had been intended as a short shopping trip into something more interesting.

"Once we get what we need, we can pile it into the SUV and maybe grab something at a restaurant. How does that sound? It can be nice eating something I haven't cooked."

Jase turned to beam a smile at him. "That's sounds wonderful, Chef. Thank you."

"It's a date, then," he said with a firm nod. He instantly regretted his use of the D word, but honestly, after what had happened a few nights earlier, his word choice hardly rated as an issue to fret over.

By silent agreement, neither he nor Jase had mentioned the jerk-off session in the bathroom. Emil had had to bite his tongue to keep from begging forgiveness. That was only going to make him feel better and serve to force Jase to relive the experience. That couldn't be healthy for the boy, so Emil plastered a smile on his face and went about business as usual.

Their unexpectedly shared lives had fallen into a decent rhythm. Every day, Jase helped Emil in the kitchen, learning new skills and proving to be a hard worker and an adept learner. At night, Emil would help Jase settle down with a back rub while they sat in the chair. Once Jase was asleep, Emil moved him to his bed. Then Mackie or Quinn watched over him while Emil continued to work. Hours later, Emil would slip in, often after jerking himself in his office, like a dirty old man. It helped him keep his sanity while he was with Jase, however, and it ensured that there would be no chance that the boy would feel obliged to help.

And Emil slept on the floor. As big as his bed was, nothing was wide enough when it came to keeping him from the temptation that was Jase.

So he had a good plan and stuck with it. Part of it included that—it being Saturday—it was market day. If he was going to teach Jase cooking, there was no better lesson than where to go for good, fresh food and how to pick out the right stuff. He'd driven, as usual, although this time he was sure he was being tailed by someone. Duncan had been right about being surveilled. He didn't care. He had nothing at all to hide. This wasn't a ruse. He really did go every Saturday to buy fruit and vegetables in Haymarket.

The Faneuil Hall area was bustling with people, despite the cold weather. Given the proximity of the garage where he'd parked, he estimated that the walk back and forth wouldn't be too taxing for Jase. They could catch an early dinner at one of the local spots easily, as well. It wasn't exactly waterfront, but it had its own charm.

The explosion occurred in the next instant, a deafening sound followed by a split-second of utter silence and a sense that time had actually stopped. Then it was chaos, a rain of debris with people screaming and running for their lives. Emil grabbed Jase and raced to the side of a building, not caring if his superhuman speed was noticed. Crouching down, he covered Jase with his body while he scoured the area for the source of the blast. He didn't spend a moment analyzing the what or the why — or even the who. He had those answers already. What mattered now was keeping Jase safe.

Or so he thought. Through the carnage, the smoke and the frantic humans, he spotted the source of the evil. Marius stood on the top of a nearby building, holding up a phone with his one hand and grinning wickedly.

He's filming it. Whether it was for Dracul's edification or Marius' own dickless jerk-off session later on, the sight of it infuriated Emil. And it was a chance for him to do something to stop it. He was torn between protecting Jase and protecting all the people of Boston. There could be yet another explosion and Jase was far from out of danger. But there was no choice here, none at all.

Bending down, Emil shouted into Jase's ear to make himself heard. "Stay here! Do not move until I return. I will be angrier than you've ever seen me, than you've ever seen anyone, if you do. Understand?" The boy turned a frightened face toward him and nodded.

As sure as he could be that he'd done all that was possible to keep the boy from harm, Emil launched himself from his position and took off through the crowd. He had to be careful not to give himself away or to bowl over the delicate humans he dodged. He hardened his heart to the bodies lying mangled near him as he sprinted around the center of the blast. The dead were beyond his help and the dying needed more than he could give anyway. Getting Marius was his goal, and no one other than him was going to be able to do it.

If luck had been with him, he would have reached the guy's position without detection. It wasn't. Emil happened to look the moment Marius spotted him. The man's grin didn't fade as much as he turned from his position and disappeared from sight. Emil poured on his speed, heedless now to being observed. He headed for the side of the building he judged Marius must have leaped down from. As he rounded the corner, he spotted his quarry climbing into an SUV with tinted windows.

A roar escaped him as he jumped the remaining distance and onto the hood of Marius' vehicle. At first surprised, the guy recovered to grin maniacally. With his half-ear and some missing teeth, not to mention scars from long-ago burns, he looked every inch the monster humans would think him to be. He stared straight into Emil's eyes and gunned the SUV forward. Emil had to clench his fingers around the bottom edge of the windshield. Marius swerved as he drove effortlessly with his one hand, not only down the crowded streets but on the sidewalks, too. The explosion had sent chaos throughout the area as people tried to both stop to gawk and flee from the scene.

Emil swayed with each turn, but he didn't let go. This was his best chance to bring Marius down. He spread his legs to hug the hood better before releasing one of his hands. Then he punched at the glass in front of him. It held, sending a shock of pain up his arm. He ignored it and punched again, throwing as much of his strength into his arm as he could. On the fourth try, the windshield cracked but it didn't shatter, a safety feature of newer vehicles that he would have admired in any other circumstances.

Through the spidery lines, he could see that Marius was no longer grinning. That was some comfort. It was short-lived. With a sudden jerk of his wheel, the guy sent the SUV careening into a wall. He braked right before it crashed fully. The impact, though, was sufficient to jolt Emil's hold. He yelled as much in frustration as anything else as he tumbled off the hood and onto the sidewalk. By the time he picked his battered body off the pavement, Marius had sped away.

Only the presence of a few frightened humans kept him from roaring in frustration. Thoughts of Jase sent him loping back to where he'd left him. In the log jam of people, cars and emergency vehicles, one large man with a scraped jacket, ripped jeans and a bloody hand hardly registered. He forced himself back into the war zone and stopped only when a cop corralled him.

"I'm sorry, sir. You can't go past this point. We need space to help the wounded, which you look to be one of. We have EMTs right over here."

Emil pulled up short and glared down into the earnest young woman's face. To her credit, she didn't back down, even though he was sure his expression must be terrifying. He knew this because that was how he was feeling about Jase being alone in the carnage.

"I'm fine. My boyfriend's over there. I have to get to him." He didn't question his use of the B word, not for a moment.

"I'm sorry, sir," the cop began.

Emil stopped listening to her. Over her head, he saw something that made his heart skip. Out of the smoke-filled air and swarming emergency crews, Jase came running. He didn't stop until he'd plowed right into Emil's waiting arms.

"I'm sorry, Master," the boy sobbed against him. "I couldn't stay. I needed to know you were all right. I don't care about the punishment."

Emil pulled him into his arms, indifferent to any stares. Who cared what two men did when so many people lay dead and dying? "It's okay, baby. It doesn't matter, so long as you're safe."

He carried the boy away from the scene of death and his own failure. "We're going home now."

* * * *

"Mr. Stelalux, you are telling me that the only reason why you chased this man you claim to not know was because he was acting suspicious?"

"Ma'am, please believe me that no matter how many times you ask that question, my answer is going to stay the same. I saw him recording the horror and it seemed to me that he was enjoying what was happening, so I went after him. I thought at the least he was disgusting, and I didn't want him uploading people's dying moments on the Internet. I wasn't thinking clearly."

"Given that you left your boyfriend where another bomb could have gone off, I'd agree."

Trey looked back and forth between Franklin's minion and the chef. The interview was being conducted in Emil's office. It wasn't as spacious as Alex's and lacked a second visitor's chair. He was stuck holding up the wall again as his only choice. Jase sat curled in Emil's lap, looking like a frightened yet secure kitten. When Agent Markey had started to insist that they be interviewed separately, a short, intense stand-off had ensued. There had been threats lobbed back and forth involving "…taking you down to the station" and "Do I have to call my lawyer?" It had surprised Trey to hear that the aliens had legal counsel. Maybe they didn't and it had been a bluff. If so, it had been a good one. Emil had won the battle of wills, leading to this little party.

"And, Mr. Purdue, your testimony on this remains unchanged?"

"Yes, ma'am." The boy's voice was muffled by Emil's T-shirt.

Markey eyed Trey before sighing. She didn't seem convinced with the story, nor should she be. It was far-fetched, and Trey couldn't wait to hear what had really happened, although it wasn't hard to guess. It was surprising that anyone had noticed what Emil had done at all, given the circumstances. The agents tailing him had immediately gone running toward the blast to help victims, no longer interested in following Emil.

"You're lucky you weren't killed being thrown from the hood of the SUV like that."

"My aching body is admonishing me as we speak," Emil intoned. His hand was wrapped with an ice pack. The bruises on the knuckles of one hand looked painful, to be sure, and his palm on the other had lost some skin. Those were the *visible* injuries.

"Hmm…" Markey closed her notebook and put it away in her jacket pocket. "We have twenty-one dead and dozens wounded from this so far. We don't need to increase the body count with a vigilante."

Not surprisingly, Emil didn't respond. He simply out-stared her until she turned and left. Trey started to follow her. She stopped outside of earshot, or what she thought of it as being. Likely, Emil could hear every word.

"You seem to have a good rapport with these people. Franklin wants you to stick around and see what you can learn. Something is off here. We know none of the Stelalux family planted the bomb, because they were all under surveillance. Eye-witnesses describe the man this one pursued as looking just like them. It seems obvious they at least know who the bomber is."

"Yes, ma'am. I hate to think they are involved at all, but I know my duty. You can count on me."

"Thanks. Check in later with your report, no matter how meager."

Trey rolled his tense shoulders before returning to Emil's office. "She's gone," he said, closing the door and taking her vacated seat. "Are you sure you're okay?"

"I've had worse." The way he said it indicated he was trying to downplay his injuries to protect Jase. "Are you being imbedded as a spy?"

"Something like that."

"Well, let's go see Alex, shall we?" Emil stood, somehow detaching Jase's hold on him and setting the boy effortlessly on his feet.

Jase didn't protest, merely clutched at Emil's hand instead. He'd been forthcoming with Markey, yet withdrawn and obviously freaked out by the day's events, as well he should have been. He and Emil hadn't been that far away from ground zero. A few more minutes, a few more yards, and the boy could have been maimed or killed. So could Emil have been, for that matter.

They trudged down the hall to Alex's office where the rest of the family waited, including Quinn and Mackie. Not Lucien, though, or Demi. Harry's quiet demeanor hid a core of steel and a man determined to shield his family from everything bad. He didn't subscribe to Alex's and Val's more modern notions of equality, either. He was clearly the boss of his husband and son, and while Lucien appeared fine with that arrangement, Demi was obvious chafing at the constraint. And, God, didn't Trey know all about *that*.

"All done?" Alex asked.

"Yes," Emil answered. "I won't be surprised if there are more interviews on the subject. I'm sorry," he said to the room at large.

"There is nothing to apologize for," came Alex's stern reply. "We do need a debriefing, however." He looked pointedly at Jase.

The boy wasn't, as far as Trey knew, privy to all the aliens' secrets.

Emil grimaced before saying, "Hey, Mackie, Jase could use some fun. How about you teach him pole dancing." Jase looked at him with obvious surprise.

"You'd like that, wouldn't you, Jase? I see you bopping to the music when you're working in the kitchen."

"Yes, Master, I would. Thank you."

Mackie grinned broadly and pulled away from Val's embrace. "Sure…sounds like fun. And the club is pretty quiet right now, especially for a Saturday night. No one really feels like a party, you know? Come and help, Quinn."

"Sure thing." The other boy stood from his place on Alex's lap. "You'll love it. I do, and I haven't been doing it long. It's easier than it looks."

The two boys each grabbed one of Jase's arms and herded him away before he could get in a word to the contrary, not that he would have. He was clearly devoted to Emil and although Stockholm Syndrome crossed Trey's mind, he had bigger fish to fry. The boy was in a safe place, and that was all that mattered for the moment.

He closed the door behind them and flopped down on the couch. "What a fucking awful day. I wasn't even in the thick of it and I'm still sick to my stomach." He glanced at Emil. "It was this Marius guy, I'm assuming."

"Yes." Emil's tone and posture spoke of fatigue and failure. "I nearly had him."

"Markey was right about your almost being killed. You guys are immensely strong, but an SUV is like two tons or more. Add in a few laws of physics and you're lucky to be alive and walking."

Emil cracked his neck. "I'm fine."

"I wish you'd let me be the judge of that," Harry said peevishly.

"There's no time for fussing over my booboos, old man. I need your help downstairs." He changed his attention to Alex. "With your permission, I think we need to make some assumptions about what Marius is doing and work to counter his explosive materials. Tracking him down isn't going to do us any good if we can't stop this destruction, once and for all."

"Agreed." Alex flicked his gaze toward Trey. "Would you mind helping on this? Your forensic training may come in handy, whereas Val and I are useless with this stuff."

Trey climbed back to his feet. "Sure. My experience with explosives is very limited but anything I can do to help. My people are dying. I need to stop it. And I've sniffed around to see if I can get you some of the evidence. No dice, I'm sorry to say. If I'm of any use on this end, let me have at it."

"I'm happy to have you," Emil said. "Come on."

Trey followed the chef and the doctor to that secret door and staircase where they kept stuff that no human should see. This time, instead of going into Harry's lab, they went through the opposite door. The front part of this room contained an impressive, and highly illegal, array of weaponry. The back end was a sea of greenery. Well, not in the literal sense. Many of the plants growing on stands were different colors, although they were embedded in water instead of soil. The smells they gave off were indescribable from a human reference. Some of them were pleasing, others not so much. Trey had to cup his hand over his nose at the barrage of scents.

"Sorry," Emil said. "Not all of this is human-friendly." He took in a deep breath and let it out slowly. His expression revealed how much he enjoyed it. "This is our last bit of home."

He walked around the long table, running his fingertips across the leaves and flowers. "I carry the seeds we were able to rescue wherever we go. I can only grow them in a place like this, hydroponically and sealed. None of this can be allowed to spread in your world. They would choke out natural vegetation and poison wildlife.

"There are a few potential candidates here, stuff that can sicken and kill humans, certainly. Some of it is caustic to material, as well, such as cotton and wool." He stopped in front of a plant with vividly red, spiky leaves. "I think this is the one, though. Don't you, Harry?"

The older man joined him. "Yes. It has the right chemical composition to create an explosive. Marius was definitely focusing on the potential for it to combust centuries ago."

Trey walked cautiously closer to get a better look. "You use that thing to blow shit up?"

Emil chuckled mirthlessly. "Not exactly. It's a spice, by your viewpoint, although a human esophagus and stomach couldn't tolerate ingesting it. It would be like eating acid."

"But your kind can?"

"Yes. It's a wonderful flavor enhancer for blander foods like pasta."

Harry wrinkled his nose. "Too much for my tastes."

Emil plucked off a few leaves. "In any case, Marius was experimenting with it. And he is like a dog with a bone, as you humans would say. Once he sinks his teeth into something, he doesn't like to give it up." He frowned. "There's no way he grew it somewhere and imported the leaves into Boston, though."

"Yeah, well, Customs would have caught it," Trey observed.

The aliens shared a look. "We have our own private planes and can find out-of-the way landing strips. Customs wouldn't know he'd entered the country. No, the real issue is that it deteriorates quickly once plucked. He would have had to bring in a lot of whole plants, given the size of the explosions. Surely, he's not finished, either. I don't see his importing that many. A plane-load is possible, but then he'd have to transport it over land somewhere and contain it while processing it."

"So, what are you saying?" Trey felt stupid, until a thought occurred to him. "He brought in seeds."

Emil nodded. "Yes, seeds that he then grew in a hydroponic garden like this one. He must have established a grow room and a lab somewhere in the area."

"Okay, we need to find that." Trey couldn't think how, of course, not at the moment.

"And in the meantime, we go to the lab and figure out a countering agent. It's a gamble because we could be wrong. It's all we have," Emil added with a quirk of his brow.

"Let's get to it," Trey said, already heading out of the room. His growing ease with his alien buddies and their environment surprised him less and less with each new crisis. It didn't matter in any event. Stopping this Marius fucker did.

* * * *

Jase giggled as he tried to emulate the enviable way Mackie made his butt dance. "I can't get it right."

"You're overthinking it, sweetie. Twerking is a state of mind."

Quinn smiled and nodded. "He's right. You have to let go and stop worrying about whether you look silly."

The three of them were standing on one stage in G-strings. Mackie had given a brand new one in silver to Jase. He liked the color because it was one that Master favored, given the décor of his bedroom. The familiar way that the fabric divided his ass and contained his dick and balls was almost comforting.

The main room of the club was pretty quiet, but a couple of the other stages contained go-go boys. The few members in residence that night were clustered around them. Jase was glad he wasn't attracting any attention, not that he wasn't used to being half- or fully naked in front of strange men. His job at the moment wasn't to entertain them, however. It was nice to let go and enjoy himself after the horror of the day.

As he'd clung to the side of the building, the realization of what had happened dawning on him, he'd learned something unexpected. He wanted to live. As miserable as his life had been, he had hope for the first time in years that it was getting better. He was glad to have escaped the death that had claimed so many. His only fear during those long, horrible minutes had been *for* Master, not *of* him. The threat of punishment hadn't made a dent in his worry, so great was his terror that Master would die and never come back to him.

In the end, the man had been safe and not mad about Jase's disobedience. He'd seemed happy, relieved even, and had carried him all the way back to the club. Jase had felt cherished. He would have learned to dance, only to make Master happy, but found he loved it for himself. There had been a time when he'd considered taking dance classes, except he'd never asked. Money had been scarce and something like that would have been an indulgence. These were free, though, and he intended to surprise Master later with what he'd learned.

Grabbing the pole, he spread his legs wide and pumped his hips as fast as he could.

Mackie clapped. "That's it! You've got it."

Jase stopped on a gasp and pressed his cheek against the cool metal. "Really? Give me a second and I'll try it again."

"Let's put on a better song," Quinn said. "I'll go ask Kitty."

"Is that okay?" Jase didn't want to upset the members.

"Sure," Mackie batted the question way. "The men don't care what we dance to. They just like to watch us move."

"Okay." He took a deep breath and waited for the change of music. "Oh, I love this song!"

Thirty Seconds to Mars' *Walk on Water* started to play. It wasn't the heaviest beat to twerk to, but he didn't care. After a few seconds of bouncing his butt, he released the pole and let the rhythm take him away. It didn't matter who watched or how good he was. It was awesome simply to rock his hips and twist in time to the music. He closed his eyes for a few seconds to allow his mind to drift. When he opened them again, he found men were crowding around him with avid gazes.

His steps faltered a moment before he remembered that these men couldn't hurt him. They couldn't even touch him. His master wouldn't allow that. He knew how to keep Jase safe. Still, he hadn't forgotten the act of flirting with men. He could tease, and it was easy this time because no one was making him do it for their own avarice. This was something he was enjoying. Smiling down at them, he emphasized the swing of his hips. Then he turned, spread his legs, put his hands on his knees and jiggled away.

There were claps and whistles, and soon money was being stuffed inside his G-string. The attention once more flustered him until he remembered that it was all a game. He liked how the positions had been reversed for once, where men had to fight for his attention and were rewarding him, not someone else, for his efforts — with actual money, not something he needed like food and rest. They weren't ones or fives, either, but twenties and, holy shit, a hundred-dollar bill was tucked in by a man who winked at him. Jase's cheeks get hot. He wondered if Master would allow him to keep any of it.

He grinned and batted his eyelashes at the guy before flitting his gaze to one side. That's when his lungs froze and his heart started pounding with dawning horror. Master stood by the bar, his gaze homing in on Jase. Even at a distance, he could see the red. A gleam of white showed fangs descending past his lower lip. Then Master's mouth opened. Whatever sound he made — and Jase knew it only too well — was drowned out by the music being suddenly cranked way up.

The bouncer, Val, raced to Master's side and grabbed him by one arm. The club owner, Alex, latched on to the other one. The doctor joined in and so did the cop. They tugged and pulled Master backward. It was a replay of what had happened with Washburn days ago in the playroom, only this time, Jase was to blame for causing it. The bartender, Kitty, swooped in to block the view of the struggle. And still, Master's gaze never left Jase. He kept staring until he'd been dragged out of sight.

Jase sobbed and, jumping off the stage, ran after them.

He'd fucked up. Master had told him to learn how to dance, not flirt with other men or allow them to put their hands on what belonged only to Master. Terror rose in him as he chased the man. It wasn't fear of punishment that drove him. It was worse than that. He'd disappointed the one person in years who had treated him like something more than a hole. Being beaten bloody was nothing compared to the pain he'd experience if Master cast him aside. Surely he would, too. No one wanted a slave who was stupid and arrogant enough to entice others right under his nose.

Down the hall he raced. The farther he got from the main room, the softer the music was. He could hear it now, the roaring and bellowing of an enraged alien vampire. It would serve Jase right if the monster inside Master was released. He'd regained his desire to live that afternoon, but without this man in his life, he wasn't sure he wanted it anymore.

"Master!" he screamed out the moment he entered the room. It was still taking four men to keep Master pinned to the couch. Jase slid in between them, burning his knees on the rug, desperate to reach his goal. "Master, please!"

He was crying now, as he wrapped his arms around Master's leg and pressed his face against the rock-hard thigh. "I'm sorry. I'm sorry. Please don't be mad. Please!"

He wailed in great gulping spurts. Tears ran down his face. Some dam of emotion had let loose and he couldn't hold it back. All the fear and pain and misery, the disbelief, the sense of betrayal—everything he'd been forced to bottle up and push down in order to survive escaped and spilled out of him.

He babbled in between racking sobs that shook his body and made him feel as if he were breaking into a million pieces. He didn't stop, either, when strong hands pried open his fingers, pulled him and held him close. His tears soaked the cloth he pressed his face into, something that smelled familiar. He took in gulping breaths of the scents, and they slowly eased his sorrow.

Nonsense words flowed over him until they started to make some sense. "Hush. You're safe. I'm not mad. Easy, baby. Don't make yourself sick. Forgive me. I didn't mean to scare you."

Eventually, the primitive part of Jase's mind gave way to rational thought. The meaning of Master's words filtered through. His tears dried, and his weeping slowed to an occasional hiccup. He forced air into his lungs with steady breaths. Master rubbed his back, easing him down from the crying jag.

"There now, that's better." Master's voice was low and steady. The monster was gone again, leaving the man who baked sweet bread and took care of everyone.

Jase dared to press a kiss to the chest he laid against. "I'm sorry I made you mad, Master. I shouldn't have let those men touch me."

"No, baby, you don't owe me an apology—not for that, not for anything. You did nothing wrong out there. The blame is mine." He took a deep breath. "My reaction was out of line. You have every right to dance for those men, if that's what you wanted to do. It's a good way for you to make a lot of money, actually— more than you would working in a kitchen. I should have thought of that before. And you're not mine, so my jealousy is unfair."

Exhausted from the horrifying and emotional day, Jase sat up and did something that would have been unthinkable only a week ago. He contradicted his master. "I *am* yours."

Master's head reared back, a look of astonishment on his face before he replied, "No, Jase, you've been trained to think that."

Okay, now he was plain mad. Folding his arms, he glared back, unconcerned over what trouble his behavior might cause him. "You think I'm so broken that I don't know my own feelings?"

Master's face fell. "Oh, no, baby. You're not broken."

"You act as if I am."

"I don't want to cause you pain the way those others like Washburn did. That's all." He ran his fingers down Jase's cheek before cupping his face. "You deserve to get your life back. I don't have a right to tie you to me. I can't claim you, Jase. You belong to *you*, no one else."

A sadness stole over him, and he slumped back down against Master's chest. "I'm tired. And it hurts all the time here." He rubbed the spot between his pecs. "An ache that started four years ago and doesn't go away"—he lifted his gaze—"except when I'm with you. You ease it, Master, and I think you can banish it forever."

Master placed his large hand over Jase's, dwarfing it completely. "I don't think I'm the best person to touch this particular wound, but if you'll let me, I'll try."

"I want that, Master," Jase said with a solemn nod.

"Okay, then, I'm going to need the truth…all of it. It's going to be painful for you, but without it, I don't know what to do for you. Do you trust me with that?"

"Yes." As he said the words, he meant them. Already, though, he his stomach fluttered and his pulse quickened. He'd pushed the beginning of his nightmare as deep down as it could go. Bringing it back to the surface would be agony. "For you. For us," he amended and was rewarded with a smile.

"Let's go to my room where we'll have privacy."

It wasn't until Master picked him up and carried him out of the office that Jase realized they'd never been left entirely alone. The others stood outside, hovering with concerned looks. Embarrassed, Jase closed his eyes and tucked his head against Master's chest.

"Be careful with him," the cop said.

"I'm around if you need me," the doctor added.

"Thank you all for your help and concern, but Jase and I have it from here." Master's steady reassurance helped allay Jase's worry.

His reference to the two of them acting in concert and conquering trouble made hope rise in his heart. He knew at that moment he'd fallen in love.

Chapter Ten

Emil held Jase while they lay propped in bed. He'd only bothered to kick off his shoes, but he'd dressed Jase in one of his T-shirts. It was like a nightgown, it hung so low on the boy's small frame. The G-string was tossed on the floor, and the tips he'd earned were piled neatly on the nightstand, although Emil would have gladly ripped them to shreds, given how they reminded him of that awful moment when he'd seen those sweaty pervs leering over the boy and pawing him with their money. He had pulled himself together and was determined not to lose his shit again.

Holy fuck, it had hit him like the proverbial freight train — the fury, the bloodlust. He was embarrassed that he'd risked everyone's lives by his lack of control. Worse, he'd frightened Jase and made the boy cry so hard that Emil had worried for his health. Never again. He wouldn't harm this sweet human like that ever. He'd cut his own throat first.

They'd been lying like this for a few minutes while Jase marshaled his thoughts. "Take your time," Emil said for the second or third time. The wait was killing him. He knew he was going to hate Jase's story. It made him sick already, imagining what it was.

Jase moved restlessly before starting. "My dad died when I was four. I don't remember him much. I guess he was a good guy, and I think my mom loved him. She had trouble coping once he was gone. I know that. Money was tight and she had to leave me by myself often because she had to work and couldn't always afford a babysitter.

"When she met Jack, things got better. She smiled more and he took us both out to eat and movies. He played catch with me, which made my mom really happy. There was always something about him, though, that kind of creeped me out. I was too little, at first, to understand. Later, I avoided him as much as I could. I figured it didn't matter. I was heading into high school and would be gone in a few years. So long as he treated Mom well, that was all that mattered."

He stopped, and Emil schooled himself in patience. He rubbed Jase's back in the way he knew the boy loved, slow circles up and down.

"The summer before I was supposed to start high school, my mom got distracted with her phone and stepped in front of a bus. She died a few hours later without regaining consciousness. Jack tried to comfort me at the hospital, but I didn't like the way he held me and I pushed him away. He was mad. I could tell. I didn't care because Mom was dead. I hurt too much to worry about him.

"That was a mistake. I let down my guard. The night after we buried her, he came into my room. And—"

Jase stuttered to a halt. He curled against Emil's side. "It was agony. I'd been pretty sure I was gay for a few years before that. I'd even started sneaking looks at porn on my phone. What I saw men doing to each other looked fun until Jack did it to me. I couldn't believe anyone wanted something that hurt so much. I cried and struggled, but he was too strong. I couldn't make him stop. When he was done, he pulled my head by my hair and told me that lube was for good boys. If I wanted some next time, I'd start being nice to him."

Emil hugged him close and peppered his head with a few kisses. "Oh, baby, you'd been watching sex. What your asshole stepfather did was rape."

Jase nodded. "I know that now. At the time, I was confused and scared. He threatened to kill me if I told anyone and I believed him. That summer, he kept me away from all my friends and neighbors. I never had any family other than my parents, so there was no one to check on me. He told people I was grieving and wanted privacy."

Emil nodded. "He isolated you. Abusers do that."

"Every day, he gave me what he called 'lessons'. I learned to give him blow jobs and not fight him when he fucked me. He was right about the lube. It was much easier with it. I didn't dare gainsay him. I kept telling myself that once I started school, I would get some break from him. I never did."

Sitting up, Jase pulled away, only to sit cross-legged beside Emil's hip. "Jack gambled…a lot. I hadn't known anything about it. He was in debt big time. One night, a couple of goons came to the house and started beating him for the money he owed their boss. When he couldn't pay, they decided to take me. They said I'd be a fair trade."

He picked at the bedspread as he spoke. "I fought them, not that it did any good. I pleaded with Jack to save me because being with him was better than these strangers. I didn't understand what was happening until I found myself imprisoned in a brothel outside of New Orleans. Lots of men had me then."

Jase bowed his head and a tear slid down his cheek. Emil couldn't stand it. He picked the boy up and settled him on his lap. "It's okay. I'm here." He wiped the tears with his thumb and replaced them with soft kisses. "You don't have to tell me any more if you don't want to."

Jase wrapped his arms around Emil's neck. "I want to finish it, please. There's not much left. That's where Washburn first had me, and when the brothel decided to auction me off, he bid the highest. I was happy at first to go back to one man instead of ten or more a day.

"But I didn't understand what he intended. I learned fast how to be a slave. With him, I had to actively please him. It wasn't enough to lie there and be fucked or have a cock fed down my throat. I had to worship my master with enthusiasm. He beat my accent out of me, as well as any pride or hope I had left. He paraded me in front of other men like him and pretended I was something more than a hick boy from the south. We moved around a lot in secret social circles because of my age. He rented me out to other men as part of his business dealings. There were parties sometimes where me and other boys like me had to play sick and painful games with lots of men.

"It was also a dirty secret involving underage boys. I was one of the older ones, actually. Some were horribly little. I never knew where I was, from one day to the next. Washburn kept me in the dark, literally, when we traveled. The day I turned eighteen, he was overjoyed. I could finally be his slave out in the open."

Placing his head on Emil's shoulder, he sighed. "You know the rest, Master."

Yes, he did, and the whole thing made him murderous with rage. That wouldn't help Jase, though. He owed him a sympathetic ear and more apologies. After losing his shit the way he had, he couldn't say it often enough.

"I'm sorry I made you afraid tonight. I would rather cut off my cock than scare you."

"You didn't, not really. I wasn't afraid you would hurt me. I only feared you were mad."

"I wasn't — not at you, anyway. It was those club members I wanted to tear apart." As he said it, he realized he would have to make amends to Alex. His behavior had been unacceptable. He'd nearly given them all away with his loss of control.

"That doesn't make me feel better, actually. I still feel guilty for doing something that upset you. I want to make you happy."

Emil groaned. "Oh, baby, that's what all those men who abused you have made you think you have to do. I'm just one more guy who doesn't deserve you."

Jase surprised Emil by sitting up and straddling his lap. He whipped off the T-shirt as well. All his sweet beauty was on full display. Emil's fingers itched to run down the boy's slender, hairless chest and play with the dick that lay demurely against his fly. Balling them into fists, he held them at his sides where they couldn't get into any trouble.

Jase stared at a point somewhere around Emil's chin. "May I ask you a question, Master?"

"Anything. Any time."

"Are you really an alien vampire?"

"Yes. What I told you about my coming from another world was true. Blood *is* an important part of my diet, as you've seen. But I don't turn into a bat," he added with a grin that Jase hopefully could see. "Why do you ask?"

Jase gnawed at his lower lip in adorable fashion. Getting this up-close look at him when he was seemingly more relaxed was proving very distracting. "It's just that it makes you a monster, yet you're the least monstrous man I think I've ever known, certainly based on the men I've had to deal with in the last four years." He pressed his palm against Emil's chest. "It confuses me."

"I can only imagine." The light pressure between his pecs grabbed Emil's attention. It was almost like a brand, the heat of it seeping through his shirt and sending a spark down to his cock. He lost his control in as much as he had to touch in return. Unclenching his fists, he placed his hands on the boy's flanks and slid them to cup his ass. It was the perfect handful. He rolled his hips to ease the rising ache and bit back a moan.

Jase's breath caught. "Oh, I should have realized what I was doing. Let me take care of that, Master."

When the boy tried to wiggled back, Emil held him in place. "No. Ignore that. It's my problem."

The human frowned. "But…I don't understand. Don't you want me?"

"With every fiber of my alien vampire being," Emil confessed and tried for a grin to ease the seriousness of his confession. He failed, but he wasn't going to also fail Jase this night. He had amends to make and he had an idea of how.

"In fact," he said, reversing their positions with a speed that had the boy blinking at him in surprise, "with your permission, I think I know a great way to demonstrate the way I feel while making my apologies again."

"What do you mean, Master?"

Emil ran a fingertip down the middle of Jase's torso. He'd never truly noticed before how every inch of body hair had been waxed away. There was no treasure trail or pubic hair to play with. He stopped his progression above the root of the boy's cock.

"When has it ever been your turn for pleasure? Has anyone bothered to give you an orgasm?"

Jase's gaze skittered away at the question. "I used to jerk off like, always, before Jack, um…did what he did. After that, the whole thing disgusted me, and Washburn punished me if I got hard. Being kept in chastity all the time made it impossible, anyway."

Once again, Emil regretted nature's intervening in his efforts to kill the man. "How do you feel about it now? Would you like to come?"

Jase returned his gaze to Emil's chin. "Is that an option? Am I allowed to touch myself, Master?"

"No. I mean… Yes, you can touch yourself anytime you want. What I meant, though, is may I make you come tonight?"

Jase's eyes went round and wide. "I'm not sure I understand you, Master."

Emil grinned. This could be fun. "Let me show you."

He waited with his breath held and almost quivering anticipation for the human to give assent. Jase did with a tentative nod that was almost no consent at all. Emil decided to accept it anyway with a caveat.

"If you don't like what I'm doing at any point, all you have to do is tell me to stop and I will. I promise. You are in control of your own body, Jase. Understand?" This time, the nod was more definitive.

With mounting excitement, Emil pushed back to gain a clearer path to what he sought. Jase's dick lay flaccid still against soft, small and hairless balls. Everything on Jase was pint-sized compared to Emil's bulk. He did feel like a monster in comparison, yet was determined to bring the boy the pleasure he deserved.

He started slow and easy, using his fingers to bring the cock carefully to life. And it did take time. His gentle massage of the shaft didn't produce any effect for long minutes. It was hard not to become angry all over again at the visible proof that Jase's body had been trained into such submission that even natural biological responses were suppressed.

Patience, though, finally brought him a reward. The flesh in his grip started to swell. He encouraged it with long, sure strokes. He brought his free hand into play, caressing the sensitive skin where inner thigh met groin. Jase's breath hitched and his hips jerked as his cock became stiff.

"That's my boy," Emil couldn't help whispering. "Get nice and hard."

Jase moaned softly and his fingers twitched. When the shaft became completely rigid, Emil played with the tip some, running his thumb along the silky skin. A tiny drop of pre-cum leaked out. The sight of it made Emil smile. Finally. This was what a boy Jase's age was supposed to experience.

Once he had Jase hard and restless, he moved on to stage two. Scooting back another few inches, he bent down to suck the cock into his mouth. He moaned around the sweet-tasting shaft and swallowed it all the way down. Jase cried out and arched into him. It sent the cock in a fraction farther, until Emil's lips pressed against the boy's pelvis.

It was nothing to swallow Jase's cock, a mere morsel of deliciousness. He worked it with his throat muscles while he laved the underneath with his tongue. Sliding his hands under the boy's ass, he used it to leverage him up even more. Emil opened his hearing to focus on the whooshing of blood through the femoral artery. His own dick pulsed in syncopated rhythm, urging him to sink his fangs in and drink. He ignored it. This was for Jase and only him. Emil made sure to keep all his teeth away from the tender flesh of the boy's dick.

Jase writhed as his climax built. Normally, a boy of his age would have shot off already. Emil was sure of it. Years of abuse still took its toll and made it hard for Jase to overcome and act naturally. It didn't matter. Emil would crouch there and feast on the boy for as long as it took.

"Master, please." Jase twisted violently within Emil's firm grasp. "I need more. Something…"

Emil racked his brain to figure out what unnamed thing Jase required. It came to him, although it was fraught with risk. Pulling back, he released the cock from his mouth and fisted it instead. He pumped it hard while he wetted two fingers. Then he returned to the blow job, lifted Jase's ass up with one hand and slid his slickened fingers past the puckered ring of Jase's hole.

It unfurled for him beautifully. He tried not to think of how it had been trained not to resist invasion. That thought wouldn't help Jase. Instead, he concentrated on navigating largely unknown territory for him and fumbled to locate the boy's prostate. It was right where he hoped it would be, a ribbed bundle of nerves that their species shared. He sucked hard on the cock in his mouth, hummed around the shaft while crooking his fingers repeatedly.

"Master!" Jase's shout met Emil's ears a split-second before cum spurted down his throat.

He worked the dick over and over with fast, hard swallows and teased the prostate with fluttery scratches. Jase cried and moaned and thrashed his way through his first orgasm in longer than Emil dared to remind himself. At the very end, Emil pulled back in order to allow a splash of cum to hit his tongue. *Delectable.*

He eased onto his heels, reluctantly letting the dick go before he overworked the sensitive skin. And he slid his fingers free with equal care. Jase still clutched at the bedding and his eyes were closed. A smile graced his adorable lips, testament to how much Emil had pleased him. It made Emil feel like a hero. Such a simple thing, and yet Jase had been denied it for too long. Emil was going to have to make a list of all those men who had to pay for what they'd done to this sweet boy. When the dust cleared from Dracul's recent volley, Emil would find the time to wreak terrible vengeance. For now, though, he needed to concentrate on helping Jase heal.

"How are you?" he asked in a soft voice so as not to kill Jase's post-orgasm buzz.

Jase's smile increased and he opened his eyes to slits. "That was amazing. Thank you, Master."

"No need to thank me. I got as much pleasure out of it as you did." That was the truth. He liked taking care of people and nothing he'd ever fed anyone had achieved this kind of reaction. It was entirely gratifying.

Jase's eyes widened and he looked down. "I don't think that's true, Master. At least, you're not fully satisfied."

Emil followed the boy's line of sight. "Oh, that. It's nothing," he said, dismissing his own raging hard-on. He was a little surprised his worn denim contained the unruly beast. Now that he was thinking about it, it was painfully hard and his balls ached like a bitch. "Don't worry about it. I'll take care of it later."

Jase started to sit with his hand outstretched. "Please, let me help you."

Emil shook his head emphatically. "No. Thank you, but no. This night's for you. I don't want you to service me in any way." His dick disagreed with him violently. He ignored it and resolutely decided that a trip to the bathroom was in order as soon as he was sure Jase was settled for the night.

His determination flagged with Jase's next offer.

"Um, maybe there's something I can give you that would be different, something I've never given to another man or had taken from me."

With a sinking feeling, Emil realized what the human was saying. "Jase, no…"

"My blood."

Shit. Against his will, Emil's gaze homed in on the artery that had already beckoned him. He shook his head, as much for himself as for Jase. "No. That's too much. It would be a violation far worse than what others have done to you."

"Don't you think I should be the one to decide that?" Jase's expression turned surprisingly mulish. It was a good sign, actually. A great one. It meant Emil had already set the boy on a path where he could overcome the enforced slavery he'd lived with for years.

"Yes, normally that's true. You are an adult with a mind of your own, and I'm glad to hear you voice your opinion. But this is different. You literally don't know what you're offering."

"That's true."

"Blood sucking frightens humans. I've been on this world long enough to know that."

Jase gnawed his lip again. This time, though, it was more serious than cute. "I am scared. I admit that. I think maybe it hurts, at least at first. Mackie says it also makes him come extra hard. That sounds like fun. I mean I can't imagine coming any harder than I just did, but I think I'd like to try it sometime."

Emil really wished he hadn't said that—and with a look on his face that would drive a sane man wild. "Mackie and Val have a long-standing relationship where trust has been built. I can't ask you to do something I know will go against your natural instincts. That would be abusive of me." Emil forced the words out, even though it killed him. His cock leaked cum inside his pants in protest and he had to bite back a groan.

Jase looked at him sharply. "You need to come as much as I did." Lying back down, he added, "Please, take a little of my blood. I trust you to do it carefully and to stop if I ask."

Oh, this was too much. Emil's sense of decency and self-control had its limits. The human was laying himself out like a feast for a starving man. Who was Emil to refuse? *An asshole*, a little voice said. He ended up ignoring it as much as he had his cock. He bent down and pressed his nose against the femoral artery.

He listened to it and smelled the faint aroma of blood safely coursing through its encasement.

It could be exposed a little. It didn't have to be a bite. A tiny scratch would do it, a few licks, then reseal it. Jase would barely feel a thing and it would be nothing more than a mild cut that could happen anytime, anywhere. Except arteries were dangerous things to open. He would have to be very careful. And all of this was a big, fat, selfish rationalization. Still, he did it.

His fangs punched down, and he scored the flesh over the artery with a single tooth. Blood welled up immediately. He quickly fastened his lips around the wound and sucked. It was only a small taste, an amuse-bouche for his tongue. The warm, salty blood trickled down his throat with maddening slowness. It wasn't nearly sufficient to satiate his needs.

But it made him come, immediately, in a hard rush that was like a punch to his groin. His whole body convulsed, a ripple of ridged muscles that made him hunch and shake. He stuttered around the bit of Jase's thigh that he sucked on, breaking the seal of his lips. Fear of causing him harm overrode the high of his climax. He quickly licked the wound closed before slumping over the human's groin. He inhaled the musk of the boy's cum, pumped out more of his own into his now sticky, wet jeans and relaxed into a blissful state that he'd never known before.

A small hand landed on his head. "My *Master*."

"My Jase," he replied because there was nothing else to say. Whatever he'd thought days ago when he'd taken responsibility for this boy, he knew now that letting him go was going to be the hardest thing he'd ever done. He wasn't sure he could survive the loss.

Chapter Eleven

"Baking soda? Seriously? That's all it's going to take?" Duncan's skepticism wasn't surprising.

"You were there when we tried Harry's potions. We've experimented with a lot of different things that didn't work nearly sufficiently well. I got the baking soda idea from working in a kitchen for so long. You know it's effective for small grease fires. I also remembered that I've never used this particular plant in baking. It's too picante. The moment I dumped some on the leaves, they shriveled. Harry and I are amping it up so that it works faster and better on a large quantity of leaves, but yeah."

"Good work, Emil," Alex said. "We have something of a plan at least."

Duncan shook his head. "I'm not so sure. How much of this stuff are you going to need? And we still don't know where he's going to hit next."

"True," Emil conceded. "We're going to have to find Marius' growing room, destroy his current crop then eliminate him."

"Yeah," Val interjected. "Nothing is going to be a permanent fix unless we kill the fucker. Odds are he hasn't given his process to anyone. He was paranoid and secretive from the beginning."

The cop held up his hand. "Okay, so we all agree on that score. It still doesn't answer the question of how."

Emil nodded. "Yup, and we have a plan."

"It was your idea, Emil," Harry made the point of saying. "Credit where credit is due."

Uncomfortable with being the center of attention, Emil waved away the praise. "It's not a big deal. I just happen to be the botanist and a cook." He turned to Duncan. "See? There's this city-based movement of growing local produce year-round indoors using hydroponics. No soil, just water. And there's a local company that converts old freight cars into growing rooms."

Duncan grunted. "That's handy."

"It is. I think Marius lucked out there, but he would have had one delivered here, regardless. Given the growing time for this plant, he must have started about six months ago, even before Adrian's killing spree."

"So, Dracul has been fighting a multi-stage war from the beginning."

"He's insanely murderous, but no fool," Alex confirmed. "Go on, Emil, if you please."

He scratched the back of his head. "Well, now this is where it gets a little sticky for you, Duncan."

"Oh yeah? I'm drowning in a vat of molasses already, so lay it on me."

"I'm going to break into the company's offices tonight and look at its order records for the last year to see if I can locate where Marius has his base. If we can destroy his crop and him, we'll stop this hideous violence from continuing."

The cop winced. "Is that the only way? I have to assume this company is innocent in all of this and might not be the source of his growing facility, anyway."

"As near as I can tell, it's our best option. We have to at least cross it off our list as a viable path to Marius. You can't flash your badge or get a court order without explaining why, and we all know how problematic that is…"

Duncan held up his hand again. "Say no more, really. I don't need the details, although I'm surprised it's not Val doing the B and E."

"I'm better suited to know what to look for, and while I have no breaking and entering skills, I do have something of a secret weapon. I have Logan."

* * * *

"You don't have to do this." Emil wanted to give the woman one more chance to opt out of something that could land her in jail.

Logan rolled her eyes. "How many times do I have to tell you that I want to help? For me, this is another way to serve my country. Compared to other things I've had to do, burglary hardly ranks."

Emil winced inwardly at the reminder of how much the human had already suffered in her short lifetime. He hated adding to the list of things that might keep her from returning to normalcy. She'd come a long way in the last year since he'd first met her. She spent more time inside the club in the small storage room he'd converted into a bedroom for her. She ate his food without wariness in her eyes and accepted clothing and other small items he bought for her. That was a significant change from the hostility and suspicion she'd treated him to at first.

"You know that this isn't intended to be payment for anything I've done. I do that freely and won't think less of you if you tell me to fuck off."

Logan zippered the Eddie Bauer down jacket he'd given her a month earlier and huffed out a breath. "Can we stop talking now? 'Cause it's pissing me off. I want to get a load of what it feels like to be one of you aliens."

Without saying more, she walked to his back, wrapped her arms around his neck and hopped up. Emil took the weight with ease, mentally assessing that she could use a few more pounds to be healthy. Her legs encircled his waist, and he had no doubt she'd be able to keep herself onboard while he was free to use his hands as necessary for their journey.

They stood in the tiny space between their building and the one next door. There was no way for a car to park there and a quick perusal earlier had confirmed no person lurked nearby. Val and Mackie had just started their epic and staged marital spat in the front of the club. There was a lot of yelling by the boy, his voice carrying far enough for Emil to hear. That should keep the feds busy while Emil and Logan took off.

He inhaled a deep breath and jumped. His vertical lift only got him to the third floor, but there were plenty of places for him to grip with his fingers. He propped his booted feet against the brick for extra leverage and quickly climbed to the roof. He landed with a thud then paused to see if there was any indication they'd been heard. The only sound drifting upward was Mackie's lament over why he'd ever thought marrying Val would be a good idea.

Emil couldn't help grinning before he took off and vaulted to the next building. Logan's grip on him tightened as they sailed over the narrow chasm. Then she chuckled in his ear, and he knew that she was actually enjoying herself. That confirmation gave him a boost in energy. He didn't need to hold back for her protection. So, he poured on the speed and leaped his way down the street. Once they were clear of the surveillance perimeter, he jumped off the last building and down to another vacant alley. His knees jarred with the impact and his breath labored more than it should have.

"Shit," he said as Logan slid off his back. "I'm out of shape."

Logan chuckled again. "That's you out of shape? Damn, dude, that was one sweet ride."

"I'm glad you liked it, because we'll have to travel back the same way."

"I'm looking forward to it. I'd love to traverse the whole city one night like that sometime."

Emil vowed he'd make that happen, later, once Marius had been dealt with. "It's a date. For now, we have a more pedestrian mode for the rest of the journey."

Centuries of hiding had made his people more cunning than usual. They lived with the fear of having to flee at the drop of a hat, as the humans would say. The family had vehicles stashed in lots of different locations and under various assumed names. Emil headed to the closest one, as certain as he could be that the feds didn't know about it.

Logan stayed abreast of him, asking no questions. Her trust in him was humbling and her training as a warrior was an immense benefit at the moment. She took one look at the pedestrian, four-door sedan and quirked an eyebrow. "This isn't as sweet as leaping over alleyways, but I suppose it's nondescript for our purposes."

"Exactly. I won't be breaking any speed limits, either."

The drive to their destination took no time. It was the dead of night during a weekday, and even without the horror of the previous Saturday's explosion, not many humans would have been out and about. He parked a few blocks away from the company they intended to break into and made the rest of the journey on foot.

They approached the building via the back way in order to decrease the chance of being spotted. Then they crouched behind a Dumpster to check out the security. It wasn't much, from what they could see. Why would it be? This wasn't some government installation, merely a small business trying to carve out a niche in a growing market for locally sourced food. There weren't cameras mounted on the outside or the inside. The locks were helpless against Logan's picking skills. She had them in the main office with little effort.

"Someday you'll have to explain to me why the military teaches its people how to bypass security and pick locks."

Logan raised her eyebrows as she re-pocketed her tools. "When did I ever say I learned this while serving?"

Nonplussed, Emil grinned. "Fair point. Okay, next is hacking for its customer records."

Logan sat at the big desk dominating the room and booted the computer. "Technically, this constitutes cracking, but yeah, let's see what we've got. This will take longer."

Emil busied himself by looking around the room and admiring the pictures on the walls. It was homey and obviously family-owned. He hated invading their space this way. *Damn Dracul.* He made criminals of them all one way or another. More than ever, Emil wanted this whole thing to end. He could live out a nice life on this planet given the chance. A vision of Jase flashed through his mind, the boy lying in Emil's arms, sleepy and contented. He'd been happy that morning, no noticeable lingering effects from their previous night's talk. Emil had left him working away in the kitchen, having shown him how to make a simple loaf of bread.

"I'm in."

Emil's reverie was interrupted by the more pragmatic issue at hand. He went to the desk. "Let me take over, please."

"Sure." Logan vacated the seat, yet hovered in case he needed her.

This part was easy. No exceptional computer skills needed, which was good because he had none. The customer list was in a clearly marked folder. A quick scan of the orders placed in the last year for a container gave him the information he needed. He noted the address of the delivery point and vaguely recognized it as being in a section of Boston called Brighton that was in the western outskirts of the city.

He stood. "I have it, thanks. Please erase any history of what we did and shut it down."

"That was fast. Are you sure?"

"Oh yes. Marius may be clinically insane, but his mind is easily understood. I recognized the human alias he used. It would amuse him in his own twisted way. We now know where to find him. It's simply a matter of planning the attack."

The trip back was uneventful. Logan insisted on joining him in Alex's office. She wanted in on the action and her warrior skills remained appreciated. The two of them sprawled on opposite ends of Alex's couch while the other family members ranged in their usual fashion. Duncan was MIA, undoubtedly doing cop work as the city braced for more trouble. None of the boys were present, either, a favor to Emil because he didn't want Jase to be alone but also didn't want him to be privy to what was going on. He hadn't told him about Dracul or the endless war and how the recent bombings tied into their alien group. And the boy hadn't asked any questions, although Emil could see in his eyes that he had them. In this one instance, the boy's brutal training worked to protect him from a horror that was only going to upset him.

Emil had debriefed everyone about what he'd found. It was Val who expressed what they were all thinking. "Seriously, Mars Nobel? The guy could be a comedian if he weren't so bent on murder or mayhem."

Emil nodded. "Very true." He turned to Alex. "It's been almost a week since his last hit, I think we should move on this tomorrow night or in the early morning of Saturday. He'll likely be resting at dawn. He never got used to dealing with Earth's sun and probably does most of his work at night. And you know he's not going to let the weekend go without another attack. He wants everyone to start breathing easier before acting again. It ups the terror factor. But he also can't wait too long or risk Dracul's wrath. My guess is he'll rest for a couple of hours then head out."

"I am aware," Alex intoned. "And I agree. There was a reason humans started to believe we were vulnerable to be killed during the day. Many of us did do exactly as you describe. Val, you and I will draw up the plan of attack. We have to devise a way of dealing with our federal babysitters, as well. It won't do to have them tailing us.

"Emil and Harry, get working on what you'll need to destroy his growing room and anything else he has there, plus any delivery system you might need if we find an active bomb." He looked at Logan. "Can we count on you to help with the planning?"

"Yup." Logan popped out the one word and that was it. There was nothing more to be said, anyway.

Everyone left to get started. "I'll meet you downstairs, Harry. I want to make sure Jase is settled for the night."

"Of course."

He opened his hearing and sense of smell to track down the boy. Excitement mounted as he got closer. Not a huge amount, not something that would send his heart racing too much. It was only that he was looking forward to a few minutes of interacting with Jase before getting into the dirty business of stopping Marius. He found the boys in the workout room, dressed in skin-tight clothing, doing yoga.

"This is called warrior's pose." Mackie led the small class, posing with his legs spread and arms outstretched.

But it was Jase who captured Emil's attention. Of course he did. The boy's lithe body was on full display. The way the clothing hugged his small rump made Emil salivate and his cock rise from its slumber. The sight was somehow more provocative than seeing the boy fully naked. *This way, I can unwrap him.* The stray thought made him grunt.

Jase's body burned with the effort to hold the pose, and he grimaced in concentration to mimic it perfectly. Then a deep, harsh sound caught his attention. He flicked his gaze to the doorway and instantly forgot about his straining muscles. There was Master staring at him with hunger in his eyes. Jase knew that look, knew it well. It should have scared him. Normally, it would have. Not now, not after the night he'd spent in this man's arms after he'd pleasured Jase in a way he hadn't dreamed was possible.

"Master." Breaking his pose, he raced over to him. He stopped abruptly when he wanted to leap into the man's arms. Instead, he went up on his toes and pressed a chaste kiss on Master's lips. He hoped he hadn't been too bold.

He squealed in surprise and fright in the next instant. Master grabbed him by the waist and hauled him up. Then he was kissing Jase senseless. Master's big hand held the back of his head while he slanted his lips over Jase's. The move was so surprising and so delightful that it took a moment for Jase to relax into it. Once he did, Master's tongue swept in and tasted every inch of Jase's mouth.

He'd never been kissed like this before. Sure, Jack had slobbered on him with his stinky saliva. Other men had, as well. It had been simply one more part of Jase that had been taken from him. He had never actively participated in the revolting invasion. Now, though, he shyly chased Emil's tongue with his own. His reward was Master clasping his ass and pressing their bodies even closer. By the time Master let them both up for air, Jase's heart pumped wildly and his surprisingly hard dick pressed against his soft yoga pants. Master's equally hard cock poked Jase's leg.

"And here we have the classic lover's pose," Mackie called out.

Jase's cheeks heated. Master grinned at him before setting him back on his feet. "Very funny, Mackie." He ran a finger along Jase's cheekbone. "How are you doing?"

Jase looked down out of shyness, not submissiveness, although that was foremost in his life still. "I'm fine, Master."

"Good." He kissed Jase on the forehead before letting him go entirely. "I have work to do for probably the rest of the night. Go to bed whenever you want. Soon, in fact. It's very late."

"Yes, Master."

He hated the idea of spending the night alone now. How his life had changed in such a short period of time. He didn't voice a complaint, of course. Master was a busy man with important things to do. He didn't know what was going on, but he was sure Master and his family were involved somehow with the bomber. They were trying to stop him, although he didn't understand exactly why they had to instead of the police. No one told him anything, not even Mackie or Quinn. They were in on it, though. He was certain of it.

Master nodded. "Good. Go ahead and finish your lesson."

With that, he was gone. Jase turned to find Mackie and Quinn grinning madly at him. "What?"

"You're in love with him," Quinn said.

Jase hunched in in on himself. "So? He's my master. I'm supposed to love him."

Mackie rushed forward and grabbed him by the shoulders. "No, sweetie. You, *Jase*, love him, *Emil*. This isn't about dominance or slavery, real or pretend. You truly love him, don't you?"

"Yes," Jase admitted. He could hear the defeat in his own words.

Quinn came over. "What's the problem? Isn't that what you want—a chance for a normal life before settling down? If so, that's okay. Emil will understand. You deserve to have some freedom. He won't force you into anything. You must know that by now."

"I do. I honestly do, and that's the problem. I don't think he loves me back. I'm a burden to him, a duty. He feels responsible for me, even though he shouldn't."

Mackie rolled his eyes. "Sweetie, let me assure you. That man is head over heels for you."

"You think so?" Both the other boys nodded and smiled. The news elated Jase for about two seconds before reality had him crashing down. "I don't think he'll act on it. He doesn't want to be like the men who used me. He wouldn't allow me to reciprocate the blow job he gave me, and I had to practically beg him to drink my blood."

Both boys gasped then squealed. Mackie actually jumped up and down. "You fed him?"

"I think so. He sucked on my inner thigh for a few seconds. And I know it made him come in his pants." He scratched absently at the spot Master had scored. It was a small scabbed-over area, barely detectible, as if it had happened days ago.

"Yeah," Quinn said, "the whole blood thing amps everything to an eleven. It's scary, though, huh? The first time."

"Not really." That was the truth. It might have been because of the years of brutal pain and the fear that had gone with it, but Jase could honestly say that what Emil had done to him hadn't been traumatic in the least. In fact, he couldn't wait for it to be repeated.

"Okay, um…how about we finish this lesson instead of talking about love and sex. It's getting me worked up with nowhere to go." Jase pointed at where his dick strained against his yoga pants.

"Sure," Mackie said. "Whatever you want, but I'm betting that problem of yours will resolve itself the moment you slide under Emil's sheets."

* * * *

Damn, Mackie had been right. Seconds after turning in for the night, Jase's naked body betrayed him. It had rolled over without his conscious decision and he'd humped the bed for a quick climax. Fear had washed over him the moment the last spasm subsided. His skin had gone clammy and his heart hammered away from more than the effort to come. He'd lain there worrying over how to cover his tracks before he remembered. *Master is kind. Master won't care.*

To prove it to himself, he resisted the urge to change the sheets. Instead, he stayed where he was with his eyes closed and tried to do the one thing Master had told him to do and go to sleep. Eventually, it worked. He roused, startled and muddle-headed from a deep sleep when Master slid in beside him. Naked. The man was completely undressed for the first time Jase had known him. The feel of his skin against Jase's was wonderfully cool.

He opened his eyes. "Master?"

"Go back to sleep. I didn't mean to wake you. It's not yet dawn."

"Yes, sir, except I need to tell you something first."

"What is it?" As he asked, he rolled toward Jase and slipped an arm across his waist.

"I, um, jerked myself off earlier."

"Oh, yeah?" Master sounded sleepy, not upset.

"In your bed. *On* your bed, actually. I humped the sheets." He cringed at the confession.

"Did you hurt yourself?" Master moved his hand to lightly clasp Jase's cock. The damn thing proved to be insatiable now that it had been reborn. It hardened in an instant. Master chuckled. "I guess not. Let me see if I can help you get back to sleep."

He started pumping Jase's cock with slow, sure strokes. Jase moaned and bucked into the hold. He placed his hand over Master's thick wrist then felt a steel rod brush against his thigh. No, that was Master's cock. He couldn't resist reaching for it. Given their size difference, he only managed to touch the tip, and it was as big as he'd imagined. Slickness covered it already, testament to how much Master wanted him. Jase tried to wrap his fingers around the shaft but couldn't quite get to it. He groaned in frustration.

"Here now," Master said. "If you're determined to touch me, let me make this easier for both of us."

The large man somehow contorted his body to align their two dicks. Slinging his leg over Jase's hip, he brought them closer together, too. Then he maneuvered

Jase's hand so that he could hold the root of Master's cock. Or at least he tried to. It was so big around, Jase's fingertip couldn't meet his thumb.

"You're huge," he whispered.

The shaft in his grip jumped at the observation. "It makes me crazy hearing you say that." Master's breath ruffled Jase's hair. He still smelled like he'd been baking all night. It was delicious. Master bucked his hips and, using the heel pressed against Jase's ass, made him do the same. With his hand wrapped around both shafts, the guy jerked them together. The silky skin of alien cock was no different than a human's. But it was cooler and it moved inside, as if it were a living thing in and of itself.

Jase allowed Master to lead the way, naturally. He wasn't passive, however. He had a handful of flesh to play with. He experimented with pumping and squeezing. His efforts were rewarded with low moans and a snapping of Master's hips that sent them both careening over the edge in too short a time. Once he felt his orgasm overtake him, Jase dropped his hand to clutch at Master's balls.

Master groaned. "Yes, more."

Jase obliged and forced his eyes open so he could watch the effect he was having. Master's chin jutted, straining the cords in his neck. A gleam of fangs showed past his lips, and Jase wanted to offer him a vein. He didn't know how to go about doing it without interrupting Master's current pleasure, so he didn't try. He decided to ask Mackie and Quinn the proper etiquette or strategy for achieving it next time.

Please, God, let there be a next time.

When their orgasms faded, Master released their dicks and casually wiped his hand on the covers. Jase felt dumb, worrying about his own mess in the face of the man's indifference to sleeping in cum-filled bedding. It didn't disgust Jase, either, which was another first. He'd hated sleeping in his master's spending before.

Although his passion was satisfied for the moment, Master didn't let him go and roll away. On the contrary, he hugged Jase closer. Knowing he should go to sleep and let Master do the same, he couldn't let go of a nagging concern.

"Master?"

"Hmm."

"Is everything going to be okay? I mean…with the bomber and stuff."

Master tucked Jase's head under his chin. "Don't you worry about that. It's something my family and I have to deal with, and we will. In a couple of days, it will be all over, then you and I can sit down and make a plan about what you're going to do with your life. I'll help you in any way you want."

Jase didn't care about that. His life was fine the way it was, thank you very much. He found the courage to press the issue. "But are you going to be safe?"

"Certainly I am. I'm not doing anything dangerous. I promise. Now go back to sleep."

"Yes, Master." Jase shut his mouth because in his heart he was still an obedient slave. But he had the horrible feeling that, for the first time, Master had lied to him.

Chapter Twelve

Emil set his mouth in a grim line before saying, "I don't like this plan."

"Your objections have been duly noted, my friend." Alex had on his I-am-the-captain expression, and was using his authoritative tone. He didn't typically pull rank, but Emil's objections had obviously gotten to him. "Jase will be safe. Do you believe I would send Quinn into danger? Would Val do so with Mackie or Harry with Demi?"

"No, of course not, sir."

Val clapped him on the back. "We understand how you feel. We're all on edge. We don't want our loved ones out where Marius might stumble upon them, but we need them to distract the feds. Plus, there will be four fewer people for Lucien and Kitty to keep track of when the shit hits the fan here."

"Duncan has assured us that only four undercover cops in two cars are currently assigned to keeping track of us. They may be highly suspicious of our involvement, but they have too many leads to chase. They don't have a sufficient amount of personnel to devote many resources to what may be a dead-end. That works in our favor. The boys taking off for any early morning trip will suck half of them away. Although," Alex added, "I can't imagine why they think those young humans could be of any threat when there's the rest of us to worry about."

Emil wanted to argue, yet that would be irrational of him. He'd hated the plan from the beginning and had voiced his concerns a couple of times now. Alex was getting sick of explaining it to him, and Emil didn't blame the man. There was still a deep-seated fear inside him that it was a mistake to let the boys out on their own.

Jase didn't think so, of course. He strolled into the garage, chatting with the boys. He seemed happy and relaxed — excited even, at the prospect of their boys' trip up the coast. He'd had so little in his life that even this minor event pleased him. That reaction alone made Emil conflicted about his feelings. Of course, Jase didn't understand that the jaunt was a diversion. He didn't need to know.

The boy smiled at him and came to give him a quick hug. "Are you sure this is all right, Master? I could help in the kitchen, what with Damien sick and all."

"I'm sure. Damien is fine and Kitty can help out. You go and enjoy yourself. Keep an eye on the others. They get into trouble easily," he whispered into his ear.

Jase's eyes widened at hearing those words, then he grinned. "Oh, Master, be serious."

"I am." He kissed him, hard then went back for seconds, taking his time, until a loud throat-clearing forced him to let go.

Alex jerked his head toward Mackie's Jeep, where he, Quinn and Demi had already seated themselves. Emil nodded. If the others could let their boys go, so could he. He straightened Jase's jacket to make sure it covered him well, then sent him on his way with a playful swat on his cute rump that made the boy laugh—a beautiful sound that he hoped to hear again soon.

He stood with the others, waving the boys away and forcing himself to focus on his own task at hand. Packs of jars filled with extra-special baking soda stood propped against the wall. He hoped he'd made enough to do the trick, whatever the trick turned out to be. Although he wanted to be the one to deal with Marius, he understood that of all of them, he was best suited to neutralize a bomb, if it came to that.

Harry entered a few seconds after the boys took off. "Lucien is all set. I don't like his involvement, but I trust Kitty to keep him from harm."

Emil felt vindicated by the older man voicing his concern. But he also knew that Alex and Val were right. They needed a clear shot at going after Marius. It would have been nice not to have to worry about the cops at all. Marius was to blame for that, and his very thought had always been that casting suspicion on them would hamper their efforts to stop him.

"You're right. She will. I'm sorry I've been fussing about all of this. Let's do it." He picked up the backpacks stuffed with his and Harry's baking soda mixture, hoping like hell he wouldn't have to use it. And, if he did, he hoped it would work. They were going on supposition at this point. Marius could have been employing something completely different. They'd know soon.

The screech of the fire alarm blasted suddenly. Emil took a moment to fret over his beloved kitchen. Kitty and Lucien would take care of the club members and go-go boys, but the grease fire they'd deliberately set would destroy the space he'd lovingly created. It was the best plan possible under the circumstance, and he couldn't second-guess it, either. Emil had already done the unforgiveable and spiked Damien's food in order to send him home early with a stomach ache. None of the other staff was on duty. There's was nothing for him to do about anything happening above anyway. Kitchens could be repaired. Humans, not so much.

They gave it five minutes before piling into the oversized SUV and taking off. Val was at the wheel and he navigated them out of the underground area and through the alley. A brief look confirmed that guys were milling about the front of the building with a couple of fire engines and an ambulance blocking the street. If the surveillance team rushed in to help, they were not going to be able to chase after them.

With the muted colors of a winter dawn breaking as their backdrop, Emil and the others arrived at a shabby residential neighborhood. They parked the SUV on a side street and walked the rest of the way to the dilapidated house that matched the address on the order form. It appeared to be deserted, but they knew better than to be fooled by that. Crouching in the waning darkness, they peered through the rotting fence around the back to confirm that the shipping container was there. It took up almost the entire overgrown, weedy yard. It looked like a storage area, except that an HVAC system was attached to its side. A thick cord connected the compressor to the house, running through a basement window.

With the confirmation that they had the right place, they split into two groups, as previously agreed. Emil scurried with Harry along the fence to find a place to break it open without making too much noise that would carry to the house. Alex, Val and Logan went in search of a way to get into the house itself in the hopes of finding Marius. Emil didn't give that part of the mission any thought, however, sure that his friends and family knew their job. He needed to concentrate on his own.

Getting inside the yard was easy. Marius obviously hadn't worried about that. The container was slightly harder. The lock was sturdy. Emil would have wished for Logan and her skills, except Harry had plenty of his own. He carefully, yet quickly, poured acid onto the metal and yanked it open when it was sufficiently weakened. Emil stepped inside first, watchful of traps. But Marius' hubris and contempt for humans had made him almost careless. There was nothing there to see other than a whole bunch of what they'd come for.

Emil exhaled noisily as he surveyed the rows of plants. "We were right, thank fuck."

"Yes, most fortunate," Harry agreed.

That was all the talking they needed to do. Each of them put down the backpacks and duffel bags they'd carried with them and got to work destroying Marius' killing fields.

A noise at the door had Emil whirling with a nine millimeter raised in his hand. Although he hated weapons of any kind, he knew how to use them. He'd almost forgotten he'd strapped the thing to an ankle holster back at the club. Alex stuck his head in and cocked his eyebrow at him.

"I see that you both guessed right. Unfortunately, Marius is nowhere to be found. Val and Logan are already dealing with what's in the house, but we have to assume he's left to plant more explosives. In fact, we found a map of the various locations he intends to hit."

Harry frowned. "Careless of him."

"No," Emil said with a shake of his head. "Hubris. Marius has always thought himself smarter than anyone else, even Dracul. He didn't think we'd find him."

"Or if he did," Alex continued, "he wants us to chase him down and watch him slaughter humans."

"Can I see the map?" Emil asked, uncertain of why he thought he could fathom the killer's intent. But of all of them, he was the one who'd known Marius the best because they'd been in the same department on the ship."

He followed Alex into the basement of the house and studied what Marius had laid out on a large and worn oak table that had probably come with the property. His gaze landed on one spot in particular almost immediately.

He pointed it out. "There. That's where he's gone."

Alex peered down. "Why do you think that?"

Emil turned his troubled eyes on his captain. "Children. He's only targeted space where adults hang out, or in the case of Faneuil Hall, it was chance that it was only adults. But this" — he emphasized with a jab of his finger — "is where you'll find lots of kids on a Saturday morning. He's going to hit Frog Pond. I'm sure of it."

Alex swore and called out to Val and Logan. They came racing down the stairs and a new plan was formed. Within minutes, Emil was back in the SUV with Alex and Val. Harry and Logan had been left behind to neutralize that which Marius had amassed for his murderous schemes. They'd make sure that nothing remained that would give the human authorities any notion of an alien presence.

* * * *

Jase laughed. "Come on, you guys. Stop fooling around."

"We're not, dude," Mackie insisted, glancing at him through the rearview mirror of his sporty red Jeep. "Honestly."

Jase looked to Demi, sitting next to him in the back seat. "He's messing with me. I know he is. There is no way your human father gave birth to you."

Demi shrugged. "What can I say, dude? It's true." Looking like a slightly miniature version of the aliens with a bit of Asian features thrown in, the boy certainly made his claim seem possible.

Jase shook his head. "No, I'm not buying it."

Quinn turned to look at him from over his shoulder and said, "Stick around for a while and you may see Mackie pregnant."

This story they'd been telling him on the way back from their jaunt to Rockport boggled his mind. The idea that drinking Emil's blood could turn Jase into a breeding male both fascinated and repelled him. Yet, with all that he'd seen and all that he knew so far, it wasn't that much of a stretch. He'd have to ask Master. Other than the persistent worry that Master had lied about his being in danger, Jase trusted him to be honest.

The early morning journey up the coast with the three other boys had surprised him. He could tell, too, that

Master wasn't happy about it. Still, he'd asked — not told — Jase to do it, and Jase would do anything for Master. It had been bitingly cold, yet gorgeous and fun, skipping around the large boulders on the coast while the sun rose. Mackie, acting the wheel man, had taken a leisurely way there, but was taking the faster highway back. He was obviously enjoying using his wedding present from his husband to its best advantage.

He'd also kept staring in the side mirror, as if worried about something behind them. When Jase had asked what was going on, the others had done some kind of silent assessment about what they should tell him. In the end, all Quinn said was that they were making it easier for their men to do what they had to do. Then they'd started distracting him with this tale about being turned into breeding males. Even if they were telling the truth, they needn't have bothered. It was a sufficient reason for Jase that his master didn't want him to know what was happening. He wasn't going to probe further, if only because he didn't want to get them in trouble. He hoped Master would explain things to him eventually. As long as the man remained safe, however, he would count himself lucky, regardless.

A phone rang. Quinn pulled his out and answered it. "Alex, is everything okay?" Jase and the others went completely silent while Quinn listened and nodded. "Sure, I understand. We're heading back to the club now. We're fine. It was fun.

"A fire? Is everybody okay? Yes, we'll be careful, I promise. We'll park on the street and find Lucien and Kitty. Don't worry about us. I love you. Be careful."

"Well?" Mackie demanded before Quinn said a word.

"Alex said they're good on their end and that we should go straight to the club, although there was a grease fire in the kitchen."

"The kitchen?" Jase sat forward. "I should have stayed behind."

"No!" All three boys shouted him down in unison. He got the sneaking suspicion that the fire wasn't that big a surprise to them.

"You wouldn't have been able to stop it," Quinn said. "It was just one of those things. Anyway, Alex said to go straight back. No detours and absolutely no going anywhere near the Common."

"Why's that?" Demi asked, the very thing Jase wanted to know. Although hearing that Master was safe so far eased his mind somewhat, the fire was a disturbing wrinkle. There was much more going on here than he'd imagined.

"Alex didn't say."

Mackie groaned. "And you didn't ask him."

"You know I don't question Alex the way you do Val," Quinn huffed.

"Because you don't like getting your ass beat, whereas everyone knows I can take my licks."

Quinn threw up his arms. "Don't get all I'm-a-submissive on me, *sweetie*. I know how to trust my man and get what I want without baiting him first."

"Making him crazy is half the fun," Mackie countered.

"And twice the work." Quinn folded his arms.

Jase was getting agitated with worry. "Wait. I don't understand."

Demi patted him on the arm. "It's okay. Quinn and Mackie have different styles. They still end up in the same place."

"Which is where?"

"Going to exactly the place Alex said we shouldn't, naturally." The kid didn't say 'stupid' but it was implied in his expression. "The Common wasn't part of the plan."

Jase threw up his hands in frustration. "What was the plan? What is going on here?"

Mackie shook his head. "We don't know, exactly, sweetie. The men don't confide everything to us."

"They are trying to protect us," Quinn practically sneered.

"We have some nasty relatives of sorts that need a beat-down," Demi added. "Ask Emil sometime when you've made him stupid with sex. He'll tell you."

Mackie increased his speed and started weaving among the heavying traffic. "And the men keep forgetting just how helpful we can be. They need a reminder. Hence, we go to the place they told us to avoid. We just don't know why or what we're walking into, that's all."

"Then we shouldn't go," Jase stated the obvious.

"Except there must be something risky happening to the men we love, and although they wouldn't think so, we might be the difference between them living and dying," Quinn said. "They're not indestructible."

Jase's stomach did a flip-flop of fear. *I knew Master was lying.* And maybe disobeying made Jase a bad slave. So be it. He wasn't going to lose the man now that he'd finally found him. "Mackie, drive faster."

* * * *

Trey headed for his bed with glazed eyes and was half-asleep already. He landed face down and didn't care that he was still fully dressed. After clocking more than twenty-four hours, nothing would disturb him. Then his phone started ringing and he nearly wept at the sound. He also considered tending his resignation from the force if it meant the chance of getting a few hours' sleep. In the end, he pulled it out of his pocket and answered with his eyes closed.

"Speak." He didn't care if it was a superior on the line.

"Duncan, we need you."

"Emil?" He rolled over, wide awake now. "You found Marius?"

"We found his bolt hole and his stash of explosives. Harry and Logan are dealing with that. Alex, Val and I are heading to where we think is his next bombing site."

That had Trey lurching to his feet and racing for the door. Fatigue stood no chance against terror. "Tell me where so I can get Franklin and his people to cordon it off."

"I'll tell you, but you can't let anyone else know."

"Fuck that. People are dying." He punched through to his garage, where his car sat still warm from his trip home.

"If we don't stop Marius, thousands more will be killed. If he sees any one of your people, he'll abort that plan and move to another. We're not even sure we know where he's going. It's an educated guess. Mine, actually."

"I trust that." He got in and started his motor.

"Thanks, and I hope I'm not leading everyone astray. I need your promise on this, Duncan. You know what's at stake and why this isn't like catching a human terrorist."

Trey backed out onto the street and gunned it. "Yeah, yeah. Fine, tell me where."

"Frog Pond."

"Fuck!" He glanced at the clock on his dashboard. "It will be filled with kids skating in an hour or so."

"We know. We're parking at the garage below the Common and are going to do our best to scout out the area hopefully without him seeing us. He won't know you at all, though."

"Yeah, but I know him—an alien with one arm. If I see him first, I'm taking him down. I don't care how I have to explain a pile of dust, either."

"That's fair. See you on the other side."

The call disconnected. He started to pocket his phone then decided he needed to make one more call.

"Christ Jesus, this better be good."

"Karl, I need you to meet me at Frog Pond. Please don't ask questions now. I promise I'll explain later, and I need you to come in quiet."

A noisy breath blew through the connection. "On my way."

* * * *

"Damn, it's so crowded."

"Humans are resilient," Alex observed. "It's one of the things I admire about them. In the face of terror, they go on with their lives, refusing to be cowed."

The three of them—he, Alex and Val—lurked behind the small enclosure that provided the entrance and exit to the garage. It was still early, the skating pond not yet open for business. It would be soon, however, and that's when Marius would make his move. There would be no point in bombing an empty park.

That was assuming he was right. There'd been nothing about Marius' plans to confirm it. It was merely a hunch on Emil's part. There were other possibilities, such as the bridge he'd highlighted and the airport. His gut still told him this was the place, though. It would be bad and yet a small escalation of the carnage. It checked all the boxes based on his knowledge of how his former shipmate's mind worked.

"Where is he?" he murmured.

He scanned the growing group of people. While it was cold, it wasn't frigid. Groups milled about with light winter clothing. The sun was starting to shine in earnest, making it a lovely day for spending some time outdoors. Families were arriving at the Frog Pond pavilion, looking to rent skates. A gaggle of little girls skipped up, paired off and holding hands. One at the front had a princess crown on. A birthday party… Had to be. All Emil could picture was those sweet girls being maimed and killed.

He broke his gaze from them and searched intently. "Where are you? Where are you?" He spotted a tall figure off to one side, shambling along. A homeless man, probably. With his watch cap pulled low on his face, it was hard to get a good look at him. He carried a dirty duffel bag, though, and that alone made him suspicious. As did the fact that his far sleeve appeared to be plastered to his side, as if there were no arm in it.

Emil tapped Alex's shoulder. "What do you think?" He pointed in the direction of the man, who continued to approach the rink.

Alex straightened. "Could be. It's a good disguise. Build's about right and that bag could contain a lot. Val…"

"On it." Hunching into his own coat and pulling a cap low on his brow, Val headed toward the man.

Not satisfied they'd identified Marius, Emil kept looking. Now the little girls were laughing and pulling on skates. Others had already hit the ice, the rink having just opened. The man kept going and so did Val, picking up his pace to close the distance, yet not rushing to raise suspicion. Emil's phone vibrated in his pocket.

He pulled it out and checked the caller. "Duncan."

"I'm here, over toward Boylston. And don't chew my ear about it, but I brought in Karl. We need help and he's trustworthy."

"You can take that up with Alex later." Emil looked in the direction the cop had stated and caught sight of him and his partner. "I see you. Val's on the other side of the rink. There's someone approaching who might be…

"Wait." Emil narrowed his eyes at a figure rounding the Frog Pond pavilion on Duncan's side. A musician, from the looks of him, with a long duster, a rasta hat pulled down low and a covered base fiddle slung over one shoulder. The guy sauntered over to the side of the rink and, putting his burden down, leaned on the rail to watch the skaters.

Val and his quarry hadn't quite reached the pond, the man having slowed down. He redistributed his bag, showing for the first time that he had two arms to move. At the moment when Val was realizing this and looking back at Emil and Alex, the musician turned slightly. His movement stole Emil's attention back.

"It's him," Emil said into the phone and to Alex at the same time. "Rasta hat by the railing. That's Marius."

Shoving his phone back in his pocket, he grabbed his own pack and raced. It was brutal keeping his pace to a slower, human level when all he wanted to do was fly. His gaze homed in on the bag on the ground. Death lurked inside, ready to go off at any moment. Marius' nonchalance at standing next to it made no difference. The man's blood ran colder than the arctic. He undoubtedly found it a source of pride that he didn't simply dump it and run.

Alex ran next to him, and Val, having caught on, took off after Marius. He was closest, but Marius saw him and bolted in the opposite direction, no longer so casual. Emil took a second to appreciate how they'd spoiled his fun before silently urging the guy to keep running in that direction. He was almost on top of Duncan and his partner, and their plain clothes made it impossible for him to peg them as cops. But too bad for him, because they were. They pulled out their weapons and yelled "Police" in the kind of dramatic way one saw on television. And, like in fiction, people started screaming when they noticed the guns and heard those words.

Marius hadn't expected that. He paused in a moment of indecision before trying to change course for a safe way out. That's all it took. Unlike the vampires of the lore they'd inadvertently created, their kind could be killed by bullets. Duncan and Anderson shouted for him to stop, and when he ignored them, they fired at him point blank.

Emil didn't have time to watch the scene unfold in its entirety. A bomb lay waiting to decimate the ice rink. He had no doubt it was going to be the most powerful one yet. He headed straight to it, while Alex and Val started yelling at the humans to run. Alex rushed through the rink's opening, sliding right across the ice. He swept up two girls as he passed them and lifted them along for the ride. Val did the same a half-second later. At the other side, boys stood with open arms to grab the now-screaming kids and carry them across the Common.

No, not merely boys. Mackie and Quinn. *What the fuck!* Demi was also there, taking two girls from Val before sprinting away. Other humans caught on quick. Those that weren't trying to save their own children went to grab anyone Alex and Val had scooped up on the ice. It was like a bucket brigade of kids whose skates would prevent them from running for safety. Someone would be filming it, without a doubt, but Alex's and Val's ability to navigate the ice in a way humans would have failed at was the least of their worries.

As Emil skidded down beside the bag, the back of his mind worried about Jase. If the boys had come back from Rockport to the very place they were told to avoid, where was he?

"Master." The sound of the breathless voice made Emil's heart skip.

"You were supposed to be safe!" He vented his fear through fury as he ripped open the bag and tried to make sense of what he saw.

"I want to help. Please, tell me how I can."

"The children."

"They're almost all cleared. The others are seeing to that. The cop, Duncan, is here, too."

"I know. I called him." He sacrificed a second to look at Jase. The boy stared back at him with wide and teary eyes — and determination. He wasn't going anywhere.

"Open my backpack and take out one of the jars." Marius' bag was packed with explosive material and an electrical device that was designed to set the spark. When and how were beyond his skill. He was no engineer, but he was a botanist and a cook. He knew that if he saturated the material enough, no spark would set it off. He could only hope he had gotten the measurement right.

"Here, Master."

Jase opened one jar. Emil took it and started to gingerly sprinkle it over the top of the material. His plan was to neutralize it layer by layer, working downward so as not to jolt anything. He moved slowly, afraid to make any sudden moves.

"You understand that this could go off at any moment."

"Yes, Master."

"We'll both die if it does."

"I know, Master."

He tossed the empty jar away and held out his hand for the next one. Jase was ready for him. "Do you think, given the precarious circumstances, you could do me the favor of calling me by my name? I'd like to hear it once from your beautiful lips and have you mean it man-to-man, not slave-to-Master, if you don't mind."

"Emil." There was no hesitation, no coyness, no dramatic pause. "*Emil.*"

Although he was now wrist-deep in Marius' deathly shit, he had to smile. "Thank you. I hope we get a chance for you to say that a whole lot more."

"As you please, but I'd like to call you Master, too, sometimes."

"We'll talk about that. If it's something you really want, I can't say I mind hearing it."

"Truly?" He passed another jar to him.

"Yup. Who knew? I'm a secret Dom or whatever."

They worked quietly for a minute after that, slowly incorporating the baking soda mixture into the explosive. At some point, the ratio changed sufficiently that Marius' compound started to decompose. It withered, then went slimy, turning into a disgusting goo. When Emil had used the last jar, he sat back on his heels and watched the bag's contents, looking for signs that it was still volatile.

A muffled click gave him his answer. Sticking his hand in, he felt for the electrical component, found it breaking apart. The detonation had happened but the explosion had not.

"Thank God," he sighed.

Jase grabbed his arm. "Master!"

Emil jerked and followed Jase's line of sight. The man Val had been hunting was still there, the only one who hadn't run from the scene. He was bending down and grabbing something from behind the pavilion. Emil had a split-second to throw himself over Jase and cover him before the explosion rocked the area.

Debris rained down on them, on him, pelting his back with bits of dirt and mortar. He grunted with the impact of some of it, yet moved only so much as to make sure he fully shielded the smaller human.

Terror robbed him of breath more than the stuff pelting him. He wrapped his arms around Jase's head and pressed him down as much as he dared without smothering him. He could feel the boy shaking and hear his screams, despite the ringing in his ears.

Something large clobbered him on his head and he fought a wave of dizziness. Blood trickled down his face. He ignored it. He stayed lying on top of Jase until nothing more fell from the sky. Opening his eyes, he tried to turn to look and see if it was safe to get up.

Everything appeared blurry. Then Jase shoved him off with a surprising strength. Emil toppled over and blinked at the boy's worried face that now peered down at him.

"Jase? Why are there two of you?"

The boy burst into tears. It was the last thing Emil saw.

Chapter Thirteen

"Keep the ice pack on, Emil."

He eyed his nurse, Jase, who was taking his assigned role very seriously. The fact that the boy was carefully using his name and had dropped the 'Master' in front of the feds was a good sign. So, Emil shot him a smile and said, "Yes, sir."

He settled back in the booth where he sat and adjusted the pack to cover the lump. He winced because it did hurt like a bitch. Everyone was clustered at one end of the main room of the club, the separate interviews having been concluded. No one had been spared the grilling, from Kitty and Lucien, to Logan and Harry — and, of course, the boys. Emil had worried about Jase being by himself, but he seemed unfazed when he left the upstairs room the feds had been using. Only Demi had been spared, being a minor. Harry had insisted that any questioning had to be done with either him in the room or someone from social services.

Franklin had elected to cut the boy loose entirely, although he had joined them for the grand finale.

Even though his team had left minutes ago, Franklin was still there, eyeing them like a disapproving schoolmarm. Man, was he pissed. He wasn't buying their story, yet with two cops backing it up, he had little choice. It was a minor miracle everyone had absorbed the hastily concocted explanation as well as they had.

Plus, some unknown homeless man had now been identified as the unsub. The poor bastard... At least his identity might never be known, so his good name wasn't going to be sullied with Marius' horrific deeds.

The acrid smell of the fire lingered and would for weeks, likely. Lucien and Kitty had done an excellent job at a diversion. The kitchen was in shambles, and while the rest of the club was unscathed, the smoke damage alone would require substantial renovations of the first two floors. Emil tried not to pout about that. In the larger scheme of things, having to redo his kitchen hardly ranked as a tragedy.

Franklin tapped his notebook and grimaced at the crowd at large. "Well, this has been quite the day. While I was happy to report that another tragedy had been avoided and that the unsub appears to have been neutralized permanently, there are still a lot of loose ends that I don't think I'm going to be able to tie up soon. I don't like *loose ends*."

He paced away before confronting them again. "I also don't like appearing to be an idiot in front of my superiors, like the President of the United States, for one. So, here's what I'm going to write in my official report. Most of the Stelalux family headed out this morning before an unfortunate grease fire broke out. The boys went to Rockport to frolic about the rocks in the freezing cold, for some reason, then decided ice skating at Frog Pond was in order. Husbands and lovers left separately to join them, somehow without my people outside noticing."

"I find the fact that you had us under surveillance disturbing, to say the least," Alex interrupted."

"I'm sure you do. The timing of your departure vis-à-vis the fire is astounding. You missed it by minutes at most."

"They do say timing is everything."

"Yeah, anyway... Sergeant Duncan, acting on an anonymous tip, contacted his partner and they went to the Common, as well. Quite the coincidence."

Duncan coughed. "Sometimes police work is about getting lucky, sir."

Franklin glared at him. "Indeed. Regardless, a suspicious man dropped a bag by the rink and started running. After due warning, Sergeant Duncan and Detective Anderson opened fire. Then, thinking they'd killed the unsub, they proceeded to evacuate the area. They were wrong. He somehow went from where they'd dropped him and decided to make himself a casualty of his own bomb. He won't be the first perp to end it that way, I suppose. We're lucky he was the only one to be hurt."

"My head would like to disagree with you, sir," Emil said. He winked at Jase, who smiled back at him. The boy was sitting as close to him as possible without being on his lap, which is what Emil would have preferred.

"Yes, my apologies, Mr. Stelalux. Although I appreciate how all of you worked to save those kids in particular, it was monumentally stupid for you to open that bag. You had no idea it was filled with some gunk."

Emil smiled sheepishly. "I know. I think Jase and I were thinking it would be like in the movies. All we had to do was pull the green wire or something and stop the bomb, except that's not where the bomb was."

"No, that was a few yards away, in a smaller bag, for some reason. Then there is the mystery of what all of those mason jars filled with baking soda had to do with anything."

"I was going to do a science experiment as a form of street performance, remember?" Emil asked.

"How could I forget," Franklin ground out.

"I dumped it in the bag, thinking it might help in some way—again not knowing the bomb was elsewhere."

Jase put his hand in Emil's and leaned against him. "You saved my life." He didn't say 'Master', yet Emil heard it anyway.

"I'd say that's true," Franklin agreed. "I'm sure you'll show him your appreciation soon."

Emil growled at him, the sound close to human, yet something that made the federal agent blink.

"My apologies. That was rude and unprofessional of me." He flipped his notebook shut and stuck it in his pocket. "Okay, here's the thing—my real thoughts that are not going into the report…yet. I have no idea what happened, but I don't buy what I'm forced to sell to my superiors. At least part of it is bullshit. You all were up to your eyeballs in something. What? I don't know."

He focused on the cops. "Duncan, I'm asking you one more time to give it to me straight."

The cop stood and hitched his pants. He looked dead on his feet. "Sir, I've told you the truth, and part of it is that thanks to some of the people in this room, Karl and I were able to get dozens of people, mostly kids impaired by having skates on their feet, away from the blast zone." He pointed to Alex, Val and the boys. "They literally saved lives, at great risk to their own. Honestly, sir, that's all that needs to go in your report. The rest is simply noise."

He stared at the man with his mouth shut tight after that. A few seconds later, Anderson stood beside him. "What he said, sir."

"Fine," Franklin fumed. "You all may not be murderers or terrorists, but you're *something*. Know this. I've got my eye on you."

With that parting shot, he stormed out.

The room was quiet for a few minutes. Val followed Franklin to lock the door, probably, something that hadn't been done much since opening. The fire was going to put the place out of commission for a few weeks.

Val returned. "He's gone."

"Well," Kitty huffed, "this has been fun. I need a drink. Want one?" she asked Logan.

"Sure. This is not a day for sobriety."

"No more than two," Emil called out.

"Yes, Dad."

"Time for bed, Demi." Lucien stood and gave Harry a quick kiss.

"It's early yet," the boy whined.

"Not after a day like this. And it's not up for debate."

"I was old enough to help save those kids."

"I know, and I couldn't be more proud – or angry. Now, come before I take away your screen privileges." Lucien sailed off for the elevator with his usual grace, a belligerent Demi stomping after him.

Emil looked from Harry to Val to Alex. "Now what?"

"I'm tired of playing defense," Val said, tugging an unusually quiet Mackie into his arms and sitting down.

"As am I," Alex agreed. He stroked Quinn's hair and gave him an encouraging smile before saying, "I'm going to call Malcolm. It's time to take this fight to Dracul for a change."

"Who is he?" Quinn asked.

"He's a navigator," Emil replied, "who loves the stars."

"More to the point, he's a highlander now," Alex countered. "And he's the kind of dog we need in this fight."

"He doesn't like it," Emil reminded his captain. "He only wants to make his Scotch and raise his salmon."

Alex grinned. "Which is why Dracul will never see him coming."

* * * *

"Fucking hell!" Dracul screamed out his fury before delivering another blow to Brenin's already-battered face.

It sent the boy sailing across the room. He hit the wall with a sickening thud. He'd been taking the brunt of Dracul's rage for the last few minutes. Someone had to. That was how the monster worked.

Dracul turned his twisted face toward Petru. "It can't be true. Marius has to be alive. No mere human could have killed him and he would never blow himself up."

"With regrets, sir, it is true. I've studied all the reports and viewed the video put on the Internet by witnesses. There's one that shows Marius being felled by bullets, then disintegrating, proving that he did indeed die, not that anyone believes the footage isn't doctored. I think the victim of the bomb was some stupid human. In any event, this volley is over. Marius never shared his formula for the explosive with anyone, and the only other botanist among us is Emil. His loyalty to the captain is steadfast."

"Don't tell me shit I already know!" He whirled around and advanced on Brenin. The poor boy was barely conscious and cringed in the approach of more violence.

Dafydd couldn't stand it anymore. With a speed he wouldn't have thought himself capable of, he stumbled off the bed and threw himself in Dracul's path. "No." He put one hand on his belly and one palm up as if that could actually stop the monster. "Leave him alone. This isn't his fault."

Dracul roared in rage and bared his fangs. With his heart lodged in his throat, Dafydd stood his ground and shook his head. Dracul advanced with his fist raised. It took everything Dafydd had not to flinch.

"Go ahead and beat me instead. Kill me and your son. I don't care. But I won't stand by while you vent your spleen on this innocent boy." His heart pounded and his stomach turned as he saw his own death in Dracul's eyes. He wanted to care, to cling to his hope of getting free. But he was so damn tired, and if protecting Brenin for a few precious minutes was all he accomplished by this, it would have to be enough.

Then the threat of death was gone. Dracul lowered his arm and retracted his fangs. He actually smiled, although Dafydd knew from long experience that it meant worse was coming. "How bold you've become, my dear. You're right, of course. Beating that little slut won't bring back Marius or advance my plans. It would bring me pleasure, however. I suppose I can think of another way."

That was all the warning Dafydd got before Dracul grabbed him by the arm and shoved him against the bedpost. Dafydd knew to take hold and brace himself with his arms. The first thrust was a brutal reminder of what he'd escaped during the long months since Brenin had been imprisoned. He clamped his lips shut to keep from crying out.

"Oh, I have missed this hole of yours, my dear. Maybe fucking you will speed up your delivery." He shoved his way into Dafydd's resistant body and ground his hips against his ass. "Once my son is free of you, I will show you how truly angry I am."

Dafydd shuddered at the warning. He closed his eyes and suffered the assault because there was nothing else to do…yet. *Not if I get free of you first.*

* * * *

"He turned to dust right in front of my eyes."

Karl kept going over the events at the Frog Pond rink over and over like a broken record — or a man who was in shock. How he'd kept it together during Franklin's interviews, Trey would never know. He appreciated it, though. When it had counted most, his partner had come through for him.

"It was like Christopher fucking Lee burning up in the sun, except that wasn't it at all. It was only after we shot him that he disintegrated."

"Yeah, it happens when they die — that's all — no matter how that occurs. They can go out in daylight, but they prefer the dark. Our sun's too close to the planet or something." He'd told him this already. He'd told him everything he knew. Exhausted as they both were, they sat in Trey's living room, swilling beers. Eventually they were both going to pass out. For now, he needed to let Karl work through the unbelievable in his mind.

"They don't look a thousand years old."

Trey took another hit of his beer. "No, they age differently."

That reminder had him thinking of Demi—the mixed-breed boy who was both older and younger than he appeared. At the height of the crisis, Trey had still had time to notice that the brat had somehow ended up in the middle of the war zone. And he'd acquitted himself with admirable bravery. When others were sensibly fleeing danger, Demi had run straight toward it. He'd carried at least four young children to safety without flinching.

Knowing that Demi was at ground zero for an imminent explosion had sent Trey's stress level into brain-exploding territory. He knew that once the beer did its job, his nightmares were already cued up to feature the boy as a central character. Worse, it was getting harder to see him as too young and untouchable. Right before Trey's eyes, Demi was becoming another warrior in Alex's army. That fact made it all the more imperative for Dracul to be stopped.

"But Kitty's not one of them," Karl continued making his endless loop.

"Nope, she's human."

"That's good. I like her, but I'm not sure I'm progressive enough to get involved with another species, assuming I have a shot there." He eyed Trey over the rim of his bottle. "Do you think I do?"

That was probably the fifth time he'd asked that question. "I don't know, Karl. Maybe. I could ask Alex what he thinks." He'd made this offer, as well, an equal number of times.

"Nah, that's too middle schoolish."

"I agree. She's in a tough spot. Like me, she's trying to help without giving the game away to the rest of the world. Becoming involved with someone in the know is definitely in the plus column where you're concerned." He hated manipulating his partner and friend this way, but after the day's events, he'd become more committed to helping Alex defeat Dracul. The stakes were high and his people weren't equipped to deal with the danger.

"People aren't ready for this," Karl observed…again. "An alien war being waged for centuries on our planet would freak even Stephen Hawking out—you know, if he weren't already dead."

"That's right." He could sense Karl was winding down. His speech was slurring and he swayed where he sat. Or maybe it was Trey's vision that was moving. "I know it's hard, Karl, but I believe it's in our planet's best interest to keep this secret."

Karl drained his bottle and put it on the end table. Or, he tried to. The thing fell off the edge and bounced on the carpet before rolling away. He turned bleary eyes on Trey. "I manipulated a crime scene. I used the chaos to move evidence to frame some poor bastard who was too stoned to realize he was picking up a bomb. I lied to Home-fucking-land Security. That's a federal crime that could send me to jail for the rest of my natural life, which I feel the need to point out is a whole lot shorter than your alien vampire friends'. If you're worried I'm going to change my mind and spill the beans, don't. I'm up to my chin in this shit and all I can do is try to tread so I don't drown."

He slumped over to rest his head against a throw pillow. "Now, if you don't mind, I'm going to pass the fuck out."

Trey smiled, a gesture lost on his friend, whose eyes were already closed. "Thanks, Karl. Sweet dreams."

The man barked out a laugh. "Like I'm ever going to sleep well after this."

Yeah, don't I know it.

* * * *

"Right this way."

"Thank you, Master, but you didn't have to escort me down."

"Of course, I did. This is a date, and a gentleman always picks up his date."

The idea of having a date night with Master flustered him. He didn't know what to do with himself or how to dress for such a thing. He'd never had the chance to do it before, which was the point, he supposed. Master wanted to give him something special. And it already was to Jase. Quinn and Mackie had dressed him head to toe in Dolce & Gabbana, with a fitted light-gold patterned cotton shirt and tight black pants. He'd never worn anything half so fine. They'd tamed his hair, as well, slicking it back with some gel. He felt a little like Cinderella.

Master looked equally fine, if simple, in his charcoal-gray slacks and off-white button-down shirt. His hair was its usual spikey self, so he looked sufficiently like Master that Jase wasn't overly nervous about the evening. It was not too different than the times they'd spent eating in the kitchen. He felt a prick of sadness over how that space had to be redone because of the fire. It would never be quite the same in his mind.

"Close your eyes for a moment, please."

Jase did as requested and almost giggled at the courtly way Master ushered him into the bedroom with a slight pressure at the small of his back. He suppressed it, though, knowing how much trouble the man had gone to set up this evening.

"Okay, you can open them now."

He gasped instead at his first sight of what awaited him. "Oh, it's lovely."

Although the big bed was still there, most of the other furniture had been removed. In its place was a dining room setting, complete with a sideboard loaded with domed dishes, a small square table covered in a snowy white cloth and set with china and crystal and shiny cutlery. Flowers and squat, lit candles festooned every hard surface. A sweet smell of lavender permeated the room, as well. It was a fairy-tale setting, and Jase couldn't take a deep breath from the beauty of it all.

"You like it?" Master seemed nervous.

Jase beamed at him so that there would be no doubt. "It's amazing. Thank you."

"It's nothing more than what you deserve."

Master escorted him to the table and helped him with his chair. Then he shook out a napkin and placed it over Jase's lap. "I'm afraid you'll have to put up with my being both server and date this evening. I'm selfish enough not to want to share you with anyone."

Jase didn't know what to say, so he smiled and nodded and tried not to be too nervous. Luckily Washburn had taught him table manners, along with his harsher lessons. Jase felt comfortable with how to comport himself, not that he believed Master would judge him regardless. He felt safe with this man, this monster, who was nothing of the sort, as it turned out.

Master went to the sideboard. "I know the Commonwealth of Massachusetts would object, but would you like some wine?"

Jase wrinkled his nose. "No, thank you, Master. I don't like alcohol." It had been poured down his throat a time or two, but those awful memories had no place here.

"How about a Coke?"

"Yes, please, if that's not going to clash with the meal."

"You should always drink what pleases you, no matter what you're eating."

Master brought an iced and frosty tall glass of Coke over and poured himself some wine. He held up his glass. "To your first date." Jase shyly completed the toast with a soft clink before taking a sip of his drink.

Master drank some of his wine before putting the glass by his setting. "First course is lobster bisque." Master carried over two bowls, placing one in front of Jase and the other at his own place. "Please be honest about what you think of everything. I want to always serve you what you like."

Jase had no doubt he would love it all. Master's food was delicious, and Jase wanted to try new things. The moment the first taste of creamy soup hit his tongue, he moaned. "It's fabulous."

Master grinned. "I'm glad you like it. I had to use Alex's tiny kitchen to prepare our dinner, and that space is wholly inadequate."

"I would never have known."

They ate in companionable silence for a while before Master said, "I have to confess this dating thing is new to me. It's a pretty new concept on this world and doesn't exist at all on mine. I think, based on what I've seen in movies and the like, we are supposed to get to know each other."

Jase stared at his soup. "Oh, well, I think we know pretty much everything by now."

"No, we don't. We know a lot of the bad stuff, the scary parts. I'm sorry, by the way, for not telling you about Dracul and the others. You should have been forewarned."

"It's fine. I don't know that I could have handled the truth until it had reached a crisis point for me. I'm not afraid. I have faith in you and the others to keep my world safe."

Master seemed pleased with that statement. "Okay, so I want to know nice things about you. For example, what did you want to be when you grew up? I know you were forced out of school early, but before that." Master tried to keep his tone even, yet Jase heard the sadness underneath it.

Not wanting the evening to be marred by the past, Jase racked his brain for an answer. "Honestly, I don't know. I didn't think about it much. I liked video games, so maybe I thought I could become a software engineer."

Master nodded and picked up a covered basket sitting between them. "I almost forgot... Roll?" he asked, unfolding the napkin on top.

Peering inside, Jase sniffed and smiled. Then he took a warm, soft white one. He pulled off a piece and dipped it into what remained of his soup before popping it into his mouth. "Oh," he moaned. "Awesome."

Master nodded again and smiled some more before tossing an entire roll into his mouth. "So, maybe you want to go back to school. There are online courses you could take if you don't want to sit in a classroom with younger kids."

"I thought, maybe, I was going to be a chef, like you." Was this date a break-up one? A spike of panic shot through him.

Master reared his head. He grabbed one of Jase's hands. "Easy, baby. I'm only trying to help you figure out how to get your life back on track. I'm not kicking you to the curb." He chuckled ruefully. "I'm not that noble. I want you, but I also want what's best for you. You're the only one who gets to decide what that is from now on."

Jase instantly relaxed and managed to turn his hand in order to intertwine their fingers. "What I want is to stay with you. And I like cooking. Maybe I can do both for now, take lessons from you in the kitchen and take classes online for other things."

Master squeezed his fingers before letting go. "That's an excellent idea. Are you ready for the second course?"

"Yes, please."

Arugula salad with goat cheese, candied pecans, beets and raspberry vinaigrette came next. Everything was perfectly balanced and seasoned. Jase savored each bite and tried to unravel its mysteries. Even if he never became a professional chef, he still wanted to be able to cook well for himself—and for his man. He asked Master questions about it, and he answered them all with patience and obvious delight.

Petit filet with hollandaise sauce, escalloped potatoes and roasted asparagus came after that. As small as the portions were, Jase didn't dare finish his plate, given how his stomach was already starting to feel full. He wanted to have room for dessert.

He relaxed sufficiently to ask a few questions of his own. "So, did you always want to become a botanist?"

"Yes, I like plants, and fortunately, the hive needed someone new with that skill."

Jase frowned. "What if it hadn't?"

"Then I would have been assigned something it did need."

"That doesn't sound fair." Jase paused, worried his criticism of Master's culture wouldn't sit well with him.

But naturally Master took it in stride, like he did everything. "It's not, by modern human standards. But, within my people's system, we have hives within hives that have to fit perfectly. Everyone works to the greater good in order to allow the Great Queen and her lesser queens to reproduce without worry. Even though almost all females can birth at least one offspring, the queens are the most fecund."

"How many babies does a queen have?"

"Hundreds." Master gave the answer as if it were no big deal.

"Hundreds?" Jase thought of bees, then mammals, and couldn't imagine how that was possible.

Master grinned around his mouthful of food. "Remember. We live a lot longer than humans and we gestate differently, as well. Plus, there are far more males than females. That's why we evolved so that a male could change into female when our population was under stress."

That reminded Jase of where Demi had come from and how Mackie's body was changing in order to someday accommodate a growing fetus. The boys had insisted when they helped him dress that although they had been trying to distract him, the information was nevertheless true. He fiddled with his fork as he considered it. "Are… Are you going to want me to do that for you, Master?" He honestly didn't know how he felt about it.

Once again, Master took his hand. "I can't say I'm all that thrilled about the boys explaining that part to you at this stage. I certainly don't want you thinking it's a condition of your being with me. All I ask — all I hope for — is what you are willing to give me now. Whenever that 'now' may be. Tonight, it's a date. Dinner and companionship. It's more than I ever thought I'd find on this planet.

"I can't believe that an exquisite boy like you would agree to spend time with me, and I still worry you do it out of misplaced duty."

"No!" Jase rose and went to Master's side. He wrapped his free hand around the back of his neck. "I'm here because I love you."

The shocked look on Master's face would have been comical if the stakes hadn't been so high. "You don't have to say that."

Irritation rose in Jase, and for the first time in years, he felt capable of expressing it freely. "Yes, I do. I mean it and don't tell me I don't know my own mind. I'm *not* broken, remember?"

Master let out a deep breath. "No, you're not. You're right, as well, that I have to trust you when you express your feelings. Your love is a gift I prize above all others."

He took Jase's lips in a soft kiss before placing his palm on Jase's stomach. "Any room in there for dessert?"

"I'm kind of full. Can we take a break?"

"Sure. Would you like to watch a movie?"

Jase looked away. "That's fine, if you want."

Master placed the tip of his forefinger under Jase's chin and slowly turned his head back. "What do *you* want?"

"Um…" He was embarrassed and a little afraid to ask. Not because he thought Master would refuse, but because he wasn't sure how well he'd handle doing something freely that had been forced upon him.

"*Jase.*"

"Can we fuck?"

Master's eyebrows shot up, and for a few tense seconds, he said nothing. Then, "No."

Jase's heart sank.

"We will, however, make love, if that is what you truly want."

Chapter Fourteen

Don't screw this up.

Emil gave himself the stern warning before scooping an astonished Jase into his arms and carrying him to the bed. He laid him down in the middle with utmost care and took the boy's shoes and socks off to ensure he was more comfortable.

Jase blinked at him with wide eyes. "I don't understand."

"It's simple," Emil replied, toeing off his own shoes and lying on his side facing Jase. "I'm not going to fuck you. That's something that can be done quickly and impersonally if that's what people want. Humans often do, and that's fine with me, because my people also often act that way. I've done it myself, actually. You, on the other hand, deserve more than that tonight because you're a virgin. Your first time should be special."

Jase barked out a laugh. "Master, I assure you I'm not a virgin."

The casual way Jase accepted his abuse pained Emil right down to his marrow. "Of course you are, baby. You've never known sex. Rape doesn't count. Tonight is the first time for you, and I'd be honored if you'll give me that privilege." The tears forming in the boy's eyes nearly undid him. "Please, don't cry," he begged, using his thumb to wipe a drop away.

"It's from happiness, Master. I swear."

Leaning down, Emil placed a chaste kiss on the boy's lips and lingered there. "Do you think you could please call me Emil?" he asked in a whisper.

"Yes. Anything for you. Emil."

"Oh. I love hearing you say it. I love *you*, Jase." The confession was hard to get out, yet impossible to keep in anymore. He felt guilty wanting someone so young. After years of contempt over other men's lusting for younger men, he understood how easy it was to fall for someone with such beautiful innocence. He couldn't imagine his life with this boy no longer in it.

He instantly regretted his impulsive honesty. "I shouldn't have said that. I don't want to pressure you."

"Oh, Emil"—Jase rolled into him and wrapped his body around his. "I want you to love me. And I want you to believe me when I say that no matter how my life changes from now on, loving you never will."

Emil hugged him back and peppered the parts of Jase's head and face that he could reach with kisses. "I hope that's so, but you have to promise me that if it does, you will tell me. Nothing would hurt me more than keeping you at my side when you'd rather be somewhere else."

"I promise." There was steeliness in the vow.

Emil had no choice other than to accept Jase at his word. If the boy's recovery was going to mean anything, he had to be believed when he voiced his opinion.

"Can we fuck now?"

Hearing a teasing tone, Emil chuckled. "Yes, we can begin to *make love*."

His experience with a human was rusty and always before, it *had* been fucking and nothing more. He was working in the dark to a large degree, so he went with instinct and started with the obvious. Rolling Jase onto his back, Emil dipped to capture the boy's mouth. He pressed firmly at first to give evidence to his passion before lightening the touch to feathery kisses. He cupped and sucked bits of Jase's plump, pink lips with his own, tugging and nibbling.

When Jase opened his mouth and shyly licked him with the tip of his tongue, Emil refused to take the hint. Instead, he moved on to the boy's jaw, then throat. He placed wet kisses up to the earlobe, sucked on it a bit, before continuing down the tight column. He swirled his tongue at the V of the collarbone. The pulse of Jase's jugular called to him. He gave it a brief moment of attention, striping it with a lick before returning to Jase's mouth. He reminded himself that tonight was about Jase's pleasure, not his own. Drinking the boy's blood would be going too far, asking too much.

Now, he was ready to take a taste of Jase's mouth. The boy opened for him instantly and gave him a merry chase. Emil cupped the base of his head to leverage him closer and control the speed of their kissing. A breathy sigh and moan told him he was doing something right. Jase's reaction encouraged him to increase the pressure, give vent to his own needs. Jase's mouth was tastier than anything Emil had ever baked. Drinking him in was better than the finest wines on Earth.

And yeah, he was getting goopy in his thoughts, but so what? In some ways, this was his first time, as well. He'd never savored another like this before, not even the queen herself, who had been the experienced one, in any event. It was heady stuff. His cock was unusually quiescent, hard and needy as always, yet not urging him to a fast completion. Jase, in comparison, seemed more anxious to move on. He moved his legs in restless fashion and gripped Emil's arms almost painfully.

Emil decided to slow things down again. He pulled away from Jase's mouth, tugging a bit of lip at the end. He unbuttoned the boy's shirt down to his waist and slid a hand under it to cup a pec. "Do you like nipple play?" The huskiness of his voice surprised him.

Jase moaned and tossed his head. "I don't know."

Emil rubbed the pad of his thumb across one nub before lightly pinching it.

Jase's eyes flew open and he gasped. "I guess I do," he said breathlessly.

"Good. Let's see how much."

Emil was enjoying this exploration. He replaced his fingers with his tongue, flicking at the hardened nipple. He was rewarded with more moans and restlessness by Jase. Then he wrapped his lips around the nub and sucked. Jase arched into him with a cry.

Oh yes, this is great fun.

Encouraged and aroused beyond reason now, Emil shifted to straddle his lover. He tore open the rest of the shirt to gain access to Jase's torso. All that creamy, soft skin, no longer marred by anything except the faintest of bruises, was laid open for his pleasure. He ignored the bit of discoloration. That would fade soon, and Emil promised himself that nothing would mark the boy ever again.

He placed more open-mouthed kisses all the way down to the waistband of Jase's slacks. He unfastened them with a force that rent the cloth. It didn't matter. He could afford to buy Jase as many pretty pants as he could ever want. The boy wore no underwear, which both disturbed and thrilled him. Part of Jase's new life lessons was going to be that he didn't need to be naked and accessible anymore — at least not unless he wanted to be.

The boy's lovely cock was hard and waiting for him. Emil stared at it with unbridled greed for a few seconds before licking it from root to tip. Jase bucked his hips and groaned out encouragement. Not wanting things to progress too fast, Emil held Jase's pelvis down while he lavished the dick with his attention. This tiny bit of mastery was okay because it would amp Jase's pleasure.

So sweet. From the freshly washed shaft to the glistening head, it was all delicious. Emil briefly considered how he had whipped cream chilling nearby that would make the perfect topping to Jase's cock. But that would mean letting go of the boy and he didn't think he could manage that, even for a few seconds.

Besides, it would be overkill. He sucked the cock into his mouth and worked it all the way down his throat. With his lips pressed against Jase's pubic bone, he rolled his eyes to watch the boy as he brought him to his first climax of the evening. Jase didn't disappoint. With Emil's throat muscles milking the shaft, Jase shot off in seconds. He screamed and flailed his arms. He twisted in Emil's embrace and bucked. There was nowhere for him to go, however. Emil kept him anchored to the bed as he made him come.

"Oh my God! Stop!"

Emil released the boy immediately, alarm shooting through him. The dick flopped out of his mouth, not entirely soft, yet shining from his spit. Jase continued to twitch.

"Are you all right?" Emil looked down at him anxiously. Had he pushed too far?

Jase's movements were involuntary at the moment. He was devastated, wrecked, but he knew Master Emil needed reassurance. He forced his eyelids open a crack. "That was intense." He managed a smile. "Best orgasm *ever*."

Emil's face split into a wide grin. "Yeah? There's more where that came from."

Jase shook his head. "No, not yet. I need a break, and I want more to eat."

"Oh. I have chocolate mousse waiting."

"Hmm, yum. Later, though, please. I had something else in mind."

For once, Jase didn't overthink what he wanted to do or ponder how much his life had changed in such a short time. It was a minor miracle, one that had been wrought by an otherworldly creature. So, maybe that wasn't surprising. The changes within him weren't bound by Earthly laws.

Calling up the reserves of energy he'd developed over the years, he sat up and tackled Emil. Momentum and surprise were on his side. The big man toppled onto his back and sprawled with his head lying by the end of the bed. Jase went straight for the man's belt. He had it undone and his pants open in record speed. He was quite pleased with himself when Emil's huge dick sprang out.

"Jase, you don't have—" The man's words died the moment Jase covered his cockhead with his lips. "Oh, fuck."

Jase grinned around the bulbous, satiny flesh that spread his mouth open as wide as it could go. There was no way to deep-throat this monster dick, but he would do his best to take what he could. Already pre-cum dribbled out. It tasted not quite human, yet he found he still liked it. His previous experience hadn't been a trick of his mind to cope with his situation. He would gladly give Emil blow jobs for the rest of his life and swallow every drop of his cum with a smile.

It took nearly both sets of fingers to grasp the cock. Taking it inside his ass would be hard. He was determined to do so, regardless. Emil might see him as a virgin, and Jase understood that he sort of was. Still, his ass had been forced open hundreds of times. He knew he could do no less for Emil. Jase was sure the alien cock would fit into his pliable body. He'd make it.

He took the shaft down as far as he could, getting it nice and wet and making Emil as wild and ready as possible. The man quivered nicely under his touch and uttered breathless grunts. His big hands clenched at the bedding, further testament that Jase was bringing him to the edge. As he readied the dick, he wiggled out of his pants. His own cock had gotten hard again, a thing that delighted him. His sexuality hadn't been taken from him. He could feel pleasure and he was ready for another round of it once he'd taken care of Emil. He had no doubt he would get it, too.

With Emil's cock as wet as he could make it, Jase pulled off it with a long, slow suction until it popped out of his mouth completely. He knee-walked to position his ass above it. Before he could sit on the dick, though, Emil grabbed him and deftly reversed their positions.

Jase gasped and glared at him. "Why did you do that?"

Emil frowned. "You were going to take my dick up your ass. That's why."

Disappointment crashed over him. "Don't you want to fuck—? Penetrate me?"

A fierce look stole over the man's face. "Sure I do. More than anything. But not like that. Haven't you noticed how big I am? You need some prep and we're going to take this *slowly*."

"Oh." Emil was looking out for him, taking care, as always. That was because he was Master, and in the privacy of his own thoughts, he could think of him that way.

Master Emil tore off his clothing, heedless of the damage he did to what had to be multi-thousand dollars' worth of designer goods. His urgency was ego-boosting, and the man could probably afford whatever he wanted. He favored Canali, Jase had noticed, not that he would ever be able to buy something so expensive for the man. Still, it was the little things that mattered in a relationship. And, he realized with a joyful jolt, that's what this was now.

Master pulled lube out of his nightstand drawer and something else familiar to Jase—a butt plug. His heart sank before he realized that it made perfect sense to open him with the toy before he attempted to take Master's dick. It again showed caretaking, not dominance.

"Are you okay with this?" Master asked, holding the thing up. "I figured we'd get around to this at some point. Or, at least, I hoped we would," he added with a quick grin. "I wanted to be prepared and Val suggested this would be a good way to prep you for taking me inside. He's the Dom and has been playing with human boys for years, so he should know."

"Yes, please, it's fine with me, and thank you. Val was right. It will help open me."

"That's the idea." He didn't slick it and shove it inside Jase right away, however.

Instead, Master gently tugged Jase's legs apart before kneeling between them. He cupped Jase's ass to push his hips forward, then did the most extraordinary thing. He pressed his mouth to Jase's hole.

"Oh," Jase gasped at the delightful sensation of wet lips and tongue licking and swirling against the puckered ring. He was no stranger to rim jobs, except he'd always been the one forced to give them. And, little wonder. It was amazing. His hole unfurled with ease at the soft probing. Soon, Master's tongue fucked him with soft, shallow thrusts.

Jase sighed and relaxed. His cock lay heavy on his thigh, while his balls curled close to his body. He could come from this alone. Master's fingers grasping his dick and tugging ensured that he did. The climax caught him by surprise, making him sit halfway up with the intensity of it. He flopped back down immediately, gasping for breath, his head swirling.

He almost missed when the plug replaced Master's tongue. It stretched and burned, but no more than he could handle. Master pushed it in, pulled it out again, then back in. He fucked him with it a few more times before seating it all the way inside. The base pressed firmly against Jase's cleft. He didn't need to be told to clench his hole around it. This time, he liked the way it pried him open and filled him to bursting.

"There now," Master said, looming over him. "Now we can get started."

"St-started?"

"Sure. That was only the appetizer. Time for the main course."

Master proved himself to be truly a monster by beginning with Jase's mouth again, giving him short, closed-mouthed kisses. No matter how hard Jase tried, the man stubbornly refused to progress faster than he had before. Jase couldn't say he truly minded. Kissing was lovely, and who knew his nipples were so sensitive?

He made what effort he could to play with Master's body, as well. It was difficult, not because he couldn't reach the spots he wanted, although that was true. It was more that his mind and body were mesmerized by Master's attention. He could barely form a coherent thought or move in a rational way. He was utterly undone by pleasure.

By the time he'd reached the edge of his third climax, skillfully wrought by Master's clever hand, he'd almost forgotten the plug. Then, Master removed it. Or, rather, he fucked Jase with it some more before taking it out completely. It was replaced almost immediately with something far wider. Jase was relaxed sufficiently that he didn't tense more than a fraction before letting go again.

Master's cockhead breached Jase's hole slowly. It stretched the skin beyond anything he'd experienced before. But he knew how to make the muscles go slack to let it in. Then he pushed out, which made no sense, yet he understood it would help the cock to enter. His breath hitched when it became too much. Master stopped and held himself still with an effort that made him tremble. Jase could feel him vibrating through his hand and thighs.

Taking a deep breath, Jase let it out slowly and lifted his legs. Master understood and pushed in, slowly and steadily inch-by-inch. Jase's ass, so used to trying to expel someone's dick, welcomed it. Everything inside him melted, giving way. And Master didn't use his cock to conquer. He never forced Jase's body beyond the pace it could handle.

At the same time, Master's hand worked Jase's dick, bringing him back to the edge again, although careful to keep him from careening over. Jase, too, held his climax back. It wasn't time. Jase wanted to come with his master fully inside him.

And he wanted more. Greedy boy that he was, he wanted the best orgasm there was to have as the lover of a vampire.

When Master finally bottomed out, Jase opened his eyes and gazed at him. "Bite me, Master. Please."

Those alien eyes had gone black with lust. He saw how much Master wanted that, too. He also saw the hesitation. Jase decided to not give him a choice. Lifting his chin, he exposed his throat and waited with closed eyes for the strike.

It came a second later. A roar met his ears right before fangs sank deep into the tender spot at the base of his neck. Pain made Jase shout. The pleasure that followed, as Master tugged in his blood, pumped into his ass and jerked one more orgasm out of him, destroyed his senses and his mind. He collapsed into a limp puddle.

He was dead. He was alive. Nothing could ever hurt him again.

Emil drank and drank, taking long pulls of Jase's unexpected gift to him. He'd forgotten how it was supposed to be. No microwaved bags or animal blood could match this life-affirming drink that coated his throat and slaked a thirst that he'd long since learned to ignore. He could never do so again. As he thrust his cock deep inside his boy and brought him to climax once more, he knew that if he lost him, it would be the end of Emil. That man he'd made himself into would disappear forever. Life without Jase would be worse than any death.

He had him now, though, and that would have to be enough. He couldn't become greedy or needy. Jase had to stay with him of his own free will. Emil intended to devote every moment of every day to showing his love. He'd ply him with food and help him however necessary. He'd protect him from Dracul and the Washburns of this world. Nothing and no one would hurt the boy again, least of all Emil himself.

And if that meant letting the boy go eventually, then so be it.

He thrust his way carefully to orgasm, the intensity of it catching him by surprise. The exquisite tightness of Jase's channel undulated as he released his cum into it. He pumped and came as much as the tiny ass would allow and shuddered as his orgasm stuttered to its end. Then he lay still, despite his dick trying to rise for more. Jase had taken enough for one night.

Letting the vein go was harder. Retracting his fangs, he broke free of the flesh and lapped the puncture marks. Then he disentangled their bodies with the greatest of care in order to lie entwined without crushing the small human. No, his perfect-sized human. Jase fit right where Emil needed him to against his larger frame.

His kissed the boy's sweaty temple. "How was that? Did you enjoy your first time?"

Jase nuzzled into him and cracked open one eye. "It was almost perfect."

Emil frowned. "Almost?"

"Hmm. There was one thing missing."

"What was that?" Emil racked his brains for some clever sex move that he'd missed.

"Someone said something about chocolate mousse?"

It took a moment for Emil to realize Jase was teasing him. His beautiful abused boy was making a post-sex joke. With a laugh, he hugged him tightly enough to make the boy squeal.

"Whatever you want, my greedy love. Chocolate mousse coming up."

Not so long ago, Emil had helped Val and Mackie achieve their fairy-tale ending. Now he had his. Except that one thing hadn't yet happened in their story. The evil character hadn't had his comeuppance. No problem... Emil would find time to take care of that soon. His lovely boy deserved as much, although he would never learn about the vengeance Emil would wreak on his behalf. Emil would shield him from such ugliness, from everything bad.

His beautiful boy would never know pain again.

Epilogue

"That's it, you little slut. Parade around all you want in front of your window in those skimpy undies."

Jack took a slug of his beer while he tugged at his dick. The damn thing didn't work as well anymore, and living in a shithole trailer park was a new low for him. His luck at the track and at the tables would change, though. It had to. He wasn't meant for this white-trash life. But things weren't all bad. He had a nice, close view of the slutty boy next door. The kid was too stupid to turn off his lights or close his blinds late at night. He gave Jack a nice eyeful. Maybe he could entice him over with the promise of a beer someday. Boys like that were always itching for a man's dick, even if they didn't realize it.

A sound behind him had him whirling around. A huge man with red eyes stood there. No, that couldn't be true. "Who the hell are you? Fuck off!"

He got nothing more out because in a blur that left him dizzy, a large hand wrapped around his throat. He dropped his beer as he was lifted and banged against the far wall of his trailer. Jack kicked his feet and clawed at the fingers. It was like touching something dead-cold and unmoving.

"Who are you?" he croaked out, although he didn't want an answer. He wanted *air*.

The man's mouth opened. Gleaming fangs protruded. "I'm a monster." The voice struck as much terror in him as the sight of those sharp teeth getting closer.

Jack pissed his pants then and there and didn't even care that he'd done so. "Why?" He saw his death looming and was desperate to understand how his life had suddenly come to this horrific point.

The monster brought his mouth close to Jack's ear. He whimpered at the feel of oddly cool breath blowing against it. He struggled more.

"Jase." The one-word answer was almost like a lover's caress.

It took Jack's befuddled mind a few seconds to remember what that name meant. The monster gave him that time. And Jack knew then, as he remembered the boy, the one who should have been his forever but for that bad luck, there was no escaping his fate. He opened his mouth to scream as the monster struck, but those fangs caught it and tore it from him, along with his throat and his life.

Want to see more from this author?
Here's a taster for you to enjoy!

Alien Slave Masters:
The Captain's Pet
Samantha Cayto

Excerpt

Wid Bryant wrapped his arms around his waist in a futile attempt at warmth. The hangar he stood in was even colder than the transport ship, and without the limits of the confined space, no body heat from others stopped him from shivering. Of course it wasn't the cold alone that made him tremble. Fright contributed to his state. He had been scared for the last forty-eight hours or so, since he and his cohorts had been detained by the Travian security force.

What had he been thinking joining Joel and the others in vandalizing the administrative building of the occupying force? Nothing, except a deep-seated hatred for the aliens who had invaded their colony. His parents had warned him to keep his head down and hope that hostilities between the two races would be settled diplomatically. Seriously? As if there were a prayer of that happening. How did you negotiate with beings who had the superior power to wipe you off the face of any planet and with the certainty they were in the right? The battle between Earth and the Travians for the colony had ended before it began. Conquerors had no incentive to bargain. Harassing them seemed like the best way to go. Irritate them enough and maybe they'd figure the small planet wasn't worth the effort.

Or, they could simply round people up and exterminate them. That's what he had assumed would be his punishment when he'd been caught. Now he wasn't so sure. He couldn't understand why they'd bothered to ship him and eleven other guys up to a battlecruiser. Yet, here they were, standing around, freezing and waiting to learn their fate.

"Do you think they're going to kill us?"

Wid glanced at the trembling red-headed kid next to him—Stuart. He'd been shoved into the transport next to Wid, after being detained for throwing rotten fruit at a Travian convoy—a prank as stupid as the one Wid had tried to pull. The poor guy was only eighteen and more scared than Wid, if that were possible. In fact, all of the other boys that had been brought were no older than Wid's twenty years or so, and most couldn't hide their fear. Thank God there were no girls. Surprisingly the Travians had let the one girl who'd been with them, Joel's girlfriend, go immediately. His mother had scoffed over the Travians being patriarchal, but right now it seemed like a good thing.

"No," Wid finally answered. "What would be the point? I mean, if they wanted us dead, why bring us all the way up here?"

He mostly believed what he'd said. It didn't make sense that they'd be dragged so far when it was easy to blow a laser hole in their foreheads back on the planet. Still, something bad loomed. How could it not? As if in answer to his worst fears, the hangar suddenly filled with a dozen Travians. These males were even more imposing than the security detail that guarded the boys. Each one stood particularly tall, close to seven feet, clad head to toe in red leather. Their shiny black hair fell to their shoulders or below, braided in places to keep it off their harsh faces. He couldn't lie and say that the Travians were an ugly race, but they were unsettling with their pale skin and completely black eyes.

As the aliens filed in and lined up opposite the boys, Stuart let out a little whimper. Wid spared him a glance.

"Don't let them think you're scared," he advised in a low tone.

"Seriously?" Stuart murmured back. "I *am* scared."

Wid suppressed a shudder. "I know, just try not to show it. It's all we have left."

"Quiet!"

One of the guards barked out the order in the guttural language of the Travians. God, he hated being able to understand what they said. Once the occupation had been completed, the aliens had forced every human over the age of five to be implanted with a translation device. The foreign words rattled around his head until they made sense to him. The one word was easy to translate. Longer sentences spoken quickly were harder to get. Not that the Travians were patient when a human struggled to understand.

He shut his mouth, however, his bravado long gone.

The tallest of the males stood a foot in front of the others, staring down the line of human boys. When he got to Wid at the end, his gaze lingered. Wid tried not to squirm under the scrutiny. He felt invaded in the more personal sense of the word by the piercing look. After a few seconds, the male glanced away and gestured to another of them. The tall one said something short and quick that Wid didn't catch. When the other male stepped forward, he headed straight for Wid. Before Wid could even think of recoiling, the taller alien barked out one word.

"No!"

The steps of the second male faltered. His expression turned sour for a second before he changed course a fraction to go to Stuart. His hand shot out and he grabbed Stuart by one arm. The male's eyes took on a feral look as he yanked the boy to his body. Stuart cried out and tried to pull away. The male bared his teeth in what could — in an alternate and ugly reality — be called a grin. Then he turned and dragged a struggling and begging Stuart away.

Silence reigned once they'd cleared the hangar. Wid and the other boys were frozen as they digested what had happened to Stuart and what was going to happen to them. The aliens were quiet too, although that seemed to be more about discipline, waiting for a command. The tallest, who was obviously in charge, gestured to another of them. Once again the boys were perused, and Wid recognized the behavior for what it was — they were shopping, picking out which boy they wanted. He didn't dare think in terms of what they wanted the boys for.

Some of the boys struggled when taken, others acquiesced in silent misery. Joel made Wid smile in grim satisfaction when he punched the male who reached for him. The alien barely reacted, as if he'd been bitten by an insect. The disparity between the races physically meant the humans had no hope of fighting them off. Instead of hitting Joel back, however, the alien simply grabbed the swinging arm on the downstroke and used it as leverage to pick Joel up and toss him over his shoulder. The captured boy howled in outrage all the way out of the hangar.

Minutes later, only Wid and the commanding alien remained. Even the guards filed out. Putting his arms down by his side, Wid straightened to stand as tall as he could. Pride was all he had left and he was determined to hide his fear. The alien approached him with unhurried steps. When he came within a foot of Wid, he stopped and stared down. With an expression of as much defiance as he could muster, Wid stared back. Given the foot or so difference in their heights, he had to crane his neck back.

For a few seconds, they looked each other in the eye. The alien's thoughts and emotions were impossible to read within the endless depths of his black eyes. Wid wondered if the alien could read him, or were the species too different to communicate in subtle ways? Despite the coldness around him, sweat trickled down his back. He suppressed a shudder and silently goaded the male to go ahead and do whatever he intended. The waiting was agony.

Suddenly, as if in response to the unspoken challenge or plea—Wid wasn't sure which it was—the alien lashed out to grab Wid's arm. Instinct made Wid pull away, but it was as futile an effort as it had been for the others. The fingers around his biceps were like a steel vise. Nothing could break that hold. Not wanting to be dragged along, Wid suppressed the urge to struggle and instead picked up his feet to match the long strides of his captor.

They left the hangar and strode down a corridor. The ship held a dark and cold atmosphere. The few aliens they encountered as they wended their way, stared briefly at Wid even as they bowed their heads in quick obeisance of the male who had him. It had to be the captain, or whatever rank they recognized as the one in charge of the ship. Great, just his luck that he had gained the attention of the most powerful and, he assumed, the most ruthless of them all. Then the reason for his destiny popped into his head. Of all the boys standing in that hanger, he'd been the only one with blond hair. A shiver ran up his spine at the implication of why his looks mattered.

Many corridors and one lift ride later, the captain led him through a set of sliding doors into what had to be the male's quarters. Wid only had a second to digest this fact before he was pulled past the first room and into a second one with a large, firm-looking mattress-type thing lying in the middle of the floor. His feet stopped suddenly of their own accord when he realized they'd entered a bedroom. He stared at a bed. What else could it be?

"No!" The word was out of his mouth before his brain thought it. He tried to pull his arm free.

The alien tightened his grip and stared down at Wid with his head cocked to one side. He didn't look any happier than Wid felt, yet instead of letting him go, he reached out with his other hand and ripped Wid's T-shirt from his body. It came apart as if made from tissue paper. In the face of obvious evidence of where things were headed, Wid fought back. Twisting, punching and kicking, he tried to free himself and escape his fate with all the strength he possessed. It was like striking granite—the alien's body so hard and unyielding. If he caused the male any pain, it wasn't evident. The only sounds were coming from Wid and he was the only one showing any sign of strain.

His resistance did him no good. Everything he'd been wearing when captured was torn from his body. As soon as Wid was bare-assed naked, the alien lifted him up by the waist and tossed him onto the bed. Wid bounced a few times while he caught his breath, then tried to stand up to run. There was nowhere to go, of course, because the alien blocked the way back to the other room. But rational thought had abandoned him. Pure instinct made him try to flee. Gaining traction on the mattress proved difficult, and by the time he managed to put one foot on the floor, the alien had moved to catch him and toss him back.

Wid tried again and again, each time failing to get himself more than a step or two from the bed. The Travian said nothing. He merely methodically removed his own clothing and kept snatching Wid up and throwing him down. By the time the alien male was completely nude, Wid lay exhausted and badly winded. It didn't help that he'd been given hardly anything to eat and little water to drink since his capture. The alien, damn him, wasn't even breathing heavily as he approached the bed.

Wid crawled away backward like a crab in a last futile effort to escape. The alien looked somehow bigger without his clothes, his pale skin almost pearlescent in the ambient light of the room. There was no discernable hair on his body other than his head. The massive cock of the being stood out easily with nothing to hide it. Long and thick, it gleamed with wetness that dribbled slowly from the head. With his eyes glued to the weapon coming toward him, Wid shook his head.

"No. Please, don't," he begged in a voice choked with fear. Any bravado he'd ever felt disappeared in the face of being raped.

The alien knelt on the bed and reached for Wid. Grabbing him by the ankle, he dragged him closer. With the last of his energy, Wid kicked out with his free leg. He knew a moment's satisfaction when the Travian grunted from the solid blow that Wid landed on his chest. The creature wasn't immune from pain after all. The gratification was short-lived, however. The alien's fingers clamped down on Wid's arms and hauled him up.

Their gazes locked for a second. "Please," Wid pleaded one more time before he found himself face down on the bed.

A heavy, hot weight pressed him farther into the mattress. Warm breath tickled his ear before a bass voice rumbled, "Lie still! There is no choice for either of us."

It took a second for Wid to realize the alien spoke in English, not Travian. Before he had time to process the meaning of the words, however, something wet and warm and hard slid against his ass. The strange declaration be damned, fear gave him the strength to struggle, albeit futilely. A knee forced its way between his legs, spreading them wide. The blunt head of the alien's cock pressed against his hole, slid up his crack, then returned. Wid couldn't keep the whimper from escaping his lips. He clawed at the slippery cloth he lay on and closed his eyes tight. The alien pushed to gain entrance. Wid squeezed his sphincter tight in a vain attempt to keep him out.

"Don't resist. I'll make it quick."

Again, Wid's mind tried to process the intent behind the alien rapist's version of pillow talk. He sounded almost apologetic, which made no sense. No one hovered over the bed with a weapon to the creature's head, making him do this terrible thing. And did he really believe Wid would just acquiesce to this horror without complaint? Fucker! Wid renewed his effort to keep the alien cock out. He was no match for the creature's strength, however. The thick rod breached his hole. The searing pain of it robbed him of his breath. The cock bore into him, stretching his rectum with relentless pressure. Too stunned to even scream, he could only do as the alien had commanded — lie there and take it.

The alien's copious pre-cum slicked the way, but God, the burning as his body struggled to accept the girth and length brought tears to Wid's eyes. There was no chance to grow accustomed to the invasion. As soon as the alien had sheathed himself fully, he began his thrusting. Hard, long strokes drilled Wid into the bed. Strong fingers held him in place as if the piercing cock was not already enough to do so. He wanted to cry, would have without shame given the brutal assault, if he'd had the breath to do so. Instead, he panted to the rhythm of the pounding and prayed that, as promised, it would be over quickly.

And so it was. With a guttural growl, the alien seated himself deep inside Wid's ass. Wid could feel fluid pulsing into him. Thinking it was over, he bucked up against the heavy male. But the alien didn't get up, rather he rolled over to his side, bringing Wid with him. The cock stayed embedded. Wid tried to expel it with a strong push of his rectal muscles. The damn thing didn't budge. It remained hard and unmovable. The alien's harsh breath wafted onto Wid's head while his arm encircled Wid's chest to hold him close. Wid squirmed to free himself to no effect. Then a heavy leg was thrown over him to anchor him more firmly in place. So much for the bastard's assurances.

He remained trapped and there was nothing he could do about it. The laser shot to the head was looking better to him now. Then he thought of his parents and his sisters and how they must be worried, not knowing where he was or what had happened to him. Better that they not know.

He didn't so much fall asleep lying captured in the alien's arms, as pass out, exhausted by the day's events. He got no rest, however. Plagued by nightmares, he kept twitching awake. Understanding of his plight always came to him quickly and it was like the first time each time it happened. His heart raced with fear and he instinctively struggled to free himself, forgetting that it was pointless. Worse, his captor woke with him, if the creature even slept. His massive cock remained hard and rammed up Wid's ass. He fucked Wid again and again, ignoring Wid's pleas to stop and leave him be.

Eventually Wid's mind simply shut down and went blank.

About the Author

Samantha Cayto is a Boston-area native who practices as a business lawyer by day while writing erotic romance at night—the steamier the better. She likes to push the envelope when it comes to writing about passion and is delighted other women agree that guy-on-guy sex is the hottest ever.

She lives a typical suburban life with her husband, three kids and four dogs. Her children don't understand why they can't read what she writes, but her husband is always willing to lend her a hand—and anything else—when she needs to choreograph a scene.

Samantha loves to hear from readers. You can find her contact information, website details and author profile page at http://www.pride-publishing.com.

www.ingramcontent.com/pod-product-compliance
Lightning Source LLC
Chambersburg PA
CBHW021522240626
47154CB00002B/743